UNFOLLOW ME

ALSO AVAILABLE BY CHARLOTTE DUCKWORTH

The Rival

UNFOLLOW ME

A Novel

CHARLOTTE DUCKWORTH

NEW YORK

Published in the United States by Crooked Lane Books, an imprint of The Quick Brown Fox & Company LLC.

Crooked Lane Books and its logo are trademarks of The Quick Brown Fox & Company LLC.

Library of Congress Catalog-in-Publication data available upon request.

ISBN (hardcover): 978-1-64385-392-5
ISBN (ebook): 978-1-64385-393-2

Cover design by Nicole Lecht

Printed in the United States.

www.crookedlanebooks.com

Crooked Lane Books
34 West 27th St., 10th Floor
New York, NY 10001

First Edition: March 2020

10 9 8 7 6 5 4 3 2 1

I know everything about you, Violet.

I know your mother's name is Joy. I know your sister is a paediatric nurse, that she has twin boys. I know you sold your first flat—a tiny, one-bed in Blackheath with bubbling wallpaper and an illegal roof terrace—for £300k. Double the price you paid for it. I know your father gave you the deposit when you moved to London at twenty-one. I know the house you now live in cost you and Henry almost £3million, and that you also own the villa in Marbella that you pretend belongs to your parents. I know that you lie about your age; you're thirty-eight next birthday, not thirty-six. I know that 2017 was your most profitable year yet; that you've set up a trust fund for the children, somewhere to put all the money that keeps flowing your way.

I know you have hair extensions; I know the name of your hairdresser, Pablo, and that his partner is called Ian. I know where they live. I know you're loyal to him now, that you consider him "family," that you always spend New Year with him and Ian. Drinking champagne out of saucers, wearing an outfit that costs more than I earn in a month.

I know that you only got into journalism by luck. I know your ex, Angus, now married to Isabella and living in Surrey, got you a job as an editorial assistant on his golfing magazine, and that you charmed your way across one of the world's biggest media firms until you were a features writer for a woman's magazine.

I know that you were good at your job, no matter how much it annoys me.

I know that you met Henry in the bar by the office. I know that it was a work night out to say goodbye to one of the PAs. She doesn't play much of a role in your story, but even so, I know her name was Janet.

It's been so easy to find it all out. All I needed was time, and determination. You've left it right there for me. All that information—all that power—just waiting, a few clicks away.

It's what you want, after all, isn't it? Without an audience, without people like me watching, then what are you? No one asked you to put yourself on the internet. No one asked you to leave breadcrumb trails of your life across the World Wide Web, just waiting for a hungry bird like me to gobble up.

I know everything about you, Violet. But what do you know about me?

LILY

It's the best part of my day. 7.35pm. I sink on to the sofa, fish bowl of wine in hand, and reach for my laptop. The coffee table is littered with relics from a rainy Sunday: Archie's latest work of art, his bright red cup—name scrawled on the side to stop his friend Tom from using it—a half-chewed breadstick and two lift-the-flap books in need of repair. I push them to one side, and open the lid of my laptop.

I'm not usually one for organisation. James used to find it frustrating, frowning at my attempts to laugh it off. Adorably inefficient, that's what he called me. If only James could see my laptop now. He'd open it up and stare open-mouthed at the Internet history, the neatly organised bookmarks. He'd think I was a weirdo. Maybe I am.

7.35pm. It shouldn't be, but sometimes it feels like the best part of my day.

I love you, Violet.

I open the browser, my tongue ticking impatiently as the temperamental Wi-Fi kicks into life. My laptop is practically a museum piece these days. Two clicks and I'm in. I feel my body relax as I wait for the page to load, taking a satisfying glug of white wine, feeling it scratch its way down my throat. I can't afford the good stuff anymore. I can't afford the cheap stuff either, really.

As I prepare to see them again, to laugh and cry and live through their dramas, to escape my loneliness for just twelve minutes—or

3

fifteen, if I'm lucky—there's a wail from Archie's room. I feel my fingers tensing around the stem of the wine glass, the pressure almost enough to shatter it. Just me, it's all down to me. I stand up, place the glass as calmly as I can next to Tinky Winky, who's lying on the coffee table regarding me solemnly with his stupid blank face, and pinch my wrist.

By the time I get to Archie's door, he's quietened down. Just whimpers now, the worst of the nightmare over. I creep into his room, stand by his bed and stroke his hair away from his forehead. He looks so beautiful when he's sleeping it hurts. Sometimes I think there's no space in my heart for my own upset at losing James, it's too full with the agony of Archie's situation. No one deserves to grow up without a father.

"Shh monkey," I whisper, kissing him on the head. "Just a bad dream. Mummy's here."

One eye twitches, squeezing open and meeting mine. He gives a murmur of relief, and shuts it again. I wait a few more minutes, watching him as he falls into a deep sleep, and remember how I felt my heart would break every night as I tucked him in, with nothing to greet me once I left him but a living room that was both empty and full of memories, and a microwave meal for one.

And then I discovered Violet. A blonde angel. The perfect mother, with the perfect family—yet even she admitted to struggling with parenthood, making the wrong decisions. *Ballsing it up*, as she puts it. Watching her makes me feel I'm not doing too badly after all. Is it too melodramatic to say she saved me?

I tiptoe out of Archie's room and back into the living room. My laptop is humming on the coffee table. Round two. Here we go. I walk towards it, press the space bar and the screen lights up again. But something isn't right. A dead link. I've clearly made a mistake. Because on the screen, underneath the red and black header, there's just an empty blue box, filled with words that make no sense.

This channel does not exist.

I refresh the page. I double check the address, the handle, whatever you call the damn thing. But nothing. YouTube must be down, broken, something.

I click on my list of Bookmarks. My favorite sites, neatly in a row, the only thing I've ever organised. First I try her Facebook page, but am greeted by the words "This page isn't available." Then her Twitter but am told the page doesn't exist. Then Instagram, nothing. In a perverse desperation I try Pinterest. Nothing there either.

She has vanished.

Violet has vanished. As I always feared she would.

YVONNE

The sound of my husband slapping his hands against his thighs in time to "We Built This City" makes me want to crash the car and kill us both.

"Simon . . ." I say. "Could you . . . could you just not."

"What?" he replies, grinning. "It's a classic!"

"Fuck's sake!" I shout, accelerating through an amber light. "I've got a headache."

The most important day of the month, and yet my mood swings are worse than when I have my period. I read somewhere that irritability during ovulation is down to a heightened sense of competition, as women once fought over the most fertile, masculine mate.

Not much has changed there, really.

The tapping stops, and from the corner of my eye I see Simon slump back in the passenger seat. He's been drinking, as usual. Sunday lunch with the in-laws, that's what they should make every hopeful bride sit through for a month before they swish down the aisle in their layers of tulle. That'd put them all off.

Every Sunday the same. Simon's mum fawning over him, looking me up and down with a judgemental twitch in her eye, asking how he's been. *Has the stress taken its toll, he's looking a little thin? Must be so hard for him too, you know. Makes him feel . . .* and this last bit is always whispered . . . *less of a man.*

Earlier, as I stood in the kitchen, drying the serveware she passed to me unsolicited, I wanted to shout back that he *was* less of a man. That yes, it was all his fault, actually. All of it, *everything*, my whole hideous plan. The test results were clear: *male factor infertility*. His little soldiers were missing their heads and had stumpy tails, and they couldn't be bothered to swim at all, let alone in the right direction. It was nothing to do with me. My eggs were perfect. Or as perfect as they could be at forty years of age.

Three months of complicated vitamin supplements, a ban on hot baths and tight underwear . . . Simon has been trying everything to improve his sperm. But I'm not allowed to tell Jane that, of course.

Well, we never had any problems having Simon and Steve. But then I was so much younger . . .

In the living room her beloved firstborn was sitting next to his father, watching the match on the unsettlingly big television that they were so proud of. Drinking a can of beer. He refused the first two Jane offered, but then his father told him to stop being so soft, that one "wouldn't hurt." There's your answer, Jane. Stop offering him Stella, then you might get your precious grandchild.

By the time we've pulled into the driveway of our thirties semi, it's 7pm. Just a few hours left of this horrific weekend before everything goes back to normal. It'll be like yesterday never happened. Simon at the gym, me spending my days shooting happy families, my heart bursting with envy at their irrepressible matching grins and myriad nicknames for one another.

Simon's sulk has set in and he doesn't even acknowledge me as he opens the passenger door and marches up to our house. He lets himself in, makes a huge fuss of the cat and then disappears into the kitchen. I linger on the step outside, checking my phone for the thousandth time today. Nothing. Then, I follow Simon into the house, hanging back in the hallway as he opens the fridge and pulls out another can of beer. I know he's making a point, doing it to annoy me.

I shouldn't have lost my temper. It's not his fault, after all.

"Simon . . ." I say. "I . . ."

"Doesn't matter," he replies, cracking the ring pull. "Maybe you should go for a lie down."

"What do you want for dinner?" I soften my voice, consider walking towards him and giving him a hug. No, that'd be too weird. Bollocks. I always pick a fight on the wrong day.

"Whatever. I'm not really hungry," he replies.

He pushes past me and heads for the living room. Seconds later I hear a click as the television springs to life. Shit shit *shit*, it's all going wrong.

I walk back through the hall and stand in the doorway of the living room.

"*Antiques Roadshow*, huh?" I say, smiling. "Didn't realise that was your cup of tea."

His lips twitch but he doesn't look at me. His eyes are fixed to the screen.

"Simon," I say. "I'm sorry. Please. You know today . . ."

He gives a great sigh.

"Let's just wait for the appointment, Von. I'm not in the mood."

I feel a rush of sympathy for him, for his hurt male pride. It's all he ever wanted; a family. He dotes on his nephew, volunteers to babysit him at every available opportunity. When the consultant handed us his results, giving us the verdict with a sympathetic shrug, I saw the way Simon swallowed and looked away. Then later, at home, I watched through the door of the living room as he ripped the sheet of paper into tiny pieces.

"It can't hurt, can it?" My voice sounds whiny and needling, like a child. For a second I am taken out of myself and I'm looking down at the scene, hearing a forty-year-old woman beg her much younger husband to have sex with her.

He doesn't look up.

He wants this just as much as me. I just need to take the pressure off.

I take a few steps back into the hallway and look in the mirror, plumping up my brown lob with my hands. I don't look forty. But there's a bittersweet reason I don't—it's because I haven't had children.

Yet. I haven't had children yet.

This *has* to be done today. I undo another button on my blouse. Men have always wanted to sleep with me. Something to do with my pout, the fullness of my lips. And there have been so many men. It was the only power I ever had, and now it makes me want to cry. I don't want to be a whore; I want to be a mother.

I button up my blouse again and take a deep breath. I can do this. We've only been together for two years, not even seen our first wedding anniversary yet. He still finds me attractive. He's a thirty-two-year-old man, for goodness' sake.

Silently, I walk back into the living room. Simon eyes me but he's only half interested. I sit down on the sofa next to him, curling my legs up, and lean into him. He smells of beer, but I won't let it put me off. I feel him shift slightly and then he puts his arm around me.

"I'm sorry," I say, as I lie back, my head in his lap, meaning it. "Sorry for shouting at you."

I push the side of my face against his crotch. It's a cheap trick, but I feel it work almost instantly. I stay there in silence for several seconds until finally there's a shift. He puts the can of beer down on the table next to the sofa, and then I feel his hands on me, gently at first, then more insistently as he leans down to kiss me.

He's going to fuck me on the sofa, in front of the living room window, and the curtains are still open. He's going to fuck me like a whore, but today I don't care. Needs must. This has to be done.

* * *

Later I am lying in bed, phone in hand, glass of organic full-fat milk on the bedside table. Drinking it makes me feel sick but wannabe-housewife from the GoMamas pregnancy forum swears it helped her conceive. Simon is in the bathroom. He takes longer than me in there, claims he's brushing his teeth if I ever ask him. I know the truth though. I never imagined I'd marry someone who waxed his chest and used fake tan, but I understand that looking good is part of his job, and actually it makes me proud that he takes care of himself and his appearance.

I remember introducing him to Katie, the teasing arch of her eyebrow as she shook his hand. Her ironic words when he went to the toilet, leaving us alone.

Well, you two are certainly going to have beautiful babies!

Yes, we are.

I've been waiting all day for this moment, and I click on the link for Violet's YouTube channel, picking up the glass of milk and taking a mouthful as I wait for it to load. She uploads her daily vlog at 8pm every evening. The thickness of the cream furs up my tongue, settling around my lips in an unpleasant moustache. I wipe it away with the back of my hand, watching the screen as it loads, waiting for reassurance. But it doesn't come. Instead, there's the unexpected.

This channel does not exist.

The milk churns in my stomach as I close my eyes, almost as if to pray.

What does it mean?

GoMamas

Topics>Mummy Vloggers>Violet is Blue
3 December 2017

Coldteafordays
Anyone else having problems getting on to Violet's blog today? It's not loading for me?

Sadandalone
Me neither. Weird. Says page not found. Nothing on Twitter or Insta either?!

Horsesforcourses
Looks like she's deleted it!!

Coldteafordays
What?! I don't believe it. What am I going to do now!? I was so looking forward to hearing how Skye's nativity play goes next week! I was more excited about it than my own kids' . . . Lol

Neverforget
Not that surprised. Maybe her mother finally talked some sense into her. Time she put her family first.

Sadandalone
But she wouldn't just delete it without telling us why! She did a post calling out vloggers who do that just last year!

Neverforget
You're surprised that she's behaved hypocritically? *Eyeroll*

Sadandalone
I miss her already.

11

Horsesforcourses
She'll probably be back in the morning.

Coldteafordays
She better be! Not sure what I'd do without her daily updates reassuring me I'm not the only mother who breastfeeds while on the loo. Sheer desperation, you understand . . .

Neverforget
Maybe one of the trolls finished her off . . .

LILY

As usual I am running late. It's chaos working in central London, but my boss Ben is so proud of the company's W1 address—thinks it makes us look well-established—even though my friend Susie told me east is where it's at for software developers these days.

On the escalator that leads down to the Underground platforms, I find myself pulling my phone from my handbag and connecting to the Wi-Fi, my fingers tapping impatiently on the YouTube app when it connects. At 6am this morning, I did the same thing, before I'd even opened my eyes properly. I'm ashamed to say I left Archie screeching for me in his bedroom as I searched for her, my priorities skewed, my head full of grit from the entire bottle of Jacob's Creek I drank last night as I paced the living room in confusion. But still, nothing. She's gone.

Once I'm squished into a seat, I take out my book and try to read. A light-hearted Christmas love story, lent to me by Susie. But the words blur as I stare at them, wondering what's happened to Violet. Where is she?

It might sound crazy, but she's felt like my closest friend over the past three years, the one I could always rely on to cheer me up, to make me feel I'm not the only one out there struggling with grief and new motherhood. Her beloved father had fallen to the floor in Waitrose three months after she gave birth to her second baby, leaving her with postnatal depression. His heart attack came without warning while he was filling his trolley with onions.

Violet told us the story through a heartbreaking mix of tears and laughter. Giving us a glimpse of what her father was like: how he refused to use the plastic bags, how cross he got that supermarkets still provided them. "Onions have skins, they don't need to be put in plastic bags." The hospital was less than a mile away but it was too late; he died before his body even hit the floor.

When no one else could understand what it was like to lose someone that unexpectedly, she did. Some of her early posts felt like she was talking to me. Just me, and my glass of cheap wine. Telling me that it would be OK, eventually. Because everything's OK in the end.

She was the sister I never had. Sometimes I dreamt that we really were sisters, torn apart by some evil force. It wasn't out of the realm of possibility; we were both named after flowers, after all.

Pathetically, I feel the backs of my eyes begin to sting. Doesn't she care? Doesn't she realise what she's created, how much I depend on her? Doesn't she feel any sense of responsibility to her audience?

In the office, I've barely got my coat off before Nicola, head of the testing team, rushes up to me.

"Hi Lily. It's Mo's birthday today," she says. I'm glad she hasn't asked me about my weekend—it means I don't have to tell her that I didn't speak to a single adult for its duration. Unless you count the girl at the till in the soft-play centre, who only grunted at me. "Can you sort a card and a cake at some point?"

"Sure," I reply. She seems stressed. I'm about to ask her if she's OK, but she stalks back to her desk before I have the chance, leaving a twenty-pound note in my palm. Everyone here has been stressed lately. I look out of the window behind my desk, but it's started to rain, an early December drizzle setting in. I'll go later.

After filling my water bottle and making a cup of filter coffee, I sit at my desk and cross my fingers, hoping that there's nothing too taxing on my to-do list today. Ben is in Germany this week with our reseller, which means it should be relatively quiet in the office. My job title is Office Manager, but the truth is I'm a glorified receptionist. Just the phone to answer, the post to sort, and a few little admin things to attend to.

Sometimes, it feels like the hours I spend at work are pointlessly exchanged for money, like I'm being paid to sit at a desk and just exist. I have no projects of my own, no chance to be proactive. I am paid to sit here and do what I'm told, when people who are busier than me have time to tell me what to do.

It makes the days drag, but I don't mind. They could pay me to sit in the basement and I'd do it. I'm so grateful to have this job. Ben only gave it to me because I broke down at the end of my interview, told him how I was a widow with a young child. He took pity on me. He's boastful about the fact he runs an "ethical business" and worthy causes are a passion of his. I'm happy to be one. Today I'm especially grateful for the empty hours at this desk. Just me and a computer. In other words, plenty of time for me to work out what's happened to Violet.

I check again, but all her social media accounts are still missing. I didn't realise it was that easy to delete everything. I search for her username on Twitter and a few people have tweeted her, asking where she is. Some of the less clued up ones have sent messages telling her that her YouTube account doesn't seem to be working, as though they haven't figured out that she's taken it down. But none of the messages have been responded to.

I try to remember her last vlog. A normal day with the kids—Skye was at school, of course, and Lula was off nursery as it was a Friday. She had finally learnt how to ride her bike, so Violet, baby Marigold and Lula had taken off to their usual spot in Regent's Park to make the most of the winter sunshine. In fact, that was the title of the video. An unassuming day. Boring even, if you weren't as invested in the family as I am. I remember Violet complaining that Marigold had been up feeding for most of the night, but other than that she seemed on good form. No sign of the postnatal depression that had first drawn me to her, and inspired the name of her YouTube account.

Violet is Blue.

Violet isn't blue anymore, Violet is gone.

"Anyone there?"

I look up at the sound of Susie's voice.

"You were miles away!" she says, smiling down at me. Sometimes I think she's the only one here who truly sees me as a person, not just a piece of office furniture. She's holding her mug but she clocks mine, the half cup of coffee left. "Oh, you've already got one."

"Doesn't matter," I say, "I'll come with you. Good weekend?"

We walk to the kitchen together. She tells me about a disastrous Tinder date, and as always I'm wide-eyed at her antics. Our lives couldn't be more different. Her: thirty-five, single and loving it, head of marketing with precisely zero interest in pushing children out, her life a whirlwind of parties and lovely dinners out and dates with unsuitable men in their twenties. Me: twenty-seven, single mother of one, with precisely zero social life. We only met eight months ago, when Susie joined the firm. But we clicked, and I know we'll be friends for life.

"How was yours then?" she says, as she spoons three teaspoons of sugar into her mug.

"Oh fine," I say. "You know, non-stop excitement. Lots of soft-play hell. The usual. Sylvia was meant to come round on Saturday for a bit, so I could start trying to think about Christmas shopping, but she's got a bad cold."

"You know I'll always take him off your hands if you need a break, Lil," Susie says, slopping milk into her coffee. "I'm honestly not that bad with kids. I've only nearly killed my niece, like, once."

"Thanks," I say. "I'll bear it in mind."

"You all right?" Susie says, eyeing me. "You seem a bit quiet today."

"Yes," I reply. "I'm fine, it's just . . . You know that blogger I like? The . . ."

"One who makes her money by pimping her kids out all over the Internet?"

"Pimping out's a bit strong . . ." I reply. "But yes, her."

"What about her?"

"She's gone missing."

"Eh?"

"She's deleted her YouTube channel, all her social media accounts, everything. Just wiped them. No warning she was going to do it. Do you think she's OK?"

"Probably come to her senses," Susie replies, rummaging in the office complimentary fruit bowl, another of my responsibilities. "Ugh, these apples are all soft."

"Sorry. I'll get some more when I nip out to get Mo's birthday cake. I'm really worried about her. She had PND after her second baby was born, what if it's come back? Her daughter isn't even three months old yet; she said in one of her last blogs that she's not much of a sleeper . . . It must be exhausting having three children to look after."

"Oh yes, really exhausting, especially if you've got a secret nanny running around in the background making everything you do look effortless."

I swallow.

"I told you, no one proved she has a nanny, that was just a rumor on GoMamas."

"Why are you so worried?" Susie takes a bite from one of the apples, screwing her face up as she chews it. "She'll probably change her mind in an hour and bring everything back up online."

"Maybe," I say, but I'm not convinced.

Back at my desk, I Google "Violet Young," filtering by the last twenty-four hours to see if any of the news websites have commented on her disappearance. After all, she's a celebrity in her own right—one million YouTube subscribers makes her more famous than some TV stars. But there's nothing, just the post on GoMamas that I saw last night. I go to her husband Henry's Twitter page, to see if there's anything there. His last tweet is from Saturday morning, a link to his Instagram feed. I click on it.

My screen is flooded with the image of Violet, sitting propped up in their giant bed, Marigold attached to her breast, Lula on her lap, munching on what looks like a chocolate croissant, chocolate all over her face. Archie is the same. He can't eat anything without smearing it all over himself, his clothes, his hair and me.

I find it exhausting, the non-stop wiping, but seeing Lula in this picture makes me smile. She's such an adorable child.

17

Violet's mass of bleached hair is piled on top of her head in a kind of artfully scruffy bun, her almost-black roots poking through. There are dark circles under her eyes, but as always, she looks beautiful. She *is* beautiful, her eyes impossibly large and bright blue. I reach out and trace the contours of her face on the screen. I know her image so well, every millimetre of it. I've seen her and analysed her from every angle. I know she has a scar on her left shoulder, slightly raised, that she tries to hide under her bra strap. I know she has a tiny hole on one side of her nose, from a long-removed piercing. Her left eyebrow is higher and more arched than her right. I've seen her nearly naked, watched her document her pregnant stomach as it grew, taken in the silvery stretch marks that spread across the underside of her tummy like spiderwebs.

She's smiling at Henry behind the camera, one arm tucked under Marigold's floppy little body. Marigold's eyes are half closed, her lips clamped firmly around Violet's left nipple.

I read the caption Henry's attached to the picture.

Breakfast for all! #normalisebreastfeeding

There's no sign of Skye. Violet said in one of her vlogs last week that she's taken to eating breakfast at the new desk in her bedroom. A sign of maturity, she's outgrown us all. I loved that vlog. The look on Skye's face as they set up the desk in her room, overlooking the garden, was just wonderful. I must have watched it five times that evening.

I click on Henry's Instagram profile. He's not as popular as Violet, of course, but he's still got more than 100,000 followers. Mostly women, mostly mums, all a little bit jealous of her and in love with him. After all, she has the perfect life: three cherubic daughters, a husband in his forties with thick hair and an enviable job as creative director of the men's equivalent of *Vogue*, a huge townhouse in Islington, and an army of adoring fans.

Her life is perfect. So why has she left us?

YVONNE

"Beautiful," I say, beaming my most encouraging smile.

When I first met Simon, I told him I shot people for a living. It was a good test of his mental agility. Most people looked puzzled for a few seconds, but eventually figured it out. Simon took a little longer than I would have liked, but he got there in the end.

When he pulled out his phone to take my number that first day, I noticed the screensaver image on it was one of him with a small boy on his shoulders, and my heart sunk. But he spotted me looking, and told me that the boy was his nephew, Callum. His *best little bud.*

The joy in Simon's eyes as he described him, that was it for me— hook, line and sinker. Simon was so handsome, so young, and I was thirty-eight. I thought fate had finally dealt me a decent hand.

It's a typical newborn shoot: a first-time mother with nerves on the edge, a father who looks completely knackered, a tiny seven-day-old baby who understandably just wants to sleep, feed and cry. A photographer who hates the lot of them for their perfect life. No, that's not entirely fair. I don't hate them for their perfect life; I hate them for not realising how lucky they are to have it.

"Could we . . . could we try some naked ones?" the mother asks. Her name's Jackie. I stifle a sigh. Naked ones are always difficult—the second you undress the poor baby they start screaming. *It's winter,* I want to say. *Would you want to be photographed naked?*

People can be so selfish, even with their children. But I'm paid to do what I'm told.

"Of course!" I say, smiling instead. "I'll just get my blow-fan out of the car, don't want baby getting cold."

I lay my camera down on their buttoned footstool. Velvet; how long before that gets puked on, I wonder? Hello bitterness, my old friend. Outside on the driveway I allow myself a minute or two of deep breathing, looking back at their house. The sky is clear, the air invigorating. I love this time of year.

As I reach into the boot of my battered Peugeot, I feel a twinge in my stomach that brings me up short. Far too early for it to mean anything, of course, but still. I pat my tummy encouragingly. We did it doggy style on the sofa yesterday—almost less dignified than I could bear, but I'm sure it gives things an extra push in the right direction. One of the women on the forum said you should get your husband to have an espresso right before you do the deed, but Simon hates coffee. I think about the Stella he drank beforehand, and just hope the things weren't drunk.

Back in the living room, Jackie has stripped the baby down to just his nappy. I take one of the blankets from the arm of their sofa, and arrange it on the footstool.

"Here," I say. "Lie him down there. Let me just get the heater going . . ."

Once it's plugged in and blowing in his direction, I carefully remove the nappy. The skin on his little legs is so soft, he barely feels human. Thankfully he seems unbothered by his sudden nakedness— he gives a little squawk of displeasure, but then yawns and settles down to sleep, his legs and arms tucked under him, head resting on the blanket.

I resist the urge to lean down and kiss his tiny cheek.

"I gave him a quick feed when you were at the car," Jackie says. "Seems to have settled him."

"Well done, Mum," I say, forcing a smile. Does she even know what she has? "You're a natural already."

The husband—Will, I think—looks over at her, eyes wide with something I can't put my finger on. He's older and relatively attractive, although he's got a weak chin. I straighten up my shoulders and grin at him, letting my eyes meet his for a little too long. His mouth twitches into a confused smile and he looks away. It's an old habit. Sometimes, I don't even realise I'm doing it.

"Right," I say, "if you two could just step back a bit, you're reflected in the window at the moment . . ."

"Sorry," Jackie says. She shuffles backwards but doesn't take her eyes off the wrinkly baby on the footstool. I snap away, leaning over. My skirt rides up. I hear Will give a short cough behind me.

"Would you, would you like another drink, Yvonne?" he says. "We have other herbal teas . . ."

"Yes," Jackie interrupts. "Rooibos, chamomile . . ."

I stand up straight.

"I'm absolutely fine, thank you," I say, smiling at them both. "I think I have all I need actually . . ."

I hold out the back of the camera to show them, flicking through some of the shots on the screen.

"Oh!" Jackie says, tears welling. "That one's gorgeous!"

I lock the picture she's pointed at with the button on my camera.

"We've got some fantastic ones," I say. "One of my most successful shoots for a while, in fact. Well done, Mum and Dad! And baby too, of course."

I lean over him, picking up his babygrow, then pause, straightening up. Not my place.

"Er, you can get him dressed again now," I say, handing Jackie his outfit.

She's oblivious to me anyway. She scoops him up straight away and lays him on the sofa, replacing the nappy and re-dressing him. He's still asleep. I look away.

"So," Jackie says, holding him across her body. Will is lingering in the doorway to the "drawing room" as they grandly announced it when I first arrived, looking uncomfortable. I know from the tone of her voice what's coming next.

"Do you have children yourself?"

21

I sniff, zipping up my camera bag. Why do they always ask? Why do they think it's *OK* to ask?

"'Not yet!" I say, trying to sound happy about it. "Just focusing on my career for now."

"But you're married?" she says, staring at my ring. I twist it around my finger, hiding the size of the stone. Don't want her to pity me. From the corner of my eye, I notice Will slip from the room.

"Yes," I say. "So hopefully sometime soon . . ."

Her eyes narrow a little as she smiles at me. She can't tell how old I am, but she's trying to work it out. I'm grateful as ever for the roundness of my cheeks, the thickness of my hair. It was worth going through the puppy fat stage as a teenager—after a growth spurt when I was fifteen, I came out the other side curvy in a good way. Simon said I looked like Kelly Brook when I first met him. I don't particularly like being compared to other women but I know in his eyes it was a huge compliment.

"Is your husband a photographer too?"

I frown. As usual, she wants me to stay for a chat. I'm not paid for that, but since I started doing private photography I've realised that half the job is counselling. It's the reason I gave up weddings earlier this year—having to calm down hysterical brides, deal with the even more hysterical mothers of the brides and fend off drunken best men— it all became too exhausting.

"No, he's a personal trainer," I say. "Works at the Peter Daunt gym in Chiswick. The ladies-only one." We're in Richmond, she'll know how exclusive it is.

"'Oh wow," she says. "Don't all the celebs go there? How amazing, a personal trainer. No wonder you're in such great shape. What a good-looking couple you must be."

"I don't know about that." I laugh.

"It's so hard, you know," Jackie says. I look at her but she's staring down at the footstool. "I never imagined . . . I never imagined it would be this hard. You see these women online . . . I've been following them for ages, you know, since I found out I was pregnant . . . Violet Young, Mama Perkins, all those women on social media. They make it look so easy!" A single tear rolls down her cheek, landing on the baby's head.

"Last night we sat down to dinner, and Zachary started crying, and Will and I got into a big argument about whether or not we should always go to him when he cries . . . the midwife said we should, but my mother-in-law told Will it was important to get them into a routine early, get them used to settling themselves as much as possible. So long as they've had enough milk . . . I don't know. How can you ignore that sound? It's impossible."

She runs out of breath, takes a step back and slumps on the sofa, covering her face with her one free hand. I straighten up and sit down next to her, putting my arm around her. *You know what's hard?* I think to myself. *Wanting a baby so much that sometimes you think you'll die of the longing. That's what's hard.*

"It's only day seven!" I say, instead. "You're doing so well. You really are. Look at him. He's beautiful. And Will adores you, I can see that . . ."

"I don't think he adores me like *this*, all frumpy and hormonal. And he wants his mother to come and stay with us now. To 'help out'! I tried to tell him, I don't want help. I don't want all these visitors. I just want it to be the three of us . . . When Violet Young had her second baby, she didn't let anyone visit for a fortnight. I know because we used to live next door to her. They call it a babymoon—that's what I wanted to do too, but . . ."

"You used to live next door to Violet Young?"

"Yes," she says, sniffing. "In Islington. It was Will's house—the one he had before he met me. We sold it when I got pregnant. Wanted something detached, and my family are in Richmond . . . that's another thing, he's still making jokes about being dragged south of the river."

"Were you friends with Violet?"

Jackie looks up at me, confused.

"No, not really," she says. "Friendly enough, as neighbors. She was lovely though. Always rushing about, we didn't get to chat much. Why do you ask? Do you know her?"

"Oh," I say, squeezing her shoulders. "I did. Once. A long time ago. But listen, you're doing a great job. Look at him, he's happy and that's all that matters."

I stroke the baby's downy hair with my finger, and make a mental note to save Jackie and Will's details in my phone. You never know what might come in handy.

GoMamas

Topics>Mummy Vloggers>Violet is Blue
4 December 2017

Coldteafordays
Guys still no sign of her . . .

Horsesforcourses
It is super weird. I hope she's OK. Does anyone know, if you delete your YT account, whether or not you can get it back again? Cos that's a lot of subscribers to lose . . .

Coldteafordays
I'm so surprised. I was sure her next big "thing" was going to be Henry quitting his job and joining her. You know, like King Daddy and Queen Mumma. But less cringe. Not this!

Neverforget
Violet's got her book deal now. She doesn't need YouTube any-more. She's made her millions. She was becoming so boring anyway. Just her and her perfect life. She lost all relatability when she started pushing that "read to your kids for ten minutes a day" campaign. Yeah thanks, love, we all do that ALREADY.

Coldteafordays
I loved that campaign! And I don't agree her life is perfect. She was saying just last week how she was struggling with Goldie's cluster feeding.

Horsesforcourses
Oh god, cluster feeding is THE PITS! I'm so glad those days are behind me.

Neverforget

Oh right, a five minute moan squeezed in to twenty minutes of "look at my perfect life, even my dishwasher is a design classic but oh god does anyone else's perfect husband not know how to load it properly hashtag the struggle is real"

Coldteafordays

Think you're being a bit harsh, Never. She was nearly crying in that clip.

Sadandalone

That clip made me cry.

Neverforget

Rolls eyes emoticon

Coldteafordays

Henry's accounts are still active. But nothing since Saturday. What does it MEAN?

Neverforget

It means she's laughing at us all. Bet it's some kind of publicity stunt. She must be well gutted that the papers haven't bothered to report it yet. I'll bet you a hundred quid it's part of her marketing strategy for the book.

Coldteafordays

Do you think? Really? I'd be so disappointed. I was really looking forward to reading her book. I had terrible PND with my first and her blog really helped me.

Neverforget

It's obvious. She's going to pretend she's had some kind of mental breakdown, then Henry will publish a blog post saying she's taking some time off from YouTube, and that she'll be back when she's feeling better, and then she'll magically reappear to share her story of courage and survival just in time for the book to come out.

Sadandalone

I think you're wrong. She's the opposite of that cynical!

Neverforget

You're so naive. You don't think that every little "event" in their life isn't carefully choreographed to get maximum clicks?

Sadandalone

I'm not saying she doesn't know how to make the most of her content. I'm just saying, I don't think she'd do a disappearing act as a publicity stunt. It doesn't feel like "her."

Coldteafordays

I agree. But then again I suppose we don't really know her. We just think we do . . .

LILY

Anna opens the door as soon as I press the bell. She's been waiting for me, as usual.

"Sorry, so sorry," I say, breathlessly. "Hello monkey!"

Archie barrels towards me, burying his head against my legs.

"Mummy," he says, standing back and regarding me seriously. "I did a cat drawing."

"He did indeed," Anna says, smiling and passing me his bag plus a crumpled piece of paper. "A cat in a neckerchief! Quite the artist."

"Oh it's fabuousous!" Archie giggles at my mispronunciation. "Thanks," I say, smiling back at Anna. "I'm so sorry, the Piccadilly line was down . . . God, I've had a right nightmare, three buses it took me, and . . . well you don't want the details."

"Oh don't worry," Anna replies. I know she's taken pity on me, that really she should be charging me five pounds for every five minutes I'm late, as per her contract. "Pete's taken the kids to karate anyway so it was just me and we've had some lovely quiet time reading. How are you?"

"Good," I say. "I'm . . ." I look down at Archie, who's edging closer to the gate. He's desperate to get home, of course, to feed his goldfish Spike. The only pet mummy could afford; just another sign of how I'm failing him as a parent. "Just a bit knackered this week actually. Ha, and it's only Monday!"

"Mother's prerogative," Anna says. "Well, Arch had a brilliant day, didn't you, lovely? We went to playgroup this morning, then to the park this afternoon to collect some pine cones to paint tomorrow. We'll be making Christmas decorations with them."

"And mine was the biggest!" squeaks Archie, his round eyes flashing with excitement.

I stroke the top of his head.

"How brilliant," I say. "Aren't you lucky?"

"See you tomorrow, buddy," Anna says, closing the door.

As we walk the short distance back to our flat, my thoughts drift back to Violet, wondering where she is now. I wanted to ask Anna if she had ever seen her YouTube channel, but something held me back, thought she might find me weird. She probably doesn't have time, to be fair. Too busy looking after children to watch videos of other women looking after children. I quite often find myself wondering why I prefer watching Violet playing with her kids rather than playing with my own, but the guilt stops me digging too deeply.

"All the houses have lights up," Archie whines, pointing at the windows. We pass the cute alms' houses that were originally built for the poor. There's no chance I'd be able to afford to buy one now, despite being poor. This part of Acton is pretty enough, away from the high road with its garages and chicken shops. Just living a few streets back makes such a difference to the noise levels. I wonder if I'd be able to sleep somewhere as quiet as this—I've got used to the dull rumble of trains in the background, the sirens that blare past our flat, the drunk and disorderly shouting outside our door. To anyone else, the noises would be annoying, but to me they're strangely comforting. A reminder that I'm not completely alone.

"I told you." My voice comes out harsher than intended. "We'll get some at the weekend."

Archie gives a dull mumble of acceptance then races ahead of me as we turn into our street.

"Careful, Arch!" I run after him and he comes to a sudden stop at the edge of the pavement as a van hurtles past, making my heart lurch. "Jesus Christ! How many times have I told you!"

"Sorry, Mummy," he says, looking down at his feet then back up at me. I shouldn't have shouted. He points. "I wanted to see the lights."

I look over at the tiny house opposite. The entire thing is covered in Christmas lights—from a wonky inflatable Santa perched on the roof, to a sprightly reindeer leaping across the front door. In the minuscule front garden a man is standing on a footstool, carefully wrapping illuminated icicles around a naked tree.

"Wow," Archie says, his tiny mouth a perfect "o."

I stand for a few minutes, transfixed myself. It's tacky, over the top and an eye-watering waste of electricity, but like all mothers, the things my child finds magical I do too, and I can't help but smile. The man spots us, looks up and gives a little wave. Archie bows his head and wraps his arm around my legs, suddenly shy.

"Looks great," I call to the man across the road, but he's turned away, back to his job. In the window I see a woman with hair pulled back in a tight ponytail, carefully positioning a candelabra in the middle of the windowsill. Behind her is a Christmas tree, and reflected in the mirror on the side wall, a sofa, two small children wrapped under a blanket, gazing at their parents as they create their very own Winter Wonderland.

I tug on Archie's hand and pull him back down the road towards our empty, lonely flat. Christmas is without doubt the worst time of year.

* * *

When Archie is in bed after an unmatched number of reads of *What the Ladybird Heard*, I take my glass of wine and open my laptop. A surge of hope floods through me and I cross my fingers that she's changed her mind. It's been at least an hour since I last checked Instagram on the sly while preparing Archie's bedtime snack: "Twiglet bread"—toast with Marmite.

The sense of hope and optimism evaporates instantly as I load Violet's YouTube page to find the same blank screen again. I click on Henry's Instagram but there's nothing new there either. Again, I

Google her name, and finally there's a tiny piece about it on one of the trashiest gossip websites. Still not mainstream enough to be of interest to the newspapers, but I read it in a rush.

Violet Young, of Violet is Blue, *shut down her popular YouTube channel this Sunday 3 December. The mummy vlogger, who gained legions of fans thanks to her honest and frank discussions around the issue of postnatal depression, deleted all her social media accounts with no warning in the early hours of Sunday. Earlier this year, Violet went offline for a month, explaining to fans that the pressure of daily vlogging had become too much. Tubers contacted Violet's management at Dream Big, who declined to comment. Violet's husband Henry Blake, who works for glossy men's magazine* The Edit, *has also not updated his social media since Saturday, although his accounts remain live.*

I Google the Dream Big agency. The staff call themselves Talent Enablers. It takes a few clicks before I find Violet's manager, a pencil-thin-faced chap called Noah. He's wearing a polka dot bow tie in his picture.

He only represents a handful of clients, and Violet is clearly his star. Her profile photo is one I recognise: her looking sombre in black and white, taken by one of the world's leading fashion photographers. It's from an interview she did last year for a fashion magazine running a feature on the "celebrities of the future," as though they were the first to discover the power of influencers. They were so behind the times, really. I try to look away from her doleful eyes and focus on the biography underneath.

Violet, thirty-five, lives with her husband and three children in north London. A successful magazine journalist for years, she turned to daily vlogging when suffering from postnatal depression, following the birth of her second daughter, Lula. Frustrated by the lack of support from the NHS, she set out to change the way mothers with PND are treated, setting up unique peer-based support strate-gies to connect struggling women to others in their local area. Her popular coaching sessions providing practical support to mothers sell out within minutes. She spends her days recording her attempts to keep the family alive and clothed, while resisting the urge to drink gin at lunchtime.

YouTube: 1.7m subscribers
Instagram: 800k followers
Twitter: 400k followers
Popular videos:
Let's talk about sex
Making time for me
Baby turns three!

I click on the link for her "Let's talk about sex" video. I remember it well—mostly because Henry was in it too. It was a big thing for him; he doesn't usually like to feature in her more personal face-to-face videos. It was a sponsored post though, by a condom company, and I'm sure the money was huge. The two of them had a frank discussion about their lack of sex life since Lula was born, but in some ways it just made me think how fertile they both must be to have three kids if they're only doing it on "special occasions," as they claimed. I remember there was a lot of awkward chat about Violet's breasts—how breastfeeding had taken its toll. At the end there was an even more awkward few minutes where they discussed whether or not to have a proper snog on screen to round things off, claiming the last time they'd done so was back at their wedding (Carwell House in the Cotswolds; Skye was bridesmaid). As far as I remember, they gave it a good shot, but both dissolved into giggles after a few seconds.

I miss the sound of her laugh: that slightly sarcastic, resigned cackle that reassured you that she was making it all up as she went along too.

The screen flickers as the link loads, but takes me to the same Page Not Found error. I don't know what I was expecting really; I suppose I

32

was hopeful that it might have been hosted elsewhere, that some part of her was still out there on the Internet, that I'd be able to see her one last time, if this really was "it."

I sigh, picking up my phone and opening Instagram again. I scroll through my feed, and Henry's last photo from Saturday appears again. I stroke Violet's face in the picture with my hand, then thumb down to see the comments.

Hey, are you guys OK? Why the radio silence?

Come back we miss yoooooouuuu!

Where are you guys!!!

And then the more earnest.

Hi Henry. Hope everything's all right with you all. I know Vi has been having a tough time with Marigold's cluster feeding. I had the same with my son. If you need to have a week off, some time to yourselves, we totally understand. It would be lovely if you could update us all, just to reassure us that everything's OK, but of course, take all the time you need. We'll be waiting for you when you get back. Lots of love xxxxxxx

I baulk slightly at the number of kisses, my eye tracing backwards to see who's left such an over-the-top comment, and so late at night. There's a second of confusion when I see the username in front of it, and a split second of denial before I accept that it was me.

I have completely forgotten I wrote it.

I grab the wine glass from the coffee table and march towards the kitchen, throwing its contents in the sink. Enough. I need to get a grip. I think back to earlier this year, how close I came to losing everything. The way I let Archie down. I can't end up there again.

Over in the corner of the kitchen, the bottles are huddled around the over-flowing recycling bin, guilting me. I switch the kettle on, reach at the back of the cupboard above it for some herbal teabags. I know I have some somewhere, from when my friend Vicky stayed. They were fancy: beetroot, ginger and green tea. Eventually I find them, and decide to ignore the sell-by date that tells me they went off a year ago.

Back in the living room, I blow on the surface of the tea as the steam settles on my nose. I cradle my laptop again, and I type. It might not be appropriate, but I have to know what's happened to her. I have enough going on in my life without this nagging unease following me around all the time.

There's a delay as the words I've typed appear in the search bar. I'm not sure it'll be easy to get an answer, but it's worth a try.

Where does Violet Young live?

YVONNE

I'm upstairs in the bedroom, examining my chest in the wardrobe mirror, when Simon comes home.

"Von!" he calls up the stairs. "You all right, babe?"

My left breast is definitely aching a little more than normal. I cup it with one hand. It feels heavy, doughy, tender. But that might just be my bra, which has left red welts in the side of my skin. Perhaps I should go wireless.

"Up here," I say, grabbing my bra. "I'm coming." I put it back on and pull my t-shirt over my head, glancing at the bedside clock. 8.42pm. He's late, but that's normal these days. He's taken on extra personal training shifts to help pay for our IVF. After our three rounds of NHS IVF failed, every spare pound we have goes into the ISA. Simon thinks it's amusing to say it stands for "infertility savings account."

Downstairs, I find him in the kitchen, a pan already sizzling on the hob.

"Hello," I say, wrapping my arms around him and pulling him towards me. He kisses me. "Good day?"

"Better now I'm home," he says. "Tuna steaks all right?"

"Amazing," I say. "Let me give you a hand."

"How was your shoot?"

I chop a leek, thinking of tiny Zachary and his impossibly soft skin.

"Oh it was fine," I say, swallowing. "Standard. Their house was amazing though. Double-fronted, with a proper walled driveway at the front."

I pause.

"How much?" Simon says, looking up at me. "Richmond, was it?"

I sometimes forget how naive he is. But at the same time, I don't want him to lose that—it's what makes him special. Pure, almost.

"Oh, God knows. Millions. It was a nice house. How was your new client? You were back later than expected."

He shifts slightly, pushing the garlic around in the wok.

"Yeah, good. Sorry, she was a chatty one. Tried to get away as quickly as possible . . . She booked in for ten sessions at the end though. She's just had a baby actually."

"How old was she?" Simon doesn't notice the edge to my voice.

"Dunno, maybe thirty? She used to be relatively fit, but she had a Caesarean and she's upset about the state of her abs."

"What's her name?"

Simon stops stir-frying and turns to look at me in surprise. I'm not usually this interested in his clients.

"Sarah. Why?"

I ignore his question. Younger than me, *and* she has a baby. I close my eyes and allow the bitterness to subside. "I'll set the table."

After we've eaten, Simon disappears for a shower and I take the opportunity to check his phone, which had been lighting up repeatedly on the radiator cover behind him throughout our meal. He doesn't know I have the password—I watched him tap it in once and never forgot it. Our wedding anniversary. He's such a romantic.

There's a message from his brother giving details of the football class Simon has apparently volunteered to take Callum to, and then one from this *Sarah Price*, of course.

Thanks so much for such a great session! I feel a million times better than before—you're a genius. Can't wait for next week x

I delete the message, replacing Simon's phone in the exact spot he left it, then follow him upstairs.

* * *

After we've made love, I lie there with a pillow under my bottom, my head awkwardly wedged against Simon's armpit. His chest is hairless and brown and perfectly taut. I'm keen to update my app with all the details of tonight's attempt, but he says it's unromantic and gets sulky if I do so. He's got a big thing about cuddling after sex, when I usually just want to get up and go to the loo. Perhaps that's where I've been going wrong.

"I love you," I whisper, breathing in the smell of his shower gel. He's the only other man I've ever said it to. Three little words, but they were always out of reach before I met him. It was like a tap that had been stuck for years and when I finally turned it on, I found I couldn't turn it off again. What is it that makes me love him so much? I hope it isn't just gratitude; gratitude that he loves me back, that he treats me well, that he doesn't play games with my feelings.

I can't lose him.

"Love you too, babe," he replies. His eyes are half closed. He usually falls asleep straight after sex, but tonight I feel more insecure than normal, and want to chat.

"Do you think it worked?"

He shifts slightly, turning round to face me, regarding me with his big brown eyes. His hair, usually so meticulously styled, is messed up, but it just makes him look better. I imagine lucky postpartum Sarah when she first met Simon, realising that yes, he was as handsome as you'd expect a personal trainer to be; all her dreams come true.

"I don't know, baby," he says. Does he really mean "I don't care?" "We've got the appointment in a fortnight. I've got loads of extra PT work coming in. Try not to worry."

Another wave of guilt. I allow it to wash over me, then I swallow and take a deep breath. I've done it for him, just as much as I have for me.

"I just . . ." I reply. "I just want us to be a proper family."

It's not too much to ask, is it?

"Yeah, me too." But his voice is soft and unfocused, and I can tell I'm losing him to sleep already. I lie there watching him as he relaxes, feeling his chest rise and fall underneath my palm.

Once he's deeply asleep, I untangle myself from his arms, pulling the duvet away from him and staring in the hazy light from the streetlamp outside at his body.

I hope we'll always feel this way about each other. My biggest fear is us growing old and complacent, like so many of my friends seem to have done.

I roll over to my side of the bed, and pull out my iPhone. Simon sleeps through anything—the advantage of an untroubled mind, I suppose. I haven't had a chance to check since he got home, but as suspected, Violet's social media accounts are still missing. I check Henry's Instagram, but there's nothing new there either. Just tons of comments from the sycophants, begging them to return. I hesitate for a few minutes, wondering whether or not to do it, but in the end I can't resist adding my thoughts. I need to know what's happened.

Yes, Henry, how are things?

14 January 2017
From: gottheblues@hotmail.com
To: violet@violetisblue.com

Life's not fair.

That's what I tell myself.

But it's more fair for some people, isn't it, Violet? It's more fair for you. I wonder if it's because you were born beautiful? Is that why everything in your life has slotted into place so perfectly? First the cool job, then the handsome husband, then the beautiful children, then your struggle with bereavement and PND and that clever decision: to monetise it by talking about it online. Why not? When life gives you lemons . . . It was a stroke of genius.

And that's why I admire you so much, Violet. But there are people who don't believe that your "struggle" was genuine. You do know that, don't you? They think you made it all up—that your postnatal depression was just a front, a clever marketing ploy to launch your YouTube channel, after the internet came and swallowed up your magazine career. I'm not so sure. I've seen the way you cry sometimes on camera and I can tell that you're not faking it.

But the weird thing is, no one would watch if I spilt my guts to all online. No one would care. Why is it that some people are born under rainclouds not rainbows? No matter what we do, nothing goes right for us.

I hope you sometimes think about us, Violet, as you sit there in your beautiful house surrounded by your beautiful family. The unlucky ones. You do know there are people out there who would kill for what you have?

What I wouldn't give to swap places with you, Violet. What I wouldn't give . . .

GoMamas

Topics>Mummy Vloggers>Violet is Blue>Violet's Whereabouts
5 December 2017

Sadandalone
Anyone know where Violet lives? I'm really worried about her.

Horsesforcourses
Nope, only that it's somewhere in north London. Why, what are you going to do?

Lasttotheparty
She lives in Islington. Not sure where exactly—one of the roads off Upper Street I think.

Neverforget
I was going to ask the same thing. How can we find out?

Horsesforcourses
You can check on Companies House—Violet is Blue is a registered brand, right? So they must have a listing there. Might have their home address details on.

Sadandalone
I tried that, but it's just some address in Essex. I Googled it and it's an accountant's office.

Horsesforcourses
Bugger.

Sadandalone
What about Skye's uniform? Any way of identifying it and

working out what school she goes to? Might help narrow down the area?

Horsesforcourses
Are you mad? What are you going to do? Hang around outside her school until the end of the day and follow her home?

Lasttotheparty
Not such a bad idea! Ha. Would that technically be stalking though?

Coldteafordays
Jesus. You can't do that!

Lasttotheparty
Look guys, I've blown up that image Henry posted of Skye from last year—her first day at school. You can definitely recognise the badge from it—it's an oak tree with St Edward's written around the top.

Neverforget
And the prize for biggest stalker of the day goes to . . . Last!

Lasttotheparty
Ha ha, very funny. I've looked it up and it's just up by Essex Road station . . .

LILY

My phone flashes in my hand. A text message from Susie.

Where are you really? If you're actually sick and not just skiving, I'll pop over after work and cook you some soup! Sus x

I shove my phone back in the pocket of my navy coat. Susie wouldn't understand, she'd think I was crazy. It's taken three different Tube lines to get me here, but finally, I emerge at Angel station. I haven't been to Islington for years. Upper Street is packed with creative types, headphones firmly stuck in ears, heads down over their phones, rushing past as though there's just nowhere near enough time in the world for them to get to where they need to be.

I've been up since five, mulling over my plan in my mind, trying to decide whether or not to go through with it. I decided, at about 6.05am, just before Archie the human alarm clock screamed for my attention, that I had to. I owe it to them, especially after everything that's happened. And I need to know that they're all right. If everyone stood by and did nothing when they thought someone might be in trouble, then what kind of world would we live in? As well as that, having a mission—to find out what's happened to her—has given me a sense of purpose I've been missing. But it's a positive one this time.

I stop off at a tiny cafe just opposite the station for a cup of coffee and a chocolate croissant. As usual, I haven't had breakfast today, but the adrenalin from what I'm doing has made me hungry. My eyes continually scan the people around me, just in case I might spot her. Is this her local? Does she come here often? I looked at all the different

42

restaurants and bars she followed on Twitter when they first moved to Islington, Googling each one in turn to see what they were like. I don't remember this place being on the list.

There was a pub though, a really cool pub that had a microbrewery attached, down one of the back roads. Somewhere only locals would find. There were pictures of them all there too, before Marigold was born. Skye, Lula in her buggy . . . she was so young then, so cute, the spit of her dad. Violet sitting on one of the picnic tables outside, her feet on the bench, swigging from a plastic half pint cup. Those wide blue eyes twinkling, a nose of sudden freckles, enjoying the best stretch of sunshine in London we've had for years. I can't remember the caption—something about the beer. I'll admit I was upset about the beer, as she was breastfeeding. But then someone left a comment chastising her for drinking it, and she replied that it was alcohol-free.

I should have trusted her, known she knew what she was doing. I let her down.

"Where are you now?" I mutter under my breath.

"Sorry, love?"

I look up. The man behind the cafe counter is holding out my change.

"Oh, nothing," I say, taking it from him. "I was miles away."

Back on the street, I stand and eat the croissant in three giant mouthfuls, trying not to think about the three pounds that sixty seconds of pleasure cost me. I sip the coffee slowly, taking my phone out of my pocket and using Google Maps to guide me. It's a bit of a walk to St Edwards but thankfully I should be just in time. I'm grateful again to have a childminder who's prepared to take Archie from 7am. I don't know how people who send their children to nurseries manage it.

As I draw closer to the school, I feel my heart beginning to throb in my chest. I don't know why I'm so nervous. I wonder if she reads all her comments, if she has her favorite fans. Usually she just replies to one or two, with bland things like "thanks very much xoxo" and "you too! X." In fact, there's no proof that she leaves those comments at all. They're so generic they could easily be done by her management team. The thought makes me want to cry.

I can tell I'm close when I see them all: small people in green uniforms, being tugged along by harassed parents. My heart begins to thump. Am I really about to see her?

Following the directions on my phone, I round a corner and suddenly the school is in sight: a redbrick building, dating back to Victorian times no doubt, with several incongruous modern additions jutting out from each side of it. The gates are open, the small square car park at the front filled not with cars but with people. Parents chatting, kids running about. Noise, so much noise, but smiles too, blazoned across tiny faces, lighting up this winter morning.

I cross the road and linger next to a postbox, watching the coming and going. I've set myself an impossible task—the place is so crowded, the likelihood of me spotting Violet and Skye is minuscule. But I'm here now, so I try to think positively. If I don't see them this time, I'll just have to come back at 3.30pm when the kids get collected.

But then I turn around, leaning against the postbox and suddenly, there they are. On the other side of the road. I spot Skye's crazy ringlets first, bobbing along as she skips down the pavement. Slightly behind her is Henry.

Henry is doing the school run?

I swallow. He's too far away for me to make out the expression on his face, but he's alone. No sign of Violet, or the other kids.

I catch my breath, pull myself upright and wander towards them. I need to hear their conversation when they get to the school. Will one of the other parents ask how Violet is? I don't know how friendly she is with them all.

As Henry comes closer, I notice how terrible he looks. His face is dark as thunder, the bags under his eyes deep. Spurred on by curiosity, I find myself walking straight up to him, buried in a crowd of parents going the other way after dropping their kids off.

He's a few paces away now, and finally he looks up and speaks.

"Skye, come back!" he says, but his voice is a bark. Aggressive, irritated, threatening. Nothing like the man I've seen in the background of so many of Violet's videos. *King of the sarcastic eyebrow lift,* that's what she used to call him. But there was always a cheeky glint in his eye, the confidence that comes from growing up with money, and that same gaze of adoration whenever Violet was centre stage of proceedings. I suppose he did luck out—he's handsome, but she's a beauty. A beauty with brains too.

Skye stops short at her father's voice. They're just a metre or so away from me now, so I stand still on the pavement and fiddle with my phone, looking up and around me, pretending to be lost.

"Yes, Daddy," Skye says, and the sound of her sweet voice floods me with relief. She's the same Skye we all know and love. I want to jump on the forum and tell everyone, but I'm being ridiculous. Why wouldn't she be? She's only five. Whatever's going on with her mother's work is of no interest to her.

Oh Skye. You poor angel.

"You can go in yourself, can't you?" he says, but his voice is weary now, the anger gone. "Just go straight in, like I told you."

"Yes, Daddy," Skye says, but she's looking down. She gives a tiny sigh.

"I'm not sure about this," he says, but he's looking over her head. Several of the mothers seem to be staring at him, clearly as surprised as I am.

"Please, Daddy. It's the first rehearsal today!" she squeaks. "It's SO important! Please!"

He ruffles her hair, but I would have expected more: a hug and kiss at the very least. Violet and Skye have a sequence of hand gestures for a greeting, it's the cutest thing.

I turn away as Skye skips past me and races into the school gates, her bag swinging from her gloved hand. I can't believe he's let her go in alone, but to give him some credit, he does wait to make sure she's safely inside. Then he looks up, and there's a split second where our eyes meet. He frowns at me, a puzzled look on his face, but then he rolls his eyes and turns around, walking back in the direction he came.

* * *

I know this is what I came here to do, but I'm still quite surprised to find myself actually following him. It helps, of course, having an anonymous kind of face. Mid-length mousy brown hair. Average height, average looks. Nothing to make me stand out from the crowd.

I keep a few paces behind Henry, following him all the way back to Upper Street. I expect him to head for the Tube—after all, presumably he should be at work today—but he walks straight past it. Maybe he's getting the bus. If he gets on a bus, I won't bother to follow him. I know where he works anyway: everyone does. *The Edit* offices are in Mayfair, just off Berkeley Square. But he walks past the bus stop too.

Eventually, he stops outside a glass-fronted building. I hang back a little. It looks like a really posh cafe, or restaurant, on the ground floor of a relatively newly built office block. He fiddles with his phone and then puts it to his ear. My breath is coming quickly, steaming in the cold December air.

"I'm here," he says, but in sharp contrast to the anger I heard in his voice earlier, his tone is now resigned, pitiful even. "Where are you? I'll go in . . . See you in a bit . . . Skye was desperate to go to school. Probably for the best . . . bit of normality for her. OK . . . No, of course I haven't told anyone what's happened. The taxi is coming in twenty."

He hangs up, pushing open the door of the cafe. I wait for a minute or two before wandering past, hoping that he isn't looking out of the window as I do so. Inside, the cafe is almost empty. He's taken a seat in one corner, shrugged off his heavy winter coat and is gazing down at the menu.

There aren't enough people in the cafe for me to get away with going in there. If he sees me, he'll remember me from earlier. It's not beyond the realm of coincidence that I might be going into the same cafe as him, but I don't want to risk him getting suspicious.

Instead, I perch my bottom on the ledge at the corner of the cafe window, watching for whoever he's waiting for to arrive. It doesn't take long before a woman hurries past me. She's dressed head to toe in black: black high-heeled court shoes, black tights, a black woollen skirt and an oversized black coat. The only thing that isn't black is the huge

46

grey scarf wrapped around her neck. I can't see her face clearly, but her hair is cropped at her shoulders. Even from the back, she looks nothing like Violet. Violet is cool, edgy, the type to look good in dungarees. This woman is sophisticated, expensive looking, someone who'd never have chipped nail polish or greasy roots.

She walks into the cafe with a confidence you don't see very often. I hold my breath as I stare through the window—all shame gone now—and watch as Henry stands to greet her, inexplicably wiping away tears with the back of his hand as he pulls her towards him in a hug.

YVONNE

Simon's gym doesn't smell like your average gym. Probably because it's women-only, and women actually wash their workout gear more than once a month.

He's standing next to some over-coiffured, overweight woman on a treadmill. She's barely doing anything—not even a light jog, but he's all smiles, full of encouragement, and she grins back at him in between her gasps for air. She must be in her sixties, clearly never done much exercise before in her life: what's the point? If I was her, I'd sit at home eating chocolates and drinking champagne and make the most of it.

I know the session is nearly over so I leave them and make my way into the changing rooms. Today is an up day, and I'm feeling good, determined to push aside thoughts of Violet and focus on my own life. No news is good news, after all. If something really bad had happened, we'd all know about it by now.

I still feel a small thrill every time I punch the code into the huge anonymous door outside the gym. The best bit of Simon's job: free membership for me. This place charges nearly £300 a month. It's a long way from Isleworth, but I'm often nearby for work and I get to exercise and see my husband at the same time.

The changing rooms are one of my favorite things. More dressing rooms really, with a shower and toilet in each. The lighting is flattering, there's tasteful music piped over integrated speakers, and the towels are thick and plentiful. I take my time getting changed, folding up my skirt and jumper carefully, making sure my make-up is perfect, and then I head out to the main workout area.

"Babe!" Simon says, when he sees me. "Did you text me? My phone's in the staff room charging."

I kiss him, making sure the ridiculously young girl at the juice bar in the corner gets a good eyeful.

"Don't," Simon says. "I'm at work . . ."

I kiss him again.

"You're outrageous, Mrs. Hawley. My next client is watching."

I pull away. Don't want to lose him his job.

"Sorry, I'm just happy to see you. I'll leave you in peace."

"We can go for lunch in a bit if you want?" Simon says. "I've got a break at one?"

"It's a date, come and find me."

Physical fitness is obviously key to fertility, but now I've officially started the Two Week Wait, I'm careful not to overdo things. I read an article last night that said at this point in my cycle, any burgeoning embryo is microscopic in size, so unlikely to be too affected by my pounding the treadmill, but still, I don't want to take any risks.

After I've done my forty-minute workout, a mixture of high intensity interval training and weights, I head back to the changing rooms for a shower. I'd usually finish things off with a sauna, but I know they're not recommended for pregnant women, and I have to treat my body as though I'm already pregnant.

I sip a bright green smoothie in the juice bar area and wait for Simon to come and find me, watching the women wandering around. Most of them are in pairs, gossiping as they move from each area of the gym, barely breaking a sweat. They're all too thin, too made up, and most of them look the opposite of physically healthy. When I was younger, I envied these stick insect women, but as I've aged, I've grown to appreciate my curves, the way my face hasn't sunk into my skull like it does if you're slim.

As I watch them, I think of Violet. The way she's climbed the social ladder so effortlessly and so successfully. Brought up in Bristol to unremarkable if well-off parents—her mother worked in a school, her father ran an accountancy firm. How well she's done to escape this prosaic upbringing. Now she's part of the new ruling class: the social celebrity, adored by thousands of blank-faced lurkers, too busy watching Violet and her children to pay any attention to their own.

What a success she's made of things, when she could so easily have faded into obscurity, thickened around the waist with gingerish hair dyed from a box. But no, despite the three children, she's now as polished and preened as a television star.

The straw of my smoothie twists under my fingertips.

I always think of her when I come here. Not surprising, really. She's a member of the Highgate Peter Daunt gym, of course. She filmed a vlog there three years ago—sponsored of course, and dull as ditchwater. Although when I watched it back later, I did see a glimpse of Simon in the background. I'll always have her to thank for that.

* * *

"I've just got a feeling this month. It's going to work out," I say, as I tuck into my quinoa salad. All the women walking past are looking at us, wondering who I am. I reach over and ruffle Simon's hair. He hates me doing it, but never mind.

"Babe," Simon says, putting down his fork. "Let's not get our hopes up."

I feel my temper stirring.

"But we've baby danced every day for the last fourteen days, there must be millions lying in wait to do their job," I say. It's all quite predatory, when you break it down like that. "You've been taking your vitamins for three months, I've been doing everything right . . ."

"Baby danced?"

"That's what . . . that's just what they call it online in the pregnancy forums. Seriously, what if this time it's actually worked? We might not need the appointment after all. Should I postpone it?"

"Von," Simon says, sighing, but then he sits up, blinking slowly. "Look, can we try to have one meal, just one meal, where we don't talk about this?"

I push the remains of my salad away, fold my arms sulkily.

"Fine," I say. "Sorry to bore you."

"You're not boring me! I just . . . I mean, it's not how I imagined our . . ." his voice drops to a whisper, "sex life to end up. You jumping on me every night when I come home, telling a bunch of strangers online about my sperm count. I'm trying, you know? I haven't forgotten what the NHS consultant said about me. It goes round and round my head like a stupid jingle I can't switch off. I know it's *my fault* it's difficult for us to conceive. I don't need to be constantly reminded."

He looks away, and I can see his eyes are shining. I take a deep breath, and pull myself together.

"Difficult, yes, but not impossible, remember?" I say, reaching across the table and taking his hand. I remember my mother's words to me just before she passed away, telling me that a successful relationship was all about managing your partner, using all the tactics you have to get him to think what you want is what he wants too. It didn't work before, but I was young and stupid then, went about it all the wrong way. "I'm sorry. Let's change the subject, you're right."

I pause a little, and am also surprised to find tears lying in wait. To want something this badly, to be so utterly obsessed and consumed by it, is such a horrible feeling. A feeling I've only felt once before, and it nearly killed me then.

I blink.

"How's your day been?" I ask. "Busy? Any more progress on the postpartum classes you were hoping to launch?"

"Not yet," Simon says. He smiles at me, and I can tell he's relieved to be on positive ground again. It's not his fault he doesn't have the coping reserves that I've built up over the years. Thus far, he's lived a pretty charmed life. "Peter's being difficult about it. I think he's worried it'll be too successful, that it'll annoy the yoga teachers. But you know his wife has all the power anyway and Jamal said she seemed keen. I'm having a meeting with the marketing woman next week, and if I can get her on side, she might be able to convince him. So there's still hope."

"Well, that sounds promising. I'm really proud of you," I say, beaming at him. His eyes meet mine and he looks at me differently—with love, not exasperation. I push the last pieces of apricot around my plate, and think about the life I'm going to have, that's waiting for me just a few months away. Me, my husband, and a beautiful new baby. Not long now. I just have to keep the faith.

LILY

I decided not to share with the people on the GoMamas forum that I followed Henry and Skye to school. There's something about having a secret that makes me feel closer to Violet. Sometimes I feel I'm the only one who really knows her, or really cares.

When I came in this morning, I nicked a notebook from the stationery cupboard, and I'm sitting at my desk now, making notes on all the possibilities. Like a detective. I would have been a good detective . . . I pause for a minute. All those careers I could have had but didn't.

Just before I met James I was about to go abroad for a year, to volunteer on a jungle conservation program in Peru. I'd scrimped and saved for two years to afford it. But then James came up to me as I queued for my coat in a nightclub, and it was love at first sight. I couldn't leave him behind in London, and then I got pregnant, and nothing worked out how I imagined it would. Somewhere in my mind I believed—no, I still do—that I'd be able to go one day. I still had the money, and so long as I didn't touch it, it'd be there as an escape route. For four years I didn't use a penny of it. It was my security, my safety blanket.

I closed the account last week, the last of the money spent on Archie's childminding fees.

In my notebook, I neatly write down all the facts. Where and when Violet was last seen, and the details of her last vlog, as best I can remember them. Any suspicious behavior or worrying signs.

I am engrossed in my note-making when I hear a short cough. I look up. Ben is staring down at me.

"Good to see we're keeping you busy!" he says. It's a joke, but a thinly veiled one.

"Oh, I . . ." I mutter, closing the notebook.

"Pictures," he says.

"Pictures?"

"I've decided the boardroom needs them. Something black and white, a bit arty, maybe something abstract . . . nothing clichéd. Can you have a look online for me and send me a shortlist to review by the end of the day? Thanks."

He walks off, heading towards the developer team who, as usual, are looking stressed.

I pick up my mug and walk to the kitchen. Susie's in there, chatting on her phone, and she raises her eyebrows and grins as she sees me. She looks thinner than normal; another diet. Intermittent fasting, I think she called it.

"OK, babes, later then!" She shoves her phone in the back of her jeans pocket.

"Lily Peters!" she says, staring at me. "Are you wearing a dungaree dress?"

I look down at it, smiling awkwardly.

"Oh, it was on sale on ASOS . . ."

"You look great!" Susie says. "Your own age for once! Nice to see you wearing something other than those godawful trousers."

I sniff. My work trousers seemed a good purchase at the time— black, straight leg, stretchy waistband. I thought if I wore blouses over the top of them that no one would be able to see the elastic, but Susie spotted it, and was horrified when I told her they were from M&S.

"How are things?" I say, changing the subject. I feel my fingers twisting into the fabric of my dress. £12.99 in the sale. It felt good value—not too dissimilar to the dress Violet has—but it was an extravagance.

"Good, thanks!" she says. "Well, goodish. Seeing Graham for a second date tonight. I'm still undecided whether or not I can cope with dating a man called Graham, but thought he deserved another shot. I mean, Graham, what were his parents thinking? It's not even like you can shorten it. It's terrible!"

I smile. It doesn't seem too bad to me but Susie's always been a touch melodramatic.

"So," Susie says, sipping her tea. She's got that look in her eyes—a twinkle, you might call it. She's about to take the mickey out of me. I'm her pet project, I know that, but I don't mind. "How's your missing heroine? Any news?"

"No, but . . ." I pause, looking at her. "I . . . someone went to her daughter's school, to see if she would turn up. The daughter did, with the dad, Violet's husband, but no sign of Violet herself."

"Bloody hell!" Susie cackles. In many ways, she reminds me of Violet—all that energy for life, the ability to find humor in everything. Perhaps it's just a mask for the troubled waters underneath. "So someone properly stalked her kid? How did they even know what school she goes to?"

"Oh, it's easy to find these things out, if you try hard enough. Her husband had posted a photo of her daughter on her first day, and um, one of the women on the forum worked out what school it was from the uniform."

"Blimey," Susie says. "Hang on, isn't he some hotshot magazine editor?"

"Yes!" I say, enthusiasm bubbling to the surface. "He was a total cad, if you can even use that word these days—slept around with everyone: models, actresses, the lot. He was a massive party animal. But then he met Violet, and he settled down. She changed him."

"Yeah. I remember you showing me a picture of him," Susie says.

I pull out my phone, scrolling to the album where I saved all my favorite photos of Violet and her family, and show it to her again.

"Yeah, I would," Susie says, frowning slightly.

"He's not my type," I say, sternly, but as the words come out and I look back down at Henry's face, I realise I'm not sure they're true.

*　*　*

Are Andy Warhol prints hackneyed? I have no idea anymore.

Two hours of trawling Pinterest for quirky, edgy artwork that isn't clichéd, and I'm bored stiff. And there's still half an hour until lunchtime. My phone buzzes with a message from Anna—probably a photo of Archie covered in paint or sand or something similar. But I can't download it as I'm out of data for the month. I connect to the office Wi-Fi, even though it's strictly forbidden for personal use, and after a few seconds a picture of my tiny boy fills my cracked screen. He's holding a guinea pig, beaming from ear to ear.

After the initial joy that comes from seeing him so happy, the usual worry sets in. He's already asked for a dog for Christmas, it'll be a small rodent next. We don't even have a balcony, and I don't fancy sharing a living room with a miniature rat-like creature.

I stare out of the window at the rain. It's been a pretty mild December so far—I've only needed to put the heating on first thing in the morning, and for an hour when Archie gets home from Anna's. But this weekend we'll have to put up the tree, and I'm worried the fairy lights broke last year when I yanked them off the tree in a drunken strop.

I turn back to my computer. There's a new email in my personal account.

GoMamas>Inbox>Sadandalone
7 December 2017
Private Message from Coldteafordays

Hi Lily,

How are you doing? I know you're a big fan of Violet's, and so I thought I'd PM you to ask if you fancied meeting up for lunch? I'm getting really worried about her—I just have this feeling that something's happened to her. I remember you saying you work in Soho too? Thought we could have a chat and see if two heads are better than one. Text me on 07700 900363 if you fancy it, anyway. Been meaning to suggest we meet IRL for ages!

Cheers,
Ellie

I don't even hesitate. Before I know it, I've arranged to meet her in twenty-five minutes, at a cafe just by Henry's office.

YVONNE

Pineapple can help implantation. But only if you eat the core. That's where the bromelain is. There's also red raspberry leaf tea, oat flowers, and black haw. But pineapple is the easiest to get hold of, especially when you live in a rubbish town like Isleworth.

Thankfully the Tesco on the corner had plentiful pineapples yesterday and so I'm sitting at the kitchen table, munching away at the core of one. It's tough and fibrous, and nowhere near as pleasant as the outside of the pineapple, but needs must. It's only 8am but I'm alone. Simon left early for work today—he's covering a colleague's spinning class.

"Every penny helps!" he said, as I groaned when his alarm woke us at 5.30am. "Or is it every penny counts?" He's determined to raise enough so that we can afford the three-cycle IVF package, but we're still thousands of pounds off. It's hopeless.

I'm officially 4 DPO. Four days post ovulation. I keep opening my fertility app even though I know there's nothing to see yet. I've been charting my temperature every morning with a thermometer, recording the satisfying spike—or "thermal shift" as the fertility professionals call it—which confirms I did indeed ovulate as expected, on Sunday.

The doorbell rings and I carry the plate from my pineapple to the sink before going to answer it. I've been up since Simon left at 6am, and my hair and make-up are perfectly in place. *Never knowingly underdressed*, Katie always says about me. I pull down my skirt a little, wrapping my huge cardigan around me before I open the door.

The delivery man behind it hands me a parcel and asks me to sign for it.

I take it from him.

"Thank you."

"Cheers," he replies, before stomping off down the path.

I take the box through to the living room. It's exquisitely wrapped, as I thought it would be. I did a research group a few years ago when I was short of cash. It was all about customer experience, and whether or not packaging played a part in the overall impression of a company. Pretty obvious if you ask me. Everything's about packaging, from products to people. It's all how you look on the outside these days.

Before I open my parcel, I make myself another cup of raspberry leaf tea. My fourth this morning. Disappointingly, it doesn't taste of raspberries.

Back in the living room, I slice through the tape holding the box together and open the flaps. Inside is another box, in the palest grey, tied in a bow with a white satin ribbon. I lift it out and pull on the ends of the ribbon, gently easing the lid from the box. It's all so beautifully done—the perfect gift for an expectant mother. A handwritten note lies on top of tissue paper flecked with stars.

Dear Yvonne,

Thank you for your Little Stars purchase. We hope you and your baby love them as much as we do!

Love,
The Little Stars team xxx

I peel the sticker from the tissue paper and gently fold the layers back. Inside is a snow-white fleece babygrow, along with a tiny white hat in the same material, organic cotton and bamboo, decorated around the edges with silver-thread stars. It was an extravagance, and there's no way I'm telling Simon about it, but Jackie, the housewife from

Monday's baby shoot, gave me a fifty-pound tip. It's one of the brands Violet's kids always wear, and I couldn't resist. I lift the tiny piece of clothing up towards my cheek, feeling its softness against my skin.

And then I climb the stairs to our tiny spare bedroom. It's meant to be my office, but it's more of a dressing room really. I open the wardrobe, moving my collection of summer shoes aside to reach for the box at the back. It's heavier than I remembered.

I pull it out, lay it on the carpet in front of me and lift the lid. Inside are all Nathan's clothes, just as I left them—folded and washed and ready to wear. They're in perfect condition. After all, they've never been worn.

I take the babygrow and lay it over them, the little hat folded neatly on top. Then I sit back, smiling. A new start.

* * *

I've got just enough time before this afternoon's shoot, so I take Simon's laptop upstairs and get into bed. It's chilly, even with the heating on full blast, and anyway, it's important that I get enough rest during these two weeks. I try to imagine the tiny ball of cells floating—or is it bouncing?—down my fallopian tubes towards my womb, waiting to attach themselves to the inside of my uterus. Sometimes visualising things helps. Or at least, it's supposed to.

I open the lid of the laptop and start my task, the nerves heightening at the thought of what I might discover. Violet's social media accounts are still missing. I try to imagine what she's doing. Where is she now? What's happened? What's she thinking? But it's impossible to fathom. I take a look at Henry's accounts. There's a new tweet. My breath catches in my mouth. Perhaps this will be it: the answer to all my questions.

Starting the day right. Have really enjoyed the seven-day get-your-oats challenge. Definitely makes a change from my usual fry-ups, or breakfast of coffee only, and it's been great trying out all the different flavors of Johnsons Oats. They're easy to make, too—just add water and microwave. Perfect for the time-poor. Three thumbs up. #johnsonsoats #ad #spon

I click on the image underneath the tweet to enlarge it. He's holding a bowl of porridge up to his face, grinning like a monkey and holding one thumb aloft in approval. No sign of his missing wife, no mention of where she might have gone.

Cunt.

I scroll down to read the comments. People have such short memories. *Love Johnsons Oats! Apple and cinnamon is my favorite!* Hardly anyone has bothered to mention Violet, but a few people have tagged friends, to draw their attention to the image. *Look, Caz, guess everything must be OK then?*

I feel the anger start to simmer, my breathing quickening as my heart pounds. How dare he. How fucking dare he. Just publishing his scheduled posts promoting this rubbish, as though nothing's happened. How can he just ignore all the questions, all the fans wondering, worrying about where she's gone, and continue with his vacuous job as though she doesn't even exist?

I'm actually shaking now. I stare at his face, the hard set of his jaw, the way his eyes have shrunk with age and the toll of sleepless nights. But that grin is still there—those perfectly white teeth, the lopsided smirk, the glint in his eyes that says he'll always get away with everything.

And it's that disgusting grin that convinces me that I have to go to the police. Any doubts I have been entertaining over the past week evaporate. I have to do this. Men like him disgust me.

GoMamas

Topics>Mummy Vloggers>Violet is Blue>Violet's Whereabouts
7 December 2017

Horsesforcourses
So guys, a friend of a friend knows Violet's next door neighbor. Apparently on Saturday evening she heard Violet and Henry screaming at each other. Like properly screaming, through the walls. It was so bad it woke up this woman's newborn. Then—and this is the best/worst bit—an ambulance arrived. She couldn't see who it was for, and she didn't want to go outside and stare like a horrible rubbernecker. But still! WTAF has happened?

Sadandalone
Oh my god!!!!

Bluevelvet
I'm really upset to hear this. I thought they were rock solid.

Horsesforcourses
Do you remember earlier in the year though? All that business with Mandy? Maybe something did happen, she lost her temper and . . .

Neverforget
Who knows what goes on behind closed doors . . . ?

Bluevelvet
Did your friend find out any more, Horses?

Horsesforcourses
Yes, she said she hasn't seen Violet since. But weirder still, there's

been some other woman there, coming and going with shopping and stuff. Letting herself in with a key. It's not her cleaner. She's never seen her before, doesn't know her name. It's just SO weird now, Violet's been missing for four days and there's been nothing. Not even a statement from her management.

28 January 2017
From: gottheblues@hotmail.com
To: violet@violetisblue.com

I've known you for a while now, Violet. Of course sometimes you make questionable decisions, as we all do, but I always thought you were pretty morally decent. But every now and then you do something, and it makes me want to cry. And today was such a day.

I was bored, suddenly remembered your other email address. Not your official one on your website, but the one I found in the bowels of the internet, one night on a particularly exhaustive search. *Youngviolets81@live.com.* (By the way, the "81" is a dead giveaway of your real age—you might want to think about changing that.) Realised I'd never Googled it before.

In the address went, and up it came, straight away. Your eBay account name: youngviolets81. I almost laughed out loud at the shock of it. For some reason, I couldn't picture you bothering with something like eBay.

345 transactions, 100% positive feedback. What were you buying? I clicked to see.

But then my own naivety slapped me round the face. You weren't buying anything. You were selling. Selling, selling, selling. I clicked on every single listing for the past six months. There were so many things. SO MANY THINGS. I was so stupid, I didn't understand. But then I read the descriptions, and I realised. What a fool I had been.

Unwanted gift. Collection from Barnsbury, N1.

Unwanted gift, still new in box. Collection only from N1.

Never used. Collection only please, north London!

All the big-ticket items. The ones you once said you gave away to family and friends, or donated to charity. Brand-new push-chairs, the latest high chairs, immaculate Moses baskets lined with lace . . . all unwanted gifts from PRs, turned into cold, hard cash.

What a let-down. Charity begins at home, eh, Violet? In a great big mansion in north London.

LILY

I'm early, for once, and so I sit in the window of the cafe, watching for Ellie. I have no idea what to expect, what she'll look like—I didn't think to describe myself to her either, so I hope she works out who I am. There aren't many other people in the cafe, which is strange given that it's lunchtime. It's one of those tiny places tucked down a side street that you'd only know about if you were a local.

I'm too nervous to have much of an appetite, but when my jacket potato arrives I shovel it into my mouth anyway. I check my phone periodically—she's late, but she has a high-profile job at a PR agency, so I guess it's to be expected. At exactly twelve minutes past one, I hear the door to the cafe creak open and she comes in, looking around to find me.

She's far more glamorous than I ever imagined any fan of Violet's to be, dressed in a bright red dress and an ankle-length cream coat. Her hair is dark, almost black, pinned up neatly, and she has two enormous gold hoop earrings on that quiver as she turns her head.

She spots me, hunched in the corner, parka falling off the back of my chair. I pull my grey cardigan around myself. I don't want her to notice the dungaree dress—if she's as big a fan of Violet as I am, she'll know that it's just like the one she has.

"Lily!" she calls, waving over at me. "I'll just order something and join you."

I nod back, smiling, forking in the last of my potato. I'd rather not have to eat in front of her.

"Sorry, couldn't find the place!" she says, breathlessly, pulling out the chair opposite me. She's carrying a bottle of sparkling water.

"Oh, sorry it's a bit scruffy," I say. "Sure you're used to far more salubrious venues! It's just usually quite quiet, and about half the price of the places like Pret." As soon as the words are out, I regret them. I think of the lunch I'd cobbled together for myself this morning—leftovers from our dinner last night. I'd made tuna pasta, but there was no tuna left in it, so this morning I'd torn up one of Archie's cheese strings and scattered it through. How relieved I was to have an excuse to bin it before I came here.

"No, it's great," Ellie says, looking around. "I need to find more of these kind of places. Secret Soho. You know what I mean."

She pauses, staring at me.

"You look really familiar," she says, frowning. "We haven't met before, have we?"

I shake my head, give a small laugh.

"Nope, don't think so," I reply. "I get that all the time though. Must have one of those faces."

"Must do."

"Do you work nearby?" I ask.

She nods, taking a sip of her sparkling water straight from the bottle.

"Yep, just round the corner actually. Just off Dean Street. You?"

"We're above the eco-friendly shoe shop behind Carnaby Street."

"Wow, very fancy! What is it you do exactly?"

"Um . . . I work for a tech company. We mostly design apps for brands, but we do a bit of web development too."

"Gosh, you must be very clever then."

I smile, look down at my empty mug. Now that she's up close, it's obvious that Ellie is older than I thought she was. Her skin has that delicate quality about it, a collection of fine lines around her eyes.

"Not really," I say. "I've got more of a . . . support role. And you work in PR?"

"Yes," she nods, rolling her eyes. "Awful, isn't it? I'm an account director for some global healthcare brands. It's full on, but I enjoy it.

A lot of travel involved. Luckily my husband works from home, so he helps out a lot with the childcare. Although, it's not helping out when it's your own children, is it? What is it Violet always says to Henry? It's not babysitting when it's your own kids!"

"Do you think Henry wanted kids?" I say.

"No," she says, shaking her head. "I didn't say this on the forum but one of my colleagues knows Henry really well, worked with him years ago. By all accounts he was quite the party animal, certainly not the sort of man who'd settle down with a member of the breastapo and care about whether or not the yoghurt they ate was organic. He really wasn't that kind of man. She changed him. But I suppose she has that quality, doesn't she? She draws you in."

I nod.

"She's the first person I ever really watched online."

"She's the best of the mummy lot," Ellie says. "Not perfect though— do you remember that time she left the kids together on the trampoline and they ended up banging heads? God, that was so irresponsible. I can't believe she actually put that video up—did you see the comments she got? Served her right, really. And she's not always good about dis-closing things—you know they got a massive discount on Henry's Land Rover?"

"Really?"

"Oh yeah, I know the guy who works on that account. Really dodgy." Ellie pauses, staring past my shoulder. "I absolutely loved her up until then. Went off her a bit when I found out about that."

"'Do you trust Henry?" I say. "I can't believe this stuff with the ambulance . . .'"

"Well, he's certainly besotted with her." The waiter brings over Ellie's lunch and sets it down in front of her—a dressing-less salad with a sliced hard-boiled egg. "But then there's the stuff about this other woman letting herself in and out of the house . . . Could be a new assis-tant, I suppose . . . Although I thought after Mandy she swore she'd never have another. What a disaster *that* turned out to be. I never liked her. Violet's got rubbish taste in people, I have to say!"

I swallow. "Your friend, the one you said knows Henry, what does *he* think?"

My words are tumbling out, and I find I'm slightly breathless.

"They lost touch several years ago—just after Violet got pregnant. I asked him to drop him a line, find out what's going on, but he said that would be too weird. But listen, I've had a couple of other ideas. Just wanted to run them past you. I always wonder . . . my husband, he says I've got an obsessive nature, but sometimes you can't help it, can you? I love people—it's why I do what I do. And Violet has . . ." She pauses again. "Well, she's always felt like a friend to me."

"I know what you mean," I say, stroking the paper napkin on my lap. "I think we'd all get on really well in real life."

"Oh me too!" Ellie says. "So listen, I wanted to tell you a couple of things. One, I know Violet's address."

I gasp.

"How?"

Ellie's neck flushes slightly.

"Oh, she's on the media database we use. Doesn't have a PO Box like most of the big bloggers for some reason. Prefers to get stuff sent direct to her than to her agent. Anyway . . ." She reaches down and pulls her shiny black handbag on to her lap, taking out a piece of paper and unfolding it on the table in front of me.

My eyes take in the letters, my brain immediately storing away the number of the house and the postcode.

"Is that definitely her address?" I ask. It sounds posh, the number familiar. 36 Acacia Avenue. Then I remember. A year or so ago, there was some post on the table behind Violet in one of her blogs. A big brown parcel, the address scrawled in huge letters on the top. I'd screen-grabbed it and zoomed in on my phone, managing to read the number, but not the rest of the address, which was out of focus.

"Yes, one hundred per cent. I confirmed it with a friend who works in our consumer division. She worked with Violet on a campaign for Joy soap last year. Sent her loads of stuff. By all accounts she was really lovely to work with, which is a relief."

"Wow," I say, pulling the piece of paper closer towards me.

"Yeah, I know," Ellie says, resting her chin on her palm. "Anyway, I live down in Surrey now—we moved out when the twins turned two. So there's no way I can go to Islington and hang around outside her house to see if she's OK. Not that I'm suggesting anyone should do that but . . ."

"I'll do it," I say, snatching up the piece of paper.

"Are you sure?" Ellie says, surprised.

"Yes," I say. "I'll get a sitter."

"I thought you lived west?"

"I do," I reply. "In Act . . . near Chiswick. But it's fine. It's good to get out of the house—I might even try to catch a film after."

"OK, great. Well, if you're sure."

"I'll go on Saturday night," I say, folding the piece of paper back up and putting it in my handbag. "I'll report back any findings!"

"What will you do?" Ellie asks. "Are you going to ring the doorbell?"

I take a sip of my tea.

"I could do, I suppose." I shrug. "Could pretend I was lost. I'll dress up a bit, say I'm meant to be having dinner with friends, but that I've got the wrong house number."

"It might be that you see her anyway, through the window, and can tell she's fine. In which case, I don't suppose you need to do anything."

"No, exactly," I say, nodding vigorously. "Let's just see what happens."

Ellie sits back.

"God, we are a bunch of weirdos," she says, laughing a little.

"What was your other idea?" I ask, keen to change the subject.

"Oh," she says, and the tinge of pink rises to her cheeks. "Well, it's my PR head, I'm afraid, I just can't help myself. I'm friends with quite a lot of journalists. I was thinking of asking one of them to look into her disappearance. They're all a bit snobby about influencers, social media stars—they have nicked most of their jobs, after all. But there's one friend, in particular, he does a lot of in-depth zeitgeist pieces. He doesn't have kids so he probably has no idea who she is, but that doesn't mean he wouldn't appreciate the value of a story on her. Especially if she's gone missing, and even more especially if Henry has had something to do with it."

She pauses, takes a sip of her water. "I was thinking . . . I was thinking of giving him a tip off."

HENRY

Amy has gone to the hospital to see Violet, leaving me with the worst company of all: my own thoughts.

I tried to explain it all to her. Things were different back then. Before the Internet came and shat on everything. Citizen journalism, they called it when it first emerged. As though it was some kind of great movement, some emancipation of the masses.

I remember my editor at *King*, Bertie Letts, telling the Features desk to do a piece on its pitfalls, like they were somehow going to beat the phenomenon at its own game by doing so. He was so pleased with himself, thought he'd caught the crest of a wave and crushed it, when of course he'd just fanned the flames.

Twenty years on and I still think and write in hackneyed metaphors. It's a compulsion. Perhaps that's why my wife is so successful. She doesn't speak like she's swallowed a load of tired old phrases. She's honest, relatable, "one of us." I know this, because the many articles about her keep telling me so.

Like so many of its brothers, my first magazine closed five years after I left it. I wasn't particularly sad to see it go. Bit of a kicker for my mates who were still there, of course, and they all emailed me the next day, virtual cap in hand. Thankfully I'd seen the inevitable coming as *King* got steadily less regal and so I moved on as quickly as possible, managing to secure my position at *The Edit*. Not without an enormous amount of arse-licking on my part—the deputy editor was the son of a friend of my uncle's, and the old boys' club had ensured when a vacancy came up, mine was the

72

first name they thought of. My title was junior commissioning editor back then. It was an easy gig. People were so desperate to have the kudos of the magazine on their CVs that they practically begged to write for me.

Three promotions later and now I've got the best title of them all: Creative Director. I'll be here till the end now. The end of me, or the end of the magazine. I'm not sure which will come first. After last week, the odds are even.

It was there though, on *King*, that sexist old "lads' mag," that I first met the woman who was to shape my life. She was an assistant on the picture desk, when picture desks had such people. We're lucky to even have a picture editor these days, and when he walks past you can practically smell his fear and desperation. But back then they were one of the many serfs doing the hard work so their bosses didn't have to. I noticed her straight away—or the top of her head anyway, above the desk divider. Something about the way she held herself—her back ruler-straight, not a hair out of place. The other women who worked on the mag dressed like lesbians. And not the good kind.

We were a big team back then. Fifteen full-time members of staff, and at least ten regular freelancers. It was fun, what I remember of it. Lots of alcohol, weekly trips to the Corner Club. On Friday lunchtime we escaped to the pub and no one ever went back to the office. Our editor didn't care—he was rarely there, anyway. It was on one of those drunken Fridays that I first got talking to her. We were wedged up against one another at the bar, bonded over the apathy of the bar staff.

She wasn't blonde, so she wasn't really my type. But as she started drinking, she loosened up and I was amazed to discover she had a filthy sense of humor. I had been wrong about her. So very wrong. Five minutes into our conversation, she called me a pussy.

A fortnight ago, Bertie was arrested on historic sexual harassment charges. Not a great surprise given what happened. They're coming for us all now, these women we drank with.

Still, it's always a pity to see one of your idols torn down like that. And men are simple creatures—they'll take whatever they can get. That's what women always seem to forget.

YVONNE

It took far longer than I expected at the police station, and now I'm running late to meet Katie. There was a lot of waiting around for the right person, and they left me sitting on a hard plastic chair in the reception area for nearly forty minutes. It was almost as though they were doing me a favor, rather than the other way round.

But at least it's done now, another thing ticked off the list. All I can do is sit back and wait, to see how things progress. I've done my bit.

While I was waiting to speak to someone, I made my notes in my diary. I'm still updating the app, of course, but I've also decided to keep a paper trail. After all, you never know with technology. It's notoriously unreliable.

> *Five days post ovulation (DPO)*
> *Temp: 36.85*
> *Symptoms: Bloating, constipation, fatigue. Dry CM (cervical mucus).*
> *Sex: No.*

It's too early for any of it to mean anything. There's a reason they call it the Two Week Wait torture. It's almost impossible to concentrate on anything but what might—or might not—be going on in your body. Whether your uterus is about to fail you or not, for the fourteenth month in a row.

Once I'm home, I tuck the diary behind the cookery books on the shelf in the kitchen. It's not the sort of thing I want Simon to find. Not that he'd go looking for it, he's not that kind of man, but still, if he needed a piece of paper he might open it to rip one out, and God knows his mind would be blown if he discovered my meticulous records. Even down to the positions each time, and whether or not I had an orgasm.

Some people think you're supposed to share everything in marriage. But I'm sure Violet's non-stop chatter about her postpartum piles didn't exactly get Henry's blood racing.

Pushka sidles up to me as I make my way through the hall. She stares at me and opens her mouth mutely.

"Oh Push," I say, putting my handbag down on the stairs. I lean down and stroke her soft head. "You're going to make me even later."

In the kitchen, I take a pouch of tuna and anchovies in wild rice from the shelf in Pushka's cupboard and spoon some carefully into her bowl.

* * *

The restaurant is a chain. A decent one, but still nothing worth shouting about on Instagram. Not like the fancy places Violet is used to, where the waiters wear matching blue waistcoats and there are bells on each table to call for service.

Katie is already waiting for me as I wander in, and waves me over to the table.

"Sorry, sorry," I say, kissing her on both cheeks.

"Not to worry, darling," she says. "You look great. Got us a bottle of red, as it's steak."

I screw my face up. It's 5 DPO; the likelihood is that the embryo hasn't implanted in my womb yet, which means we're not yet sharing a blood supply. But still, is it worth the risk? Not this month.

"Oh," I say, sitting down. "Listen, I . . . about the wine . . ."

"Oh God, you're not drinking?"

"I drove here, sorry," I say.

"Well, you can have one," Katie says, leaning forward and starting to pour me a glass. I stop her short with my hand.

"No, I can't," I say. Dammit. No going back now.

"Oh Yvonne!" she says, putting the bottle back down. "Are you pregnant?!"

I shake my head.

"No," I say. "Sorry to disappoint. But we're going to see a specialist, you know, about starting IVF privately next week, and I want to make sure I'm in top condition. I know it makes me a massive bore."

Her face falls.

"Oh, I see," she says, "of course. I totally understand. Never mind. All the more for me!"

I ask for my steak to be well done, just in case. I forgot what it was like to have to worry about these things—no soft cheeses, no runny eggs, no sushi. Violet posted a photograph of herself eating sushi when she was pregnant; she got a load of criticism for it.

I wish I could stop thinking about Violet. Will I ever be free of her?

When my steak arrives it's grey and tough, tasting of nothing. My hand rests on my stomach. All these little sacrifices, just for you.

"Are you enjoying the off-season?" I ask Katie, as we chew in unison. "I know you had a really hectic summer."

"Thirty-seven weddings in total, believe it or not," she says, taking a swig of wine. "It nearly killed me. Thank God it's over."

I met Katie on our photography course seven years ago. Both more mature than the other students, both slightly damaged by men, both looking for a new start. Katie's five years older than me, and she drinks and smokes like a sailor.

"Thirty-seven," I repeat. "That's incredible. You're a machine!"

"Yeah, well, we spent most of it on a kitchen extension, unfortunately. This is the problem with blended families, all the effing kids. The amount of food they get through! Always coming and going, like Piccadilly bloody Circus . . ." She stops short. "Oh God, sorry. How insensitive of me."

"It's fine," I say, smiling. "I don't want five kids. One would do me just fine."

Katie smiles at me sympathetically.

"Yeah. Sometimes I wish I'd stopped at one. Oh fuck, I'm getting trollied here. Sorry. It's been ages since I had a night out."

"How are things with Tony?"

"Oh, you know," she says, briefly staring off into the middle distance. "Once the teenagers have been dropped off at whatever party they've been invited to, we just collapse in front of the TV. We're so dull." She pauses, gives a sigh. "You've always been so much . . . *fun*, Yvonne."

My ears begin to burn. *Fun.* For years that's how I was described, carrying it around like a label. *The life and soul.* The one you want at your party. *Butter wouldn't melt during the day, but get a few drinks in her and she's anyone's!*

Fun was the word they used, but *easy* was what they meant.

After our plates have been cleared away, we both order pudding. Not particularly because we want any, but neither of us want to go home yet.

"So," Katie says, spooning cheesecake in her mouth. "How's things with Simon? Is the making-a-baby stuff still affecting things?"

I look down at my lap, screwing my napkin in my hand. *Focus.* The temptation to tell Katie everything—all of it, my entire plan—is overwhelming.

"It's not the most romantic of situations," I admit. "I think he's finding it tough. Especially as, you know, it's all his fault."

The words are out there and I pause, hearing them echo in my mind. Another failure to resist, another load of personal information blabbed freely.

"Oh really?" Katie says, eyes widening. "I didn't know that."

"Yeah, we had a test. He's got really rubbish sperm." Too late for discretion now, all that's left is damage limitation, making light of it. I laugh, but the sound is choked. "Wouldn't have guessed that when I picked him. He did a lot of cycling in his twenties. Might have something to do with it. Or just bad luck. He's been on vitamins to try to improve them—believe it or not, high doses of vitamin C can really help. I'm trying to stay hopeful, but what with my age and everything . . ."

"They can work miracles these days. My friend Liz just had her baby at forty-five. Third round of IVF—third time lucky."

There's always a story—always some miracle. It's all very well if you have the money, but we can barely afford one round of IVF.

"Well, I don't think the percentage chances are great," I say. "I'm just praying that the vitamins have improved things to a point where it will happen naturally. But if not, they can do this thing—sperm washing, I think they call it. Where they pick the best ones and then use them with my eggs. As I am sure you can imagine, Simon's thrilled about the whole prospect."

I feel a gut-punch of guilt. That was a betrayal of Simon's privacy that he doesn't deserve. I want to wind all the words back into my mouth and back down my throat into my lungs where they can't be heard. Why do I always do this? Keep nothing back, keep nothing sacred? TMI, that's what my so-called friends used to say as I overshared freely in the pub about my latest sexual disaster. Too Much Information. On the surface they loved the stories, thought I was *hilarious*, but I should have realised that they were laughing at me, not with me.

"Oh darling!" Katie says, reaching out and taking my hand across the table. "But remember what that nutcase promised you—pregnant by Christmas!"

I laugh.

"Yes. She's running out of time."

"We'll sue her if it doesn't happen!" Katie says, squeezing my fingers. "It'll work out. Don't you worry. You're the most determined woman I've ever met. You'll get your happy ending. I'm sure of it."

I flash her a quick smile, thinking how clueless she is. Well-meaning, but clueless.

Everyone knows there's no such thing as a happy ending.

GoMamas

Topics>Mummy Vloggers>Violet is Blue>Violet's Whereabouts
8 December 2017

Horsesforcourses
How's everyone doing today? Still no news in Violet land.

Bluevelvet
No, but you know what? I've been thinking about it more. I reckon she's just had enough of the whole online scene. Remember that thread on the forum, about a month ago?

Horsesforcourses
Oh God. THE "instamums" thread. Yeah, people were brutal.

Bluevelvet
Well, she always says she never reads anything on forums. But what if she found it? What if she saw what people were saying about Skye, about her playing up to the cameras? I think if someone slagged my kids off—especially a load of strangers who haven't even met her—then I'd just think f*** this and be done with it. Or maybe Henry asked her to stop. Maybe that's why they were fighting.

Neverforget
I think there's more to it. I think something's happened with Henry. He's got a temper on him, remember. And the ambulance!? It's too coincidental.

Coldteafordays
But he wouldn't hurt her, would he? I'm imagining all sorts now. Remember a few months ago when she had that massive

black eye? And she made a joke about walking into a street sign whilst holding Lula's hand?

Neverforget

Walking into a street sign? One step up from walked into a door. If you believe that, you'll believe anything.

LILY

"Like I say, I won't be long." I put Archie's bedtime beaker on the work surface. "Milk's in the fridge. Not too much. He might be cheeky and ask for a snack too, but he's only allowed toast at this time of day. No Nutella."

"Right," Susie says, her smile fixed. "Got it."

It feels weird having her here, in my space. It's strange to have the two sides of my life mixing like this, and I'm suddenly worried she might start poking around my things. I pause for a minute, watching her as she pulls her phone out of her back pocket and starts tapping it. No, it'll be fine. She'll probably spend the whole evening on Tinder.

Back in the living room, Archie is sitting on the sofa, thumb jammed in his mouth.

"Thumb!" I shout and he yanks it out, wiping it on his trousers. "You're spoiling your teeth." Susie looks at me. I shouldn't have snapped. Three-year-olds don't care about their teeth, that kind of discipline doesn't work. It just scares them into submission. And anyway, they're only his milk teeth. They'll fall out soon.

"Shall we . . . read a book?" Susie says, clapping her hands together. I think she's regretting her offer to babysit now, despite all the times she's insisted she'd love to.

"Ladybird heard," Archie mumbles, pointing to the pile of books stacked next to the television. "Please."

Susie looks confused. I roll my eyes.

"Sorry," I say. "It's his favorite. *What the Ladybird Heard*. He knows it off by heart, bless him. You won't have to read it, he'll probably talk over the whole thing."

"What?" Susie says. "But I thought I was going to get to do different voices!"

Archie's eyes widen and he tugs on her arm.

"You can do voices if you want to, Susie," he whispers.

I leave them to it and go through to my bedroom to finish getting ready. In order to make my story more plausible, I've put on an old dress, and clipped half my hair back. What's that expression? You can't make a silk purse out of a sow's ear. That's what my reflection says to me. My skin is mottled, the dark rings under my eyes showing through the layers of concealer I've heaped on them. It's started to congeal slightly, in the corners. I pat it with my finger, trying to blend it back in.

I might not be going on a date, as I told Susie, but there is a very real possibility that I'll see Violet, and I don't want her to look through me the way most people do. Someone's mum. That's what I am, that's *all* I am, that's all anyone ever thinks of me. It hasn't bothered me until now—I was never the glamor puss, after all, but once upon a time I was attractive, healthy, full of life, constantly kissed by the sun thanks to all my outdoor pursuits. James was the same, always tanned . . . I push the memories away.

I return to the living room fifteen minutes later in slim-fitting jeans and a black silk blouse, red lipstick self-consciously splashed across my lips, my hair loose around my shoulders. Susie looks me up and down, giving a long low whistle.

"What do you think Mummy's date will say about that, Archie?" she says.

"What's a date?" Archie asks, staring at me.

"Ignore Auntie Susie," I say. "She's being silly. Now, you, come on, it's bath time. Book away, please, let's go get your towel and pyjamas."

"You look great, Lily," Susie says. "You should wear that kind of thing more often."

I smile. The outfit was inspired by Susie, and tucked into my jeans with the top two buttons undone, the blouse makes me look about a hundred times more sophisticated than usual.

Violet would be proud.

"Thanks. Now, he should go to sleep really easily after his bath—he's worn out. But if there are any probs just give me a ring."

I linger in the doorway, my plan for the evening suddenly seeming ridiculous. I hate not being the one to put Archie to bed. What if something happens to him while I'm out?

"We'll be fine," Susie says, shooing me towards the front door. "Honestly. Now go!"

*   *   *

The temperature has fallen over the last few days and it's absolutely freezing as I make my way from Angel Tube, carefully following the map I screenshotted on my phone. Acacia Avenue is a good ten minutes from the Underground and I walk steadily, nerves heightening with every step. As I pass the cafe I saw Henry in with that woman, I pause. It's all shut up, of course, the chairs stacked on top of the tables. I still have no idea who that woman was, or why Henry was meeting her. And why was he crying? Who is this woman the neighbors have seen coming and going? Are they the same person?

As the roads grow more residential, the number of people passing me on the street thins out, although the traffic is at a standstill alongside me, belching out pollution. It's crazy that I ended up living in this clogged up, congested city, working at its heart and bringing my child up so far from nature, so far from everything I was once passionate about. It's almost like some cruel joke. And worst of all, I can't afford to escape.

The houses along the main road were grand once but now they're divided into flats, with scruffy front gardens and food waste bins pushed over by animals. I walk past them, taking in the stringy curtains hanging at the windows, every other one decorated with Christmas lights or candelabra.

My map tells me to take a left turn. Another residential street, the Edwardian houses identical, lined up like soldiers. They're getting bigger now I'm off the main road, and the gardens are tidier, the front doors painted in tasteful shades. Acacia Avenue is just ahead, a turning off the right, tucked away in the middle of this grid of roads. I pause for a few seconds on the corner, peering down the street. Violet's house is mid-way, on the right-hand side. Her garden must face south, which would explain the bright sunlight in all her kitchen vlogs.

The street is quiet, but the houses are ablaze with lights that beam from the windows. These houses are bigger still, semi-detached, not terraced, and as I make my way along the pavement I see they have basements too. Once I'm a third of the way down, there's another shift in atmosphere. Is it the cars neatly lined up on the street, that are now suddenly larger, with personalised number plates? Or the fact that the front gardens here are immaculate, all clipped box trees and window boxes full of heather? Most of the houses have closed shutters in the front windows, but a few are open, and I can see right into the front rooms.

I stop outside the first house with open shutters. The lights are off inside, but further back there's a reading lamp switched on, next to a shiny black grand piano. That's not the first thing I notice though. The first thing I notice is the magnificent Christmas tree in one corner, next to the marble fireplace. It's like something out of a Victorian painting—immaculately lit and decorated, not a garish bauble nor piece of tinsel in sight. And underneath it there are already presents, all wrapped with matching paper and enormous bows. A picture-perfect scene.

The cold December air burns my nostrils.

I continue my walk, my footsteps suddenly seeming louder in my clodhopping boots. Or maybe I'm just noticing them more now I'm approaching Violet's home. In the distance I can hear the hum of traffic, punctuated by the wail of an ambulance or police siren, but there's something uncannily still about Acacia Avenue. No wonder Violet's neighbors heard them fighting.

A few seconds later, I'm outside number thirty-three. On the other side of the road I can see her front door. I recognise the color immediately—a zingy green, standing out against the pastels and greys of the neighbors. Violet has used this front door as the backdrop to so many of her Instagram photographs—especially her "'outfit of the day" posts. The doorway is even more magnificent in the flesh, nestled at the top of a run of steps, and completed by an impressive arched window above.

There's a streetlamp directly in front of one of the first-floor windows. I wonder if that room is Violet and Henry's bedroom, and if so, if the light keeps them awake at night.

I looked up the address on one of those property websites last night. Violet and Henry paid £2.7m for this place two years ago. I knew she was successful, and that he was too, of course. But still. I can't even afford to buy myself a new winter coat.

I steel myself and cross the road. The shutters in the window on the ground and lower ground floors are resolutely closed. But the curtains are open in the room upstairs, behind the streetlamp. There are no lights on, as far as I can see. Not even in the hallway. Either they're all out, or they're all in their huge kitchen-dining-living space at the back of the house, on the lower ground floor. It's Saturday night, they're probably watching *Strictly Come Dancing*—Skye's a huge fan. She does ballet on Monday evenings, and her teacher thinks she's got real potential. She's certainly built for it—petite but strong, with long slender legs.

My heart thuds with the sudden realisation that Violet might not be OK. Something serious might have happened. Something terrible. Do I really want to know?

As I linger on the pavement, my phone buzzes in my handbag.

How's it going? Hope all ok! Ellie x

I can't let her down. I can't tell her I got this far and then wimped out. And after all, I'm not doing anything illegal, am I? I'm just knocking on someone's door, pretending to have the wrong address.

That's when I remember. I forgot the wine! I was meant to bring a bottle, to make it look more authentic, like I really *was* going for dinner at a friend's house.

Too late to do anything about it now. I push myself forward and march up the steps, pressing my finger hard on the ceramic doorbell before I have the chance to back out.

YVONNE

Still no sign of Violet. It's been nearly a week now and aside from anything else, I miss watching her vlogs. It was part of my routine. A toxic part, but a part nonetheless. Some people call what I do "hate-watching" but it's not that. There are plenty of online "celebrities" I could hate-watch—like that awful Mama Perkins and her wonky fringe. Not only irritating to look at but irritating to listen to. My feelings for Violet go beyond hate; they're something else entirely, something I don't know how to identify. There was a perverse pleasure in watching Violet and Henry, analysing each and every interaction. And now they're not here, and it's Saturday night and I'm alone with nothing to do.

I am sitting in the living room, drinking more raspberry leaf tea, trying to focus on what really matters: my own life. *Strictly Come Dancing* is on mute. The colors, lights and dresses blur before my eyes as the grinning dancers on screen whizz around the dance floor. Simon is post-match, at the pub with his mates.

It's non-negotiable, this weekly pub session after the football. He's cut back on the alcohol since the consultant's verdict but still. I hate it when he goes out without me. What will happen when the baby is born? Will he continue to bugger off to the football on Saturdays, and come home at midnight sweating booze from every pore, like he did when we first met?

Added to this, I still haven't heard any more from the police. What if they haven't taken me seriously? I put the cup of tea down on the coffee table. I always get like this in the two weeks before my period starts. Some women complain of PMT for a few days beforehand, but for me, the hormonal rollercoaster lasts almost half of the month. I am angry. At everything. At Violet. At Simon. At what happened. At my own body.

I take some deep breaths. This month is different. I need to remember that. I rub my stomach, a sense of calm washing over me as I think of my baby. It's going to be OK. I've got to focus on what I can control and not on what I can't.

I consider doing some work—I've got some editing left from my baby shoot on Thursday. I was going to do it on Monday, but it's only 7pm and I've got hours left before Simon gets home. No messages on my phone. I need a distraction.

I pick up my laptop from underneath the coffee table and lift the lid. Before I do anything else, I visit Henry's Instagram and Twitter accounts. But there's nothing new there, not since the photo of him with the bowl of oats.

I stare at his face again.

My skin starts to prickle. What has happened to her? Is she OK? Why aren't they telling people? I feel myself begin to fall down the rabbit hole and I can't bear it. I can't bear not knowing.

"Don't you care about your family at all, Henry?" I say out loud to his inane grin.

Pushka hears me and gives a little purr of approval, climbing up from the rug and settling down on the sofa beside me. I stroke her head absentmindedly, before typing familiar words into the search bar in Google. My computer remembers the page, and I click and wait for it to load.

There it is, the sales listing for Henry's old flat in Kensington. I look at it often. They sold it two years ago but the pictures are still online, for any determined stalker to find. I click on the images, enlarging the one of the living room. My heartbeat quickens. A huge space—almost warehouse-proportions—dominated by a battered leather sofa, an antique trunk used as a coffee table, a gigantic cowhide rug underneath it all. Everything was super-sized in that flat. There's a bar area off to one side, underneath an original film studio light used as a lamp, with all their favorite spirits lined up on top, each bottle almost empty. They were such party animals when they first got together. But in the corner of this overwhelmingly masculine space is something else. Tidied away, yet still sticking out like a sore thumb. A small play kitchen, painted in tasteful Farrow & Ball shades. An overflowing basket filled with soft toys. The reason they moved in the first place.

I click to load the next picture. The kitchen now: entirely made from stainless steel. Huge, again, the same proportions as the living room. Not my taste at all, far too clinical and cold. Perhaps that should have been a sign. My eyes fall on the gigantic island unit in the middle of the room, hosting the hob and an extractor fan that looks like some unidentifiable part of a spaceship.

I look away, remembering the cool sensation of the island unit through the fabric of my dress as I leant back on it.

I force my eyes back on the page, and again, in the corner, there's a splash of color. Something that wasn't there all those years ago. A child's table and chair set. Bright red, Scandinavian, expensive. When they arrived, Violet went on and on about how excited she was to receive them, not disclosing that they were gifted to her by the brand's PR team. But some followers worked it out when Mama Perkins got the same table, and there was a huge hoo-ha about it all. Leading to new hashtags, now mandatory if you want to consider yourself a respectable "influencer." Posts must be marked as #gifted or #ad depending on the circumstance.

I was full of jealousy back then, rage that it wasn't me living that life. But with hindsight I'm sure she didn't deliberately set out to mislead. She just didn't think. She's so used to sharing her life with a crowd of strangers online it didn't occur to her to tell them whether or not she paid for things herself. After all, she didn't pay for Henry's flat, did she? She moved in, behaved like it was hers as well as his. Never occurred to her to tell people she hadn't put a penny towards it.

I used to feel furious that he had let her, but any fury I felt for her disappeared for good last weekend.

It's still so new, this feeling of sympathy for Violet. I am not sure where to put it.

I move on to the next picture. The bedroom. A huge leather sleigh bed, dark green silk-lined walls, a wall of floor-to-ceiling wardrobes. Nothing else in there but another brown leather buttoned chair in the corner. The chair I used to sit in, watching him sleep.

I shut the page. I don't want to look at their bedroom, imagine them all cuddled up there, with their brood huddled around them.

The perfect family.

Not like my own. When my mother died it was as though my father unplugged himself from reality somehow. He was like a robot who could only muster up enthusiasm for his allotment and God. I was sixteen, an alien creature to him, something he could neither understand nor completely ignore. My mother had been fierce, passionate, larger than life. She brought him to life, and without her he had nothing to run on but fumes.

I always swore I'd find a warm man to father my children. Someone who loved being around them as much as I did.

I shift position on the sofa and prepare to open Lightroom. It's nearly 9pm. Work, that's what I need.

But the nagging feeling that I must find out what has happened to Violet won't leave me. I run through the options in my mind. I still have Henry's phone number. Would he reply to a text? Or I could just go to their house, knock on the door and ask. Then I'd know for sure.

But I can't—it's none of my business. The words bubble up again in my mind, popping on the surface of my consciousness. Words I can't seem to block out.

This is none of your fucking business!

Simon won't be home for another few hours. I can't bear to be alone with these thoughts any longer, and I know he'd come home, if I called him. He'd come, because he loves me. And if he's here I can't do anything stupid, I can't do anything I might regret.

I put the computer to one side and grab my phone, punching at it until it starts to ring Simon's number. It rings and rings but just before it goes to voicemail, he answers.

"Babe?" he says. His voice isn't slurred, but he sounds distracted and there's lots of background noise.

"Can you come home?" I say, my voice almost a whisper. "Please."

"What?" he says. "Hang on, I can't hear you. I'll go outside."

I wait a few seconds until the rumble of background noise has faded.

"Are you OK?" he says, and his voice is sharper now, as though he's suddenly sobered up.

"Please," I say, and even though I know this isn't fair of me, I need to know that he'll come, that unlike all the other men I've dated, he loves me unconditionally and will always put me first. "Please can you come home? Please . . . I need you."

LILY

The doorbell is louder than expected, and I step back in surprise as the sound echoes inside the house. On either side of the huge front door are two trees, and tucked away in one corner under the stained glass side panel is a brass umbrella bucket. No umbrellas in it, but imagine just leaving that here, being confident it wouldn't be stolen?

A light comes on in the hallway and I hear steps approaching. I swallow, rehearsing the lines in my head. The shadowy figure behind the door grows larger as it approaches. Whoever it is, is too short to be Henry. Is it going to be Violet?

What was I thinking? She'll never believe my story. I turn to flee but the door swings open and I freeze.

"Hello?"

I feel myself slowly exhale. The woman in front of me is not Violet. She looks like she's in her early twenties, with chin-length blonde hair. Her face is small, too small for the rest of her, with green eyes and a pinched nose. She's pretty in an unusual kind of way, and she looks strangely familiar.

Then I realise: she's the woman from the cafe. The one I saw with Henry. She must be the one the neighbors have seen, too.

"Hi," I say, my voice shaky. "Um." I try to remember my lines. "Is Susie there? I've come for the dinner party."

She stares at me confused.

"Susie?" she repeats. Her voice is cut like glass, almost aristocratic. "Sorry, I think you've got the wrong house."

"Oh," I say, cringing a little. "Is this not 36 Acacia Avenue?"

She frowns a little, but relaxes her hand on the door.

"Yes, but there's no Susie here, I'm afraid . . ."

"Oh God," I say, flicking myself on the forehead. "Oh God, maybe it wasn't Avenue! Is there an Acacia Road round here?"

She smiles at me. I peer past her into the hall, to spot any evidence of Violet—her handbag maybe, or her parka slung on the bottom of the banisters. But there's nothing. Just Marigold's buggy, which I've seen in lots of videos. The most expensive one, by Stokke, huge and grey and reassuring. Nothing like the flimsy thing I pushed Archie around in for so long. Then my eye lands on a pile of post on a small table to the left of me. There's a large brown parcel on top, Violet's name scrawled in thick felt tip above the address. It's definitely the right house.

"I'm sorry, I don't actually live here, I'm just . . ." she tails off. "I don't really know the area all that well."

"Oh," I say, "never mind." I pull my phone out of my bag, as though to check the address, and I'm about to slink away but then a new idea occurs to me. "I'll just look it up on my phone. I'm sure it was Road, now I think of it. What an idiot! How embarrassing. So sorry to disturb you."

"It's OK," she says, softening. "I wish I could help but like I said, I'm just watching the house, I'm not from round here."

Watching the house? Watching it for what reason? I strain my ears to hear any sounds of life from the back room. Lula and Goldie would be in bed by now, but Skye is allowed to stay up on Saturdays as a treat.

"Oh damn!" I say, frowning at my phone. "I'm out of data. I was going to look up the original email on my phone . . . oh God." I pause, looking around me, as though hoping for divine inspiration. "I guess I could just ring her, but it's so embarrassing! It's my boss, you see, she's just invited me round to celebrate my promotion. All a bit awkward, really—who wants to spend Saturday night with their boss?—but I felt I had to go. And now I can't remember what her address is! She's going to regret promoting me at this rate."

I'm talking too fast. The woman smiles at me again.

"Do you want to use the Wi-Fi here to look it up?" she says, and I am stunned that my plan has worked so easily. As usual, the thrill is almost overwhelming. She pulls the door open a little further. "Come in for a sec, it's freezing out there."

"Oh my goodness, thank you so much!" I say. I can't believe I'm going to get to go in!

"No problem," she says. "Don't want you getting un-promoted, after all. Here, come into the front room, I'll just get the code."

"Thank you so much, you really are a lifesaver."

She switches on the light and ushers me through. I stand alone in Violet's front room as she disappears back down the hallway to the kitchen.

I am transfixed, staring at my surroundings, trying my best to absorb every detail. I consider taking photos of everything to examine closely later, but I've pushed my luck as far as it can go tonight, and don't want to risk ruining everything. I wonder who she is, why she's so naive. Perhaps it's her age. She must know Henry and Violet have fans, and not just fans, but crazed stalkers. I swallow, suddenly nervous. But she doesn't seem to have given it a second thought. My story must have been plausible.

Maybe she's just nice. Living in London, you sometimes forget that people can just be kind, with no agenda.

The sofa is enormous and low, with a huge L-shaped section jutting out in the corner. It's blush pink, impractical for anyone with children, but Violet never lets the kids in this room, so it's pristine. It's covered in cushions that look as though they have been spattered in paint, in a clashing array of colors, but the effect is magnificent.

Violet's taste is impeccable.

Above the sofa is an equally enormous black and white photograph of Violet and Henry kissing. It's a close-up, so you can just see their lips meeting, and the curves of their cheeks. There's a glass coffee table with chrome edges, covered in books with titles like *My Vogue Home*. A stack of silver coasters sits in one corner. Everything is huge, including the marble fireplace with its enormous antique mirror.

"Here you go," she says, reappearing and cutting through my thoughts. She hands me a small card.

"Thank you," I say, taking it from her, and pretend to type the code into my phone.

"Hope it's not far," she says. She's wearing a furry gilet. Now I'm closer to her, I can tell that it's expensive, as is the watch on her wrist, which looks remarkably similar to Violet's. But she's not Violet's sister. Is she a babysitter perhaps?

"Just loading," I say, looking up at her. "Thank you so much, you are such a lifesaver."

"It's fine," she says. "The kind of thing I'd do, if I'm honest. And it is confusing round here, with so many streets with similar names."

"Yes," I say, eagerly. "So you don't live here? It's a lovely house. I did wonder how much my boss was earning when I saw it!"

"No, I live in Somerset. I'm just watching the place, like I said, for Henry. He's at the hospital tonight." She pauses, suddenly squinting at me. My heart starts to pound.

"Oh dear," I say, but I know I'm treading on dodgy ground. "Nothing serious, I hope?"

She shakes her head, looking uncomfortable for the first time. She knows she's said too much, is suddenly suspicious.

"Found the email?" she says, nodding at my phone.

It's almost agony, being so close but still so far, but it's time to leave.

"Yep," I say. I roll my eyes. "What an idiot. As I'd thought, it's Acacia Road. I'm so sorry. I'm going to be so late, it's a ten-minute walk away. Thank you so much, let me just screen grab the directions on my phone . . . and then I'll leave you in peace."

"Glad you got it sorted."

I smile at her. Where are the children? I can't ask her, I just can't. It's too intrusive.

"*Strictly*'s on now, isn't it?" I say as I walk towards the front door. "To be honest that's where I'd usually be now—glued to the telly with a glass of gin in my hand!"

She smiles again, and a flicker of sadness crosses her eyes.

Yes. We've got it on in the back room. Not really my cup of tea but the children love it."

"Oh, I didn't realise you had kids!" I say, pausing on the giant door-mat. "I'm so sorry again to have bothered you."

"They're not mine," she says. I take a long look at her again, think-ing of the rumors that circle Henry all the time. Have they broken up? Is this his new partner? Where's Violet now? Perhaps this whole expe-dition has been a mistake. I have more questions than answers now.

"Well," she says, smiling at me again. "Enjoy your dinner party."

"Thank you so much for your help," I reply, and as she shuts the door behind me, something catches the light from above, glinting at me. Her necklace. Three small gold discs, each inscribed with a letter, spelling out the name *Amy*.

20 February 2017
From: gottheblues@hotmail.com
To: violet@violetisblue.com

Hi Violet,

I have some thoughts about your new assistant Mandy.

I know why you chose her, of course. She's blonde, like you. Slim. Her nose is a little wonky, but she has big brown eyes that remind one of a puppy, and a laugh that's the definition of grating. She's "instaworthy."

But even so, Violet, she's not good for you.

For one thing, her spelling is shocking. I know that these days people think spelling doesn't matter, that text-speak has become an acceptable form of communication, but at the end of the day, Violet, you're running a business. You need to behave professionally. If you're asking people to buy into your content, then the very least they deserve is for it to be grammatically correct, and edited properly.

But the fact she's thick isn't the main issue for me. It's her lack of experience with children that concerns me. I know technically she's not your nanny, she's your PA, but we all know you leave the girls with her sometimes. I don't think you should. She doesn't know that Skye likes her toast cut into quarters, that Lula actually likes the crusts. She has no patience with them, either.

I heard her on your vlog the other day, telling Lula that if she went to nursery she'd have to be potty-trained by now or she'd be bullied by the other kids. And then she told her she was naughty when she had an accident on the floor. I know you

97

laughed it off, but do you not know that if you tell children they are bad, or lazy, or naughty, they will internalise this and believe it about themselves? You can't shame someone into being potty trained, it's unbelievably damaging.

Please don't leave your kids with this woman.

What kind of mother are you?

LILY

For the entire journey home, I turn the silver coaster over in my hands, running my fingers across its delicately engraved pattern, wondering who bought it for them, whether Violet chose it herself. I know I shouldn't have taken it, but in a house so full of *stuff* she's not likely to miss it, is she?

It takes me an hour to get back to Acton and as I approach my front door, I start to worry. I probably should have told Susie I was coming back early. What if she's invited a man round? No, she wouldn't do that. Would she? It's not that I'd *mind*, it's just . . .

I push my key into the lock, making as much noise as possible.

"Only me!" I call through the door as it opens. "It was awful."

The lights are off in the hallway, but I can hear the television coming from the living room. I follow the sound. Susie's sitting, feet up on the sofa, phone in hand. Alone. She switches off the television as I come in.

"Hi," she says, looking surprised. The make-up under her eyes is smudged, as though she's been watching a sad film and has rubbed away tears. "That's a shame."

"Everything all right?" I sit down at the armchair next to her and yank off the boots. The waistband of my jeans is cutting into my stomach, the fabric tight and uncomfortable around my knees. Skinny jeans are for skinny people; I can't wait to put my pyjamas on.

"He's been an angel," Susie says, swinging her legs round and sitting up. She sniffs slightly. "One story and then he practically jumped into bed. Fell asleep straight away."

"Wow."

"Yeah, must have really not liked me!" She smiles. "But what about you?! Hang on, let me get a glass for you, I want to hear the whole story."

I lean back into the armchair and wait for her to return from the kitchen. When she does so, she pours me a huge glass from the bottle of red she brought over and thrusts it at me.

"I haven't eaten anything," I say, taking it with mock reluctance.

"Oh God, order a pizza," she replies.

"No, it's OK," I say. I have eighty pounds left in my account until payday, and that has to cover my travel and food for the week. "I'll make some toast in a minute."

"So, tell me everything," Susie says, settling back down on the sofa, her eyes flashing with interest.

"He seemed really nervous. I don't think he'd been on many—or maybe even any—dates before. He was practically shaking." I start to warm up, remembering a date I went on once, before I met James.

"Oh God!" Susie says, giggling.

"Yes, and he was wearing a fleece. And carrying a rucksack. On both shoulders, as though he was going for a long walk in the country, not a Saturday night date in the middle of London."

"Oh you poor thing!"

"Maybe I should have given it a bit longer, but honestly, an hour of talking at him and I'd completely run out of things to say. I felt so sorry for him, but it was better not to lead him on, wasn't it? I just made noises about Archie being an early riser and snuck off before he had the chance to mention getting any food." My stomach starts to grumble. "'And on that note, I'll just put some toast on."

In the kitchen, I think again about Amy, the strange woman in Violet's house, what she said about Henry being at the hospital. What hospital and why? And who is Amy? Throughout my journey home I wracked my brains, trying to think if I'd ever seen this mysterious Amy in any of Violet's vlogs, but I would have remembered her, I'm sure of it.

As I spread butter on my toast, I feel a vibration in my back pocket. My phone. It's a text from Ellie, asking for news. I smother my toast with Marmite and grab one of Archie's Babybels from the fridge to go with it, taking the sorry supper back into the living room.

"Well, you just need to get straight back on there, I'm afraid," Susie says. "Those are the rules of Internet dating. Plenty more fish in the sea. Well done you—getting back out there after losing your husband is so brave. Is that all you're having?"

"It's fine, I hate eating a proper meal after 9pm."

Susie gestures towards the empty pizza box on my coffee table.

"You should have called me on your way back, I could have ordered you one too."

"I told you, it's fine," I say, snappily. "Sorry."

She glances at me and I shrug.

"Expensive time of year and all that . . ."

"How are you feeling about work?" she says.

"Oh you know, pays the bills," I say. *Barely*, I add in my head, washing down my toast with a swig of wine. It's delicious—so much better than the stuff I subsist on. "I like working with you."

"Do you think in the new year you might look for something new?" She starts twisting her bracelets round with her fingers.

"Don't worry, I'm not going to leave you to the world's most disorganised men, I promise," I say, smiling at her in what I hope is a reassuring way. But something's wrong. She takes a big sniff, leans forward and puts her glass down on the coffee table.

"Oh God," she says, rubbing her forehead with her fingers.

"What's the matter?" I say, reaching out to her. I knew there was something going on. I've been so caught up with all this Violet nonsense, I've not thought to find out how Susie, my real life, actual proper friend, is.

"Nothing, it's just . . . shit. Last week, when we all went for work drinks. I ended up having a few too many, one thing led to another . . ."

"And?" I say. I consider the list of possible suspects. That Susie has had a one-night stand with someone from the office isn't a huge surprise, but her reaction to it is.

She gulps air. "I went home with Ben. Abigail was away at some hen do. Oh shit, I'm such a disaster. Please don't judge me."

I swallow.

"Wow. Did you . . . what happened?"

"No, but nearly. On his sofa. It was awful. He was so drunk, he couldn't . . . you know. *Keep it up.* And then afterwards he got all emotional, started telling me he'd never done anything like it before, that the company was in trouble, that he was worried it was going to go under . . ."

My eyes widen.

"Yes, exactly," she says, noting my alarm. "I didn't want to say anything before . . . I know how hard things are for you, even though you always pretend everything is fine."

I look down. Susie continues.

"He's looking for a buyer for the firm but he mentioned there would have to be redundancies if things didn't pick up soon."

"Oh," I say, trying to work out how I feel about this news. "Did he mention me specifically?"

"No!" Susie says, squeezing me on the knee. "No. I'm just aware that sometimes . . . you say you don't have much to do. I just think it might be good to make yourself look busy, make yourself indispensable . . . just in case. You don't want to be the most obvious victim; I suppose that's what I'm trying to say."

I nod.

"I'll start applying for things in the morning," I say. I can't afford to have any gap in employment, no matter how short. I must check my contract and find out what I'd be owed in redundancy pay. I haven't been there long—just over two years—so it's not likely to be much. "Thanks for the heads up."

"Don't be silly," she says, looking down at her hands. "I feel terrible about the whole thing. I only know because he was so drunk . . . it all came out in this gush. It was awful."

"What about your job?" I say, but as soon as the words have left my mouth I realise that she'll be the last to go now. He's not going to get rid of someone with the kind of information that could ruin his marriage. Maybe I should have gone home with Ben, I think, bitterly.

"Yeah," Susie says, looking away. "It's at risk too. I think."

"Don't feel bad," I say, and her eyes meet mine. "He's the one that's married, not you."

"Yeah, but still . . . I've met Abigail and she's lovely. Like, really lovely. I've never done anything like that before. Never. It's awful, so against the sisterhood."

"Don't beat yourself up," I say. "You're not the first and you won't be the last . . ."

She looks up at me.

"Lily! What are you saying?"

I sit back. I wasn't saying anything, but the desperation in her eyes stirs something in me.

"Well, you never asked me how I met James. We met in a bar. But what he didn't tell me was that he was, er, married."

I give a short cough.

"No way?"

"Way," I say, swallowing. The adrenalin of the evening seems to have gone to my head. I never usually lie about things like this, but it's a small sin to make Susie feel like she's not the only one who's been in this situation. "Yeah, we were, er, seeing each other for eighteen months before he left his wife for me."

"Oh God, Lily. And then you guys got married? That must have been so quick?"

"Yep," I say, my heart thudding, aware that the maths probably doesn't work. "It was a whirlwind."

"What are we like?" She rolls her eyes. "Thank you for being so honest. I've just been feeling a bit low lately. Christmas, you know, all the smug couples . . . another year in my single bed at my parents' house. Alone. Just another stupid, drunken slut."

"Don't talk about my friend Susie like that!" I say, and I reach forward for the wine bottle, to refill her glass. As I do so, my phone vibrates again, lighting up on the coffee table in front of us. Susie eyes it.

"I better leave you to it," she says. "Looks like lover boy's been in touch to suggest a second date."

It's another message from Ellie. She sounds more frantic now, saying she's concerned for my safety.

"Oh, no, it's . . . just a friend," I say, locking the screen. A small part of me is enjoying keeping her waiting for the news. Just for once it's nice to be the one people are waiting to hear from, rather than it always being the other way round. "Don't worry."

"I better be off anyway," she says, standing up. "Otherwise I'll finish the bottle and then God knows what will happen. It was so awkward at work last week; he wouldn't look me in the eye. I'm such a cliché!"

I give her a sympathetic smile as I rise to my feet, too. The wine bottle stares at me from the table. I should tell her to take it home.

"See you Monday," she says, as she pulls on her coat. "Thanks for the chat. You're a good listener."

"It was nothing," I say. I hold her gaze for a few seconds, trying to imagine what would have made her go home with Ben. People are never what they seem. "Thanks for babysitting. And for the warning. I really appreciate it. As I said, things are quite tricky, money-wise . . ." I tail off and stand up straighter. She kisses me on the cheek, and I close the door behind her softly, digging my phone out of my pocket and punching out a reply to Ellie.

And then I turn back to the hall, staring at Archie's shut door. Tonight I can't resist. It's something I used to do, when Archie was little, but stopped because I didn't want him to wake up and see me standing there. Thought it might scare him. But tonight the pull is too strong. I tiptoe into his room, and stand by the side of his bed, listening to the gentle sound of his deep breaths as he sleeps. My boy, who deserves so much better than this: a huge Christmas tree, a playroom of his own, a hamster in a cage. A sibling. A father. A mother who doesn't make up pathetic fibs so that people will like her more.

A mother who can cope.

YVONNE

We're about to go to Simon's parents' for lunch and I'm dreading it more than usual. Last night, I woke up at 2am worrying about Violet and Henry, and lay there wondering if I should call the local hospitals, even though that would be hugely inappropriate. At 5am, I gave up wondering and got up, creeping downstairs to do my usual round of Google stalking. But there was nothing to reassure me, and I was left with my imagination playing the worst-case scenario on a loop.

I'm exhausted this morning. But it's Simon's mother's birthday, so even though we saw them last Sunday, there's no chance of getting out of this one. If only I was pregnant already, I could feign exhaustion, morning sickness, the potential for hyperemesis, but it's still too early. I've got another week of torture to get through before I get my reward.

We climb into the car and he whistles softly as we turn out of our tiny, uneven driveway on to the road. He's happy, staring straight ahead, his thoughts floating somewhere gentle.

It's only a thirty-minute drive to his parents', and I pass the time daydreaming about names. I've yet to broach the topic with Simon. I read somewhere that a woman becomes a mother when she gets pregnant, but a man only becomes a father when he holds his baby in his arms. Even if Simon knew what I know, it's all too abstract for him at the moment. I can't expect him to feel any kind of relationship with the bundle of cells that will be implanting in my uterus either tomorrow or the day after.

While Simon drives, I check in with the other GoMamas women in my group on my phone—my Trying To Conceive buddies. I've never met any of them—don't even know what they look like—but they know more about this than anyone in my real life. And the whole ridiculous plan was Jade79's idea. I wonder if I would have come up with it myself.

Of course I would have done, but her validation definitely made me feel less insane.

You deserve your rainbow baby, she had written. *After everything you've been through.*

My GoMamas friends are all as nervous as I am. A few are a couple of days behind me and one is testing tomorrow, even though most people would agree that 9 DPO is the absolute earliest you can POAS. Pee on a stick. The acronyms are ridiculous, but they make me feel like I'm part of a club, a secret club full of anxious but supportive women. We only turn on one another when one of us gets a BFP (big fat positive). The lucky mother-to-be gets a perfunctory congratulations after announcing her news, then she is cast out. They cease to exist; they disappear from the Trying To Conceive threads and move on to the Expectant Mother ones.

After giving advice that makes not one ounce of difference to whether one particular woman is actually pregnant or not, I open the forum thread about Violet. It's quieter than last week, when she initially disappeared and there was a rush of people posting, all sharing their various conspiracy theories. No one's updated it this morning and it's already 11am. I wonder if Violet's out there, reading all these messages, thinking everyone is an idiot for caring so much about someone they've never met before.

I quit the forum app and open Instagram instead, scrolling down my feed. It's a mix of celebrities and real-life friends, most of whom are photographers like me. I double tap each picture as it loads. Everything on social media is so fake, so contrived, it doesn't actually matter what I'm liking.

One image catches my eye. Katie took it. No surprises there—her work is breathtaking. It's a woman in her wedding dress, standing on an enormous staircase. I don't recognise the venue but I can tell it's somewhere expensive because the raw silk of her dress has been picked up by the lens, and everything about the photograph screams money. I think of our wedding, late last year. My dad had given me a thousand pounds towards it, most of which I'd spent on my dress. Simon's parents had offered to put some cash behind the bar, but the rest of it had been down to us, and we'd just bought the house, so we were broke.

I remember the tinge of disappointment that followed me around all day, the way I couldn't help but compare things to the weddings I'd photographed. And of course, my mind was inevitably drawn to the most lavish wedding I'd ever attended.

Violet's.

My first encounter with her. It was at Carwell House, of course, beloved of celebrities and media types. They'd hired the entire place—Henry was good friends with the owner, so he'd probably got it for a discount. Even so, it was extravagant by anyone's standards, and certainly more extravagant than any wedding I'd ever photographed before.

I have more memories of their wedding than I do of my own. Little details, things that have stuck. His face when he first saw me. The way Henry snapped at Violet in front of me at the reception. The way that Skye, who was only two and a half, wet herself during the ceremony. I'd heard Violet's mother telling her she had to hold it in until after the vows were made, despite her noisy protests, and so it served them all right. Poor thing. They'd laughed it off—Violet even made a video about her "wedding disasters"—but I could tell she was embarrassed.

Violet was still breastfeeding Lula, and I couldn't help but sneak a shot of her huddled in one corner of the huge banqueting room, her breast hanging out of her thin Maria Grachvogel wedding dress, Lula firmly attached to it. I thought perhaps she'd think it was a special moment. When I sent over the shots for them to pick their favorites, I was vindicated to see that Violet had circled it vigorously. *Love this!* She'd written next to it on the contact sheet. Her writing was as insubstantial as her.

But what did I expect? This was a woman who got married in bare feet.

I found out from the wedding planner that the day had cost just short of sixty grand. Sixty thousand pounds. A lot had been gifted in exchange for coverage in Henry's magazine.

My thoughts are interrupted by Simon turning the radio on. I'd been enjoying the silence.

"Just want the headlines," he says. He means the sports headlines, of course.

I stare out of the window at the row upon row of 1930s semis, wondering if Violet and Henry will ever share what's really going on.

* * *

Pat's not well, which has made everything a lot less stressful than usual. He's been in bed all morning, Jane explained as we came in.

So she has spent most of this morning in the kitchen, cooking her own birthday meal. I offered to help, but I was shooed away. I've been able to sit in their stuffy front room, reading the latest news about Violet and Henry in a copy of *The Sunday Chronicle*, which Pat helpfully has delivered, while Simon helps her with the food. The feature hasn't been published online yet, and I felt my heart race as I saw Violet's face on the front page and turned to read it. It seems that a "source" claimed Violet chose to leave social media after becoming upset by the trolling she was experiencing both in public and in private. The source went even further to claim that there were rumors that Violet's initial postnatal depression, the whole reason for her starting her YouTube channel in the first place, was an invention. That the entire story was contrived in order to prey on the misery of real women who were really dealing with it, in order to sell them her self-help book later down the line.

There was also another "source" claiming that Violet and Henry's marriage was a sham. That they were tied together by the lucrative nature of their pairing, and that in secret they hated each other. There were more rumors of Henry's alleged infidelity, claims that he had never wanted to settle down, that Violet had tricked him into marriage, the insinuation being that she was a talentless gold digger.

That one seems a little unfair.

All in all, it's the perfect tabloid story: taking up a whole double-page spread in the UK's most popular Sunday newspaper. I read the whole thing twice, not letting my eyes linger too long on the photographs they'd used—mostly taken from Henry's Instagram account. I then settle back, allowing Jane and Pat's sagging sofa to swallow me up, amazed that no one has worked out the truth.

HENRY

I took Yvonne home after that first afternoon in the pub. Home to the flat in Chelsea, that my father had bought me as some kind of obligation of aristocratic parenting. Send them to Harrow, give them all the opportunities you can, kick up a stink when they refuse to do law at university, and then begrudgingly set them up in a flat off the Kings Road, and leave them to make a mess of their lives with a clean conscience. Parenting over. Job's a (not so) good'un.

I was lost back then. Had notions of being a serious writer, but could never quite be serious enough, not when there was so much fun to be had. My father, a QC no less, thought my job was a joke. Thought I'd get it out of my system and retrain in my twenties. I'm not sure he's ever forgiven me, although Violet has done a good job of winning him over, as she does with everyone who meets her.

But this isn't about Violet. It's about her. I took her home and she was impressed with the flat, as they all were, and we made love twice, and I liked her, in a casual way. The problem was I had a girlfriend at the time. Nothing serious—not on my part anyway—after all, I was only twenty-six . . . But Camille was the little sister of a friend of mine, and he'd made jokes about breaking my legs if I ever hurt her, and to be quite honest, I thought he might.

So perhaps I wasn't quite as chivalrous towards her as my mother would have hoped I'd be. When I woke up the next morning, Yvonne was standing over me, holding my cafetière and waving it at me.

"Coffee?" she said, a bright smile plastered all over her face. There was no trace of the meek picture assistant I'd naively assumed wouldn't object to a one-night stand, no questions asked. This was a different person entirely. Lighter, more radiant. Even her hair was slightly kinked on one side, softening her features. She was attractive like this. Loosened up, like an undone tie.

I did what any man would have done. I had manners, if not morals. I stood up, kissed her, pulled out a stool for her at the island unit and made her breakfast. All the while secretly wishing she'd just cleared off while I'd been sleeping.

"Let me put you in a cab," I said, when the morning started to roll dangerously towards afternoon and she was still sitting in my shirt, bare legs tucked up underneath her on my leather sofa, showing no signs of leaving. The sunlight was streaming through the window, throwing shadows across her face. I had a vision of her then, much older. "You must be wanting to get home."

"Ugh," she said, shaking her head. Home, it turned out, was a single bed in a house share in Clapham, and she didn't have any plans that weekend. On the other hand, I was expected at Camille's by 2pm. It was August, she was having a barbecue on her tiny roof terrace, and everyone was going to be there.

Hindsight is a glorious thing, as they say. If I had thrown her out on to the street, if I hadn't made those bloody pancakes, maybe things would be very different now.

In the end, I did what all cowards do. I lied, told her with a pulled face of disappointment that I was off to visit my parents that afternoon. Thank God these were the days before social media, before your every move can be tracked and traced by the suspicious. She accepted my excuse graciously, collected up her things and left. On the doorstep, she told me it had been fun, gave me a little wink. My whole body relaxed, believing I'd got away with it, that we were on the same page.

I remember the smug feeling I had as I strolled to Camille's. Thinking I had it all: the job, the social circle and the girls I'd always wanted. It was like a warm drink heating me up from the inside. The smug self-satisfaction of the least deserving.

LILY

"Henry Blake is a smug, self-satisfied twat," Luke says, draining his paper cup. I glance around. This is not the sort of language you usually hear at the soft-play centre. Not out loud, anyway. Under harassed parents' breaths, certainly.

Another Sunday at soft-play. When Ellie's journalist friend Luke called me this morning, I had no time to arrange childcare. I'm embarrassed I had to meet him here, but it was the only place Archie was guaranteed to leave us in peace, at least for twenty minutes. I could have put Luke off, of course, but there was something in his voice that I warmed to. And after last night, I needed to get out. To spend time with other people.

Mind you, the coffee here is terrible. I look at Luke, taking in the bright blue of his eyes, the smattering of freckles over his nose. His hair is gingerish and styled in a perfect wave across his head. He's staring at the multicolored foam-filled monstrosity in one corner of the room. Ellie hadn't mentioned that he was this good-looking, and I wish I'd made more of an effort with my clothes. I don't know what I was expecting from a popular culture journalist—he was careful to correct me when I said he "did celebs"—but this handsome vision in front of me certainly wasn't it.

"Did you work with him then?" I ask, wishing I'd bought a bottle of water as well as the coffee. My throat is arid. Susie's wine was heavier than I'm used to.

"Not directly," Luke says, his eyes flicking back to mine. I try not to look away. "But I met him a few times, we had friends in common.

You could tell he was very . . . pleased with himself, let's say." He pauses, points towards the soft-play hell in the corner. "Your little lad is really going for it. Fearless."

He smiles.

There's a hint of something in his accent—not Geordie exactly, but maybe further up the coast. Northumbrian? It's gentle and reassuring and I think I could listen to him talk all day.

"So," he says. He reaches into his leather record bag and pulls out a notebook. He still hasn't taken his parka off. I wonder how he sees me. Probably as some washed-up single mother that he's planning on getting away from as soon as possible.

"How old are you?" I ask, thinking aloud. I immediately regret my own rude question, but he doesn't seem phased at all.

"Thirty-four," he replies, cheerfully. "You?"

"Twenty-seven," I say. "Sorry. You just . . . well, you look younger. I mean . . . you look, er, well, good for your age."

He gives a long laugh, his eyes widening.

"Cheers. That'll be my great skincare routine. Anyway . . . I won't take up too much of your time, I can see you've got your hands full with your little lad . . ."

"No, it's fine," I say, a little too quickly. "Honestly. He'll be happy for hours yet." It's a slight exaggeration, but Luke sits back, looking more relaxed, and I tell him about the rumor on GoMamas that there'd been a fight, resulting in an ambulance being called, and about last night and the mysterious Amy, holed up in Henry and Violet's house and secretly meeting him in cafes. I tell him what Amy told me about Henry being at the hospital. He makes notes, his eyebrows rising at the revelation that I hung around outside Skye's school, waiting to see her, but it doesn't feel like he's judging me. Not like I'd expect to be judged. But then again, he's an investigative journalist, and stalking is part of their job description. Compared to phone-tapping and goodness knows what else, what I've done is small fry.

"You might have seen," he says, when I stop speaking to take another gulp of weak coffee. "There was a big piece about them in *The*

Sunday Chronicle this morning. Nothing substantial to it though. Just tabloid fluff. I want to do a proper piece about the price these vloggers pay. It's been done before, but I like the mammy angle. So often it's focused on the teen market, you know, but Violet's a bit unusual in that she's older. You wouldn't expect adults to be so easily drawn in by these influencers, and yet they are. And of course, Violet used to be a journalist herself, so she knows how to play the game."

"Have you ever met her?" I ask.

"Hmm, yes. Once at an event."

"Ellie thought you wouldn't have even heard of her," I say.

"My sister's got a lad," he replies, "about the same age as yours. He's great. She's a single mum, gets lonely, so she's always chewing my ear off about the latest mammy trend. In fact, I spoke to her this morning about Violet and she was desperate for me to do the story."

"I'm a single mum, too," I say.

"Oh? Sorry to hear that," he says, and his mouth twitches a little. Perhaps Ellie already told him. With a fright, I realise she might have actually been trying to set us up. My brain cycles through all the things I've written on the forum in the past. Have I ever sounded needy or desperate for a man? I don't think so, but recent experience has taught me that I don't always remember what I've posted online late at night.

"It's OK," I say, feeling my cheeks redden. I shouldn't have said anything, and my words hang in the air. I must remember that he's not interested in *me*, he's interested in Violet. Time to change the subject. "So, tell me more about Henry. I'm curious. He always came across quite well on Violet's vlogs. A bit full of himself, but he seemed very charming."

"Oh, I'm sure he did. He's charming enough for the right audience. I don't know, I didn't get a good vibe from him. He seemed like there was a lot going on under the surface."

"Do you think he was violent towards her?" The words come out in a rush. "Only there are some theories on GM . . ."

"GM?"

"On the mummy forum, GoMamas, the one where someone said they saw an ambulance being called . . . they're big fans of acronyms." I roll my eyes, as though I think it's all ridiculous, despite the fact I spend nearly a third of my life on the site.

He nods, writes something in his notebook.

"A few of the women on there thought that Henry was violent. Violet quite often had bruises on her arms and legs—really visible ones—and she never bothered to hide them." I swallow. "Other people thought it was just life with toddlers; they can be amazingly boisterous, and Archie's certainly left his fair share of bruises on me."

"He didn't strike me as a violent kind of person, no," he says. "More manipulative. I don't know. It's hard to tell when you've only met someone a handful of times, and never been alone with them. In company he was always very charming, like I said, but there was definitely a feeling of superiority. Nothing unusual about that, of course. Especially not given the job he does, and his family background."

"His family background?"

"Oh yeah, they're loaded, the Blakes," he says, closing the notebook. I swallow the feeling of disappointment. He's going to make his excuses and leave. How do I get him to stay? "Old-school family money. He went to Harrow, you know?"

"Did he?" I say, genuinely surprised that there's something I didn't know about him. I thought I knew it all. "He kept that quiet."

"Yeah, well, it's all part of the façade, I guess. But his dad's loaded. He comes from a large farming family and they own half of the land in Somerset. Did you think they got that huge house off the back of his editor's salary?"

I nod.

"Not a chance. And although Violet's pretty successful—I've seen her accounts—it's only in the last year or so that the sums have got big. Like with all influencers."

"Influencers," I say, wrinkling my nose. "It's such an unpleasant term."

"Yeah."

"What will you do next?" I ask. Archie's bedraggled form is making its way towards me and I know that this civilised chat about one of my favorite subjects is about to come to an end.

Luke opens his notebook again, pushes the end of his pen to his lips. My eyes linger on them a little longer than they should.

"I've got plenty to follow up on thanks to you," he says, and I smile. "But first of all, I need to work out who this Amy is—she might be a babysitter for all we know. I'll speak to Violet's manager—they'll have to put some sort of statement out after that piece today anyway—and then I'll see if there's a publicist at the magazine company who wants to talk to me about things from Henry's point of view. There are lots of leads."

"Star Wars fan?" I say, nodding at his pen.

"What?" He looks at it. "Oh! Yeah, my nephew got it for me. He's just getting old enough to enjoy them."

"Awesome. My friend was an extra on the *The Last Jedi* actually . . . she said it was an incredible experience. Did you know they filmed most of it at Pinewood? Crazy, isn't it? That something so huge is filmed in Slough. I mean, you'd expect it to be somewhere far more glamorous . . ." I trail off, my brain scrambling for detail to add to this anecdote, anything to make him stay.

"Ha, yeah," he says, but his eyes scan towards the large clock on the wall, and I know I've lost him.

"Will you keep me posted?" I ask. My hand shoots out reflexively and rests on his forearm. There's a lump in my throat. "It's just . . . I don't know. I've got a feeling. I've got a feeling and I can't shake it. I'm scared. I'm scared he's done something to her."

"I'll get to the bottom of it." He's smiling, but there's a look in his eyes I've seen before, so many times. I let my hand fall away from his arm and rest back at my side. It was nice of Ellie to try, but he's not interested in me. Of course he's not. I'm not glamorous or rich or beautiful or engaging.

"Mummy!" I look down, startled. Archie's little hands are on my legs as he tries to climb on to my lap. I pull him up and he regards Luke with indifference.

"I wonder what she saw in him," I say, staring past Luke's head and absentmindedly smoothing Archie's hair into place.

"Isn't it obvious?" Luke replies, and I look back at him. His eyes are so very blue. "He's incredibly wealthy."

"She's not a gold digger," I say, instinctively. Still trying to defend her, despite everything. "She's not like that."

"Isn't she?" Luke says, giving me a kind of sideways smirk. He stands up, leaning down to shake Archie's hand.

"Nice to meet you, little chap," he says, and then he looks back to me. "I'll be in touch, Lily. And thanks again."

YVONNE

When they got engaged, Henry and Violet started to write a column together in his magazine. A kind of "his and hers" perspective on the whole engagement-wedding-marriage subject. I suppose Henry's editor thought it might be quite a cute idea, something to lure in new advertisers.

I knew about her by then, of course. I'd been "following" her online ever since they first got together. But there was something about the fact they were getting married—that final frontier he mockingly told me he'd never cross—that stuck a knife into me. That made me determined to meet her, and gave me an obvious way of doing so. It was a bit of an effort, with a lot of asking around, but eventually through a friend-of-a-friend I met their uber-photographer Lucio, and after quite a bit of persuading, he agreed to let me second-shoot the wedding. I had to do it for free, of course, but it wasn't much of a price to pay.

I kept all those columns—I tore them out of the magazine and filed them away carefully. They lie in plastic sheaths inside a ring binder covered in stars—one I used when Henry and I worked together. It was just an admin file then, something I kept holiday forms and freelancers' details in. When I left my job, it was the only thing I took with me. I left everything else: the arty postcards pinned to the board behind my computer, the special pen I used to mark up Cromalins, the small heart-shaped cushion that fitted perfectly into the hollow of my back.

I know why I kept the ring binder. Because it was something he gave me. A pathetic "gift" from the stationery cupboard that I imbued with more significance than it deserved.

It now lives at the back of the wardrobe in the spare bedroom, along with Nathan's box. I don't know why I kept all the columns, really. I was angry—but more than that, I was outraged. What did this woman have that I didn't? What made her so special?

I devoured them all, but they didn't tell me enough, and that's when I knew I'd have to meet her for myself. Closure, I told myself. That's all it would be.

Violet heavily promoted the columns, of course, calling it exclusive content, a collaboration she was really proud of, as though writing 400 words of drivel about your future husband was something groundbreaking. But it had the right effect. She gained a few thousand new subscribers. Probably women who read their boyfriend's copy of the mag on the loo, when they'd finished *Grazia* for the week.

The columns had run for nearly a year, and then stopped, somewhat abruptly, a month before the wedding. There was no explanation as to why. They were just pulled. Perhaps Violet got bored of writing them, perhaps the publishers decided that Henry was oversharing. Perhaps lots of readers wrote in to complain that they didn't buy men's magazines to read about the latest trends in wedding favors. Perhaps I was one of them.

I can't remember now. Sounds like the sort of thing I might have done, I guess.

*   *   *

Simon is working tonight. Another meeting with his boss about his postpartum classes, another night home alone for me. Preparing. Imagining. Tomorrow is probably going to be implantation day, when our miraculous bundle of cells burrows its way into my uterus wall and begins to grow into a baby.

As I have found myself so often lately, I am back upstairs, in the spare bedroom. Rummaging through my wardrobe for things. Mementos. The last time I got pregnant there weren't apps. No technical way of tracking symptoms. I had a diary though, of course. I have kept a diary my entire life. The sad thing is that when things are going well, I forget to write in it, which means all I'm left with are notebooks full of angst and misery. Not the sort of thing I've ever felt like re-reading, but somehow I can't bear to part with them.

But thankfully, when I was pregnant last time, I kept detailed notes.

I remember the notebook. I bought a new one especially, the day I discovered I was pregnant. It was a Tuesday. I remember because we had our cover meeting that morning, and I couldn't concentrate on any of it. I took my lunch break early—at 12pm—and took the lift down from the seventeenth floor and marched across the bridge to Ludgate Circus. It was September, one of those boiling hot days in London when pushing your way through the mass of tourists felt like walking through soup. It was only as I paused for a few seconds on the bridge, watching the Thames sparkle beneath me, that I finally felt able to breathe.

It was too soon, of course, too soon to be pregnant, but somehow I knew it was going to be all right. I was twenty-three years old. I had Henry, and everything was going to be fine.

In Waterstones, I sat for a minute in the children's book department, taking in the view. A mass of brightly colored books, all different shapes and sizes. Soon it would be me, I thought, sifting through them all with my eyes, trying to pick one that would suit my son. Because I was sure, even back then, that it would be a boy. He was such a man's man. It seemed obvious that Henry could only be the father of sons.

I was wrong about that, of course.

The selection of notebooks was disappointing, and in the end I chose a pale blue Moleskine. Slim and light enough to fit in my handbag, something I could carry with me at all times. Over the next twenty weeks I filled that notebook almost to the last page. Perhaps that's where I went wrong. I should have bought a thicker one.

I want to read it now. There's a drawer at the bottom of the wardrobe with all my diaries in it. I assume it's going to be easy to find, but my initial rummage brings me no joy. In the end, I go downstairs, make a cup of chamomile tea and bring it back up with me, setting it down on the small mirrored bedside table. Pushka follows me upstairs, curling up against the pillow on the spare bed, eyeing me curiously as she meticulously combs her tail with her tongue.

I work my way through the drawer methodically, pulling each note-book out and setting it down by the radiator. It takes a while to empty—I keep getting distracted, flicking open each book to see what year it's from, and reading a few pages from each. Remembering the past, all the men who used and betrayed me. Reliving those bleak patches when I ran home to my father, broken and disconnected from life, until the situation with him became unbearable and I escaped again. Up and down, round and round, like a woman being spun in the giant wash-ing machine of life. Picking friends up and dropping them again with exhausting frequency. And then when it all came to a head, the lazy, box-ticking diagnosis of an over-worked, under-interested doctor and his suggested treatment: a life on antidepressants.

I refused that, of course. There was only one cure for the way I was feeling.

It's all here. My whole life, thus far, laid out for anyone to discover. And in a more extreme way, Violet is doing the same. She once made a video defending her choice to exploit her children for financial gain, claiming that vlogging was her way of recording her family's story. That her children would thank her for the memories when they were older. That they were lucky—they'd always have a record of their childhood to look back on.

The fact that they might not want it didn't seem to have occurred to her.

I sit back against the bed, sipping my tea, my diaries lined up in uneven towers in front of me. The slim blue one is nowhere to be found. I must have thrown it away. Or burnt it. Who knows.

The memories after that time are still too painful, a canyon in my mind that I don't look into.

It's been seventeen years since I was last pregnant.

A surge of frustration ripples through me and I kick the tower of notebooks that's closest to me, watching it tumble into a rubble of leather-bound pages. Where could it be?

I stand up and reach into the wardrobe again, looking for Nathan's box. I only opened it a few days ago, and I'm sure the diary isn't in there, but just in case I missed it somehow, I decide to check.

I push the diaries aside with my arm, and place the box in front of me on the carpet. I wonder what Simon would think if he ever saw it. Sometimes I worry that I underestimate him, that there's more to him than his laid-back demeanor suggests. The way he brushes off our fights. It isn't just because he doesn't want to deal with them. There's something deeper there: an understanding. An understanding of me, my temper, my insecurity. I like to think I'm the smart one, but he's more emotionally mature than I give him credit for.

He married me, after all. Saved me from myself.

If he saw this box he'd be sad for me. He'd want me to let go. It's his mantra: to focus on the present, to leave the past behind. He doesn't believe in grudges. *Holding on to anger is like drinking poison and waiting for the other person to die*, that's what he always says. It makes sense, but it's just an expression and it doesn't make letting go any easier.

I take out Nathan's clothes delicately, making sure to keep them folded neatly as I lay them down on the floor. It's a strange experience, seeing them all lined up again. The white babygrow and hat I ordered just last week are already part of the group, as though they have been there all along.

Once I have laid all the outfits out on the carpet, I turn back to the box. No sign of the diary. The box is empty, except for a small white envelope. I had forgotten about this envelope. I pick it up, lifting the flap, knowing what I'll find.

Inside is a photograph of me in the hospital, Nathan in my arms. I am staring down at him, my expression hidden from view. But even though I can't see it, I know my face is a mess from crying, and as I stare at us together, the tears begin to fall anew.

That's why, I think to myself, fiercely. *That's why I deserve it this time.*

LILY

I'm in the office, applying for jobs, but I can't concentrate. I fired off some emails to recruitment agents first thing, and am now trawling the job sites for anything suitable. I'm trying to feel positive about the thought of a new job. 2018: a new year, a new career. But there's that little voice at the back of my head that keeps telling me how disappointed my nineteen-year-old self would be, asking what happened to my dreams of working in South America, saving the rainforest. How can I go into an interview and fake enthusiasm for a role I'd only be doing to make ends meet?

There's only one thing I have enthusiasm for today, and that's Violet. No, two things. Luke as well. I feel my cheeks grow hot as I think of my dream last night. It must be hormones or something. But I keep checking my phone, like a teenager, waiting to see if he's texted me. This morning when I woke up, I grabbed it, unsurprised to see that I'd sent him a message last night, after drinking the dregs from a bottle of Port that had been sitting in the back of one of the kitchen cupboards for years.

The message, thankfully, was innocent enough. No spelling mistakes, aggression or declarations of love. It read simply: *Any progress? X*

But still, there was something obsessively keen about it. People don't like keen; it scares them off. And the kiss. The kiss was entirely out of place.

He hasn't replied.

Later this week, Violet is meant to be holding another of her panel talks, this time about flexible working. I'd decided to go before she disappeared and I feel even more involved now. After all, I've finally been to her house. I've met Amy, whoever Amy is. I realised last night that she might be Violet's new assistant. Violet has been criticised in the past for having a personal assistant: someone to book her flights and sort through her post and check her content for errors. People said she secretly had all kinds of help: a cleaner, a nanny, a PA, that she wasn't representing the truth of motherhood. That her life wasn't reflective of most parents' lives. But I don't want to watch someone online who's struggling as much as me.

My phone vibrates, and I close my eyes for a second before looking at it, hoping it's him. But it's a text message from my bank, reminding me that I have fifty pounds left of my overdraft. I delete it.

As my phone is in my hand, I might as well check again. I open Twitter, my saved searches, click on Henry's name. He hasn't tweeted since last week, when he was being paid to eat a bowl of oats. I expect to see the same words I've seen the thousand or so times I've checked it since then, but there's something new there. A link to a new Instagram picture, a simple caption: *Thoughts*. My stomach turns over as I click on the link. Then I remember the news article yesterday. Of course he'll have to comment. It's out there now: truly public. I imagine what his Sunday must have been like: a non-stop flow of communication, people desperate for him to confirm or deny, to put rumors to rest.

What must it be like to have so many people caring about you?

The picture takes its time to load, and my heart pounds in anticipation. Just as it appears on my screen, I become aware of something else. I look up. Ben is standing over me, frowning.

"Busy as ever," he says, but his usual mocking tone is missing, replaced by something more subdued.

I lock my phone screen.

"Sorry, it was just . . . can I help you?" I say. My heart thuds even harder at being caught.

"A word, if you have time," he says. He's never liked me. Perhaps he can see through me, knows that I don't really want to be here. Perhaps he resented the offer, all those years ago. Just a way of helping out a widow, a nice little bit of charity, making him smile on the inside as he drifted off to sleep that night. He didn't expect me to hang around for two years, to cling on to my dead-end job for dear life.

"Of course," I say, and I follow him into his office.

"No easy way of saying this, Lily," he says. He swallows. "As you know, we didn't close as many new clients as we had forecast this quarter. We're having to undergo some cost-saving measures and I'm afraid your job is at risk."

As he speaks, I try to look upset, or surprised. I'm unable to fake either emotion. I wonder what James would think if he was here now. As the time goes by, I feel less and less able to imagine how he would feel, what he would say about things. He would probably say it was a shame, tell me that I was bright and that I'd find something else easily enough.

But that was always his problem. He didn't take things seriously enough.

"At risk?" I say. Does this buy me a few more months at least?

"Yes. We're hopeful we're going to win LogicProTech, which you may know is a big client . . ." He pauses for a second, squinting at me slightly.

"Yes, sounds promising," I say, nodding enthusiastically.

"We've had a verbal, but the MD is dragging his feet," Ben says, looking past my shoulder. "If he doesn't sign before Christmas, I'm afraid we will be looking at redundancies in the new year."

The new year. That's OK then. Just let me get through Christmas, let me make sure Archie experiences it like the other kids. That's all I want. I need to hold it together for him.

"Right," I say, blinking. "OK."

Ben leans forward on his desk.

"Christ, Lily," he says, suddenly confessional. "I never meant any of this . . . I thought . . . I wanted to help you. In your interview, when you talked about losing your husband so tragically . . . But I'm not sure . . . we're the right fit. I mean, do you even like working here?"

"I love it!" I say, wiping my eyes with the sleeve of my jumper. "Honestly! It's such a great team, and all the developers are so funny with their little quirks, and Susie and I have got a great relationship and what we're doing is so exciting, being disruptors and stuff; I mean, who wouldn't want to be at the forefront of all that and . . . and . . ."

Ben shakes his head, one eyebrow rising.

"'It's OK," he says. "Really. You don't have to pretend."

"I'm not pretending!" I say, standing. I push my chair back. "I'm passionate about this firm. We'll win LogicProTech, and everything will be OK. You wait and see."

Ben frowns at me, and without saying a word, waves his hand towards the door. I've been dismissed.

*   *   *

My breathing comes in fits and starts as I take my phone to the ladies' toilet, keeping my fingers crossed I don't bump into Susie on the way. I lock the cubicle door behind me and put the lid of the toilet down, sitting there for a few seconds, waiting for Henry's Instagram to load again.

The Wi-Fi is even weaker in here, but eventually I see him. Henry. I feel myself relaxing. That face, so handsome, so self-assured. The man who has it all. He's sitting at his desk, the wall behind him a collage of mini magazine pages. He's leaning forward on his elbows. His expression is sombre, thoughtful. He's trying to look important. Henry; the protector. Henry; every woman's dream man.

Anyone with a pulse looking at this picture couldn't help but want him, and he knows it.

The whole thing is precisely staged, and my toes twitch as I scroll down to read the caption.

Disappointed to read the stories in the papers this weekend. I know my wife and I live life in the public eye from time to time, but that doesn't mean we aren't entitled to a private life, to take some time to withdraw. Perhaps people should focus their energies on their own families, and then the world would be a better place.

If it's an attempt to silence his critics, it has backfired spectacularly. The comments are bitter.

Sorry, mate, you put yourself out there, you lay yourself open to this!

So you've bumped her off then?

Where's Violet, Henry? Not seen in public for over a week? Suspicious much?

From time to time? Don't you mean ALL the bloody time? #oversharers

I look at his face, tracing the contours of his cheek with my finger. He looks older now. Perhaps it's the shadows across his face, or the fact he's not grinning as he usually does.

"What have you done to her?" I whisper.

GoMamas

Topics>Mummy Vloggers>Violet is Blue>Violet's Whereabouts
11 December 2017

Horsesforcourses
So what do we all think of Henry's latest insta?

Bluevelvet
He's hit her or something. Definitely. He must have done—think about it, that's why she's not been able to go out. He must have done something that she can't explain away as an accident.

Neverforget
I'm glad Violet's gone. I know Skye's only a child, but she was becoming increasingly repulsive. Let's be honest here—that scene with her "singing" Tomorrow and staring at herself in the mirror while Violet told her how brilliant she was. Ugh. She wasn't even in tune!

Bluevelvet
That's pretty harsh, Never, but I know what you mean. She's certainly precocious for her age. As my mum would say.

Horsesforcourses
You can't call a child repulsive!

Neverforget
Sorry but I think they're all repulsive. Attention-seeking narcissists. Good riddance. Now, how do we get rid of Mama Perkins too? *Evil cackle*

YVONNE

9 DPO.

According to my app: Implantation day!

The blastocyst travels down the fallopian tube towards the uterus. Implantation is made possible through both structural changes in the blastocyst and endometrial wall. The zona pellucida surrounding the blastocyst breaches, referred to as hatching.

In my womb, an everyday miracle is taking place. Meanwhile, I have finally heard back from the police. They're taking me seriously, want me to come in and firm up my statement.

I kiss Simon hard on the mouth as he comes out of the bathroom.

"Hey," he says, smiling at me with surprise. I am so happy today, so incredibly happy. Must remember to write that down in my diary.

I pull his arms around my waist, staring up at him. He's tired, something he'd never admit to. He's been working too hard, taking on as many extra classes and shifts as possible. And all for nothing. No, not nothing. We can put the money to another use now we don't need to pay for IVF anymore. A new kitchen, perhaps.

Simon's got the morning off today though, finally, and we're going to go to the farmers' market shop and buy our Christmas tree. My idea. He wanted to work on his plan for this postpartum fitness programme, but I talked him out of it.

He follows me downstairs and I wait while he gets ready to go. I'm so used to seeing him in gym gear that it's a thrill to see him in normal clothes. Smart jeans, actual shoes rather than trainers and a light wool jumper that hints at the shape of his chest underneath.

Pushka comes into the hallway, her tail quivering with interest.

"All right, Push," Simon says. She purrs in gratitude as he picks her up. He'll be such an amazing father. It's all going to work out.

I need to put this Violet business behind me.

"How's the rest of your week looking?" he asks, as we pull out of our driveway.

"Um, not too bad," I say. I deliberately didn't book any shoots this week. This might be the most important week of my entire life, and I'm not going to jeopardise anything by twisting myself into unnatural positions while trying to photograph drooling newborns. "It's quiet this time of year. People are so busy with Christmas parties and stuff."

"Sure," Simon says, nodding. "Not long now until our appointment."

I glance over at him. It's so unlike him to bring it up, I suddenly feel suspicious. But he can't know that I cancelled it. The appointment was in my name, and they don't have his number.

"It's going to be great," I say. I think of the tests, secreted in my wardrobe, still wrapped in the Boots carrier bag I took them home in. I've got an excuse prepared to give Simon about the appointment: the consultant we are due to see is going to have a car accident the day before. Nothing serious, just a strained wrist and a touch of whiplash. But she's going to have a few days off and will be back in touch to rearrange our appointment.

I haven't thought beyond that conversation. I don't need to. Because before they call me back to rearrange, I will be able to tell Simon about our miracle pregnancy, and the consultant's carelessness at the wheel will be long forgotten.

I don't allow the possibility of things not working out to enter my mind. After how far I've come, everything we've been through, it *has* to work this time. It just has to.

*   *   *

Later that evening, when our tree is set up in the tiny bay window of our living room, I sit with my laptop, checking Violet and Henry's social media accounts. I can't help myself. Her situation has been on my mind all day, no matter how much I try to push it away. She keeps popping up, the memory of her huge eyes staring at me in horror, the sound she made, visceral and gutting . . . My jumper feels itchy against my neck and I tug at the collar, my fingernails scraping against the skin underneath in an attempt to relieve the sensation. How can I continue to live like this, full of joy at finally getting what I want, but not knowing if she'll ever wake up? I close the lid of my computer, look across at my phone, pull it towards me then open my messages. Then I look up Henry's name in the search bar, and begin to type.

Hello, I know I'm probably the last person . . .

"Here you are!"

I glance up, startled. Simon has come through from the kitchen, and is holding out a glass of something fizzy. He's been cooking a proper roast, at my request.

"Oh!" I say, taking it from him. "You made me jump."

His eyes fall to the ground. "Sorry."

I lay the glass down next to me on the side table.

"It's fine. Thank you for the drink."

"Appletiser. Non-alcoholic. Don't want to mess up our test results when we go to the clinic," he says. "We've been so good for months, can't let our guard down just because it's Christmas."

I smile. My phone is sweaty in my hand, and at the edge of my vision I can see Henry's name at the top of the screen. I try to hold Simon's gaze, desperate for him not to ask what I'm doing. He leans down and kisses me lightly on the lips.

"Who's Henry?" he says.

I feel sick.

"Photographer friend," I say. Lie upon lie upon lie . . . "Bit of an arse, actually. Just telling him I can't assist on his shoot next week. Patronising git."

He smiles, then turns to leave the room.

"Don't want the potatoes to burn," he calls as he disappears back through the door.

I look back down at my phone. The screen has faded to black. I throw it across to the other sofa, as though it's blistered my skin. Then, the tears start to come. I'm trapped in a hell of my own making, and there's no way out.

Simon doesn't deserve this. He's so trusting. What would he think if he knew what I was really capable of? He knows nothing of my obsession with that fucking family, of my encyclopaedic knowledge of Violet and Henry.

The only time Simon ever caught me watching her was on our honeymoon earlier this year. Being in a different place made me careless. Simon's a traditionalist in many ways, and so he booked the honeymoon. South Africa. Wine-tasting and then four nights in Cape Town. I have no idea how he afforded the trip: I never asked. Maybe Pat gave him the money, maybe he sold one of his bikes. He can't ride them since his injury, so it would have been a fair swap.

It was in South Africa that he caught me. I was lying on the huge bed, the muslin curtains billowing at the hotel's windows. We had a terrace beyond, overlooking Table Mountain. It was a blissful day. We'd just been for a swim in the pool and had returned to our room: the heat of the midday sun making us feel like true honeymooners. No contraception, of course. I had thought it would be easy. He was in the cave-like bathroom, having a shower, and I took the opportunity to pick up my phone and check Violet's page. It was habit more than anything else: we were three days in to our honeymoon and I hadn't looked before. There was something to be said for a new life washing away the pain of the old one.

But it was still there; that compulsion to see what the woman who had stolen my life was up to. As it turned out, not much: she and the two kids were making cupcakes. Simon had left the shower running and come back into the bedroom to get clean underwear. I hadn't heard him return—I was tucked up at the top of the bed, naked under the white sheet, phone on my lap. I suppose he thought it would be funny to sneak up on me. That's the downside of a younger husband. He thinks things like that are amusing.

"Who are they?" he whispered in my ear.

I remember my reaction well. I threw the phone across the bed and jumped up, pulling the sheet against me.

"Fuck!" I shouted at him. "You scared me."

"Jesus, Von," he said. "Sorry . . . I didn't . . ."

"Don't creep up on me!"

I panicked. I thought he might recognise her from the gym and start asking questions. If it hadn't been for her, I would never have even met him. Two years ago, I saw an advert for a trial day at the Peter Daunt gym in Highgate and leapt at the chance to spy on my nemesis. The irony was, she didn't even go to the gym that day, but Simon gave me the guided tour, as well as his phone number.

Eleven months later, he had transferred to the Chiswick branch of Peter Daunt, and we were on our honeymoon. I had never shouted at him before. We were in new territory, all of a sudden.

"All right," he said, frowning. "Calm down."

Then, before I knew it, the feelings I had repressed for so long all came out. In one huge tear-filled gush. How Bertie had crept up on me all those years ago, cornering me outside the toilets and pushing me against the sticky wall. Memories I had tried so hard to forget. The way I mouthed *Help me* at a man who passed us, only for him to wink and raise his hands and eyebrows, as though defenceless himself. The way Bertie's sweaty hand felt as he pushed it into my knickers. How I'd struggled to fight him off, my screams going unheard, lost under the pulsating music coming from the room next door.

I told Simon how, eventually, I just gave up, let Bertie touch me where he wanted. Anything to make it end.

He asked me if I'd reported him, and I tried to explain how I didn't feel I could, but although he tried his best, he didn't understand. Men hardly ever do, even the sensitive ones. How impossible it feels to stand up against the weight of the patriarchy, how unlikely it feels that anyone would believe you, or even care. And I was in a desperate situation—I couldn't afford to lose my job. And then there was the business with Henry. No one would have believed me. Not back then, anyway.

Simon held me as I cried, stroking my sticky hair away from my forehead, telling me he'd never frighten me like that again.

Later that evening, at dinner in a small seafood restaurant overlooking Camps Bay, he had asked me again. Who was that woman I was watching?

"Just some stupid YouTuber," I said, and my tone was enough to make him leave it at that.

LILY

James was really good at detangling Christmas tree lights. It's funny the things that take you back, sticking arrows in your throat at the most unexpected of occasions.

We're listening to Mr. Tumble's Christmas album—it usually makes me want to stuff my ears with cotton wool but today I don't mind it. Archie seems to know all the words—or approximations of them—and he's gleefully singing along as I try to untangle the mass of green cord.

"Let's just test the lights first, Arch," I say when the last bulb is finally laid flat. First job done. I try not to think about the next one— hoisting our old and sad artificial tree into place. I've had to move the huge toy box from under the window to accommodate it, and suddenly the living room has gone from looking cosy to looking cluttered.

I plug the lights in and thankfully, they all spark into life. I don't know what I would have done if they hadn't—the little spare cash I had this week went towards the set of oversized glittery baubles Archie begged me for in Tesco.

"They work!" Archie squeals, jumping up and clapping his hands.

"Yes, they do," I say, breathing out slowly. A warm glow of relief spreads through my body. I can do this. He can have a Christmas stuffed full of joy and magic, just like Violet's kids.

Last Christmas Archie was too small to have much of an idea what was going on, but he's three and a bit now, and he's been talking about Father Christmas since I first mentioned him back in September. My only worry is that he'll be disappointed with his presents.

I've been collecting bits and pieces for months, but there's no one "big" gift. At least Sylvia and my dad will spoil him—they always do. Over-compensating, I suppose.

"Tree next!" Archie says, padding over towards it. It's folded up in the doorway.

"All right then!" I say. "Let's do it."

The tree spent the year underneath my bed and looks rather worse for wear but it's lighter than I remember and I manage to click it into place and set it in front of the window without too much effort. Archie hands me the lights and I wind them round the trunk as carefully as possible, remembering James's advice about hiding the cables and setting the bulbs to rest on the foliage. It feels like just yesterday he was here with me.

I pause for a second, clutching the end of the lights in my palm. I sniff, pinching my nose and squinting the tear away. When these waves wash over me, I sometimes wish Archie wasn't here, so that I could sit down, pull my arms around myself and just sob. A good, long sob. That's what I need, on a regular basis. But I rarely have time. Not with a three-year-old around.

"Are you sad, Mummy?" Archie says, and I look down at him.

"No," I say, beaming at him. "How can I be sad with you here?"

Archie nods, his eyebrows shooting up, and then he wanders off to the box of decorations on the coffee table, rummaging through them and finding the pound shop reindeer that plays a tinny tune when you press his nose.

* * *

When Archie is in bed, I sit on the sofa, admiring our handiwork. Admittedly most of the decorations are on the lower branches, and all rather bunched up in one area, but still, it looks festive and homely. Today was a good day. I almost felt normal.

I pick up my phone, pressing the button to light up the screen. I have two missed messages from Luke. I haven't checked my phone in more than three hours—a personal record, surely—and then this happens. Typical.

Hi Lily, hope you're having a good week. Thought you may be interested to know that Violet has released a statement. Here's the link to read it. I'm still on the case with Amy, Luke

I click on the link, blinking in frustration as my phone loads the page. It's on Violet's website, the one thing she didn't delete when she disappeared nine days ago, but which she rarely updates. Once a month if that, and only ever with lucrative sponsored posts, paid collaborations with huge brands that net her more than my annual salary in just 500 words.

The headline reads:

Taking some time out

Dear friends,

I'm aware that there has been some speculation online about why I have taken down my social media accounts. I'm taking some time out to deal with a private matter. It's not my intention to be deliberately secretive, but this is something I need time and space to deal with alone, and something I cannot share with you. When I am ready, I will come back.

As always, I appreciate your kind comments and concern, and would like to assure you that I am taking the best care of myself during a very challenging personal time.

Thank you for respecting my decision.

Love and light,
Violet XXX

I frown at the message. It tells us nothing. It's a polite way of asking everyone to stop speculating, to leave her alone. But there's something else that's bothering me, niggling at the back of my mind.

I click to read Luke's second message.

Stinks of PR stunt to me. I wonder if Violet has any new products launching soon. Seems to me she wants to return with a big bang, and all this mystery is the perfect way to do it. Her Christmas baby line went on sale a while ago, so it can't be that. Anyway, we'll get to the bottom of it!

"It's not her," I whisper to myself, staring at Luke's message. I look at the time. 9.05pm. Not too late to call him. I start to dial his number and then think again. It's too weird, isn't it? Or is it?

I decide I have nothing to lose—he already thinks I'm weird, after all. I press the phone to my ear nervously, but it takes only two rings before Luke answers.

"Hi," he says, and I remember his voice, with its lovely melodic tone.

I wonder if I am blushing, sitting here on the sofa alone, in my cramped living room.

"Hi," I reply. "Sorry, I only just saw your message. It's the weirdest thing I've ever read. Her statement, I mean, not your text."

"It's a bit short-sighted," Luke agrees. "She's underestimating her fan base, just a little, if she thinks that kind of thing isn't just going to pour fuel on the fire."

"Yes," I say, nodding into the phone. "But there's more to it than that. I've read it twice. And I know it probably makes me sound nuts, but I can just tell. She didn't write it. I've read all her blogs, every single one. I know how she writes, the phrases she uses, the tone of voice. It's all wrong."

"Maybe her management wrote it," Luke replies.

"No," I say, my voice steady. "It's obvious, everything about it . . . the whole way it's been phrased . . . everything." A shiver goes down my spine and I pull the sofa blanket over my legs. "I know who wrote it. I'm sure of it. It's just like that picture on his Instagram . . . It was written by Henry."

HENRY

I wish I could make people understand that *I'm* one of the victims here too. It was meant to be a bit of fun. She made me believe she was fine with it, that it was fun for her too. She was only twenty-two or twenty-three. The sort of age where life was about experimentation, about throwing the feelers out, seeing what stuck. And I wasn't the only one she slept with. There were stories about her all the time; how she'd been to a house party with the ad team, and slept with two of the exec guys, one after another. By all accounts she was so drunk she could barely hold her head up by the time she emerged from her encounter with the second one, but we laughed it off. All good clean fun between consenting adults in their prime.

Her behavior at work was impeccable. Always on time, eager to help. Got the job done, no matter how menial. It was once we were in the pub that she transformed into this good-time girl, all fluttering eyelashes and barely concealed breasts. I came to see her as a bonus card, something to call on when I felt lonely. Like I said, I thought we were on the same page. Camille was away a lot for work—she was making a name for herself as a horse whisperer, travelling up and down the country giving advice on behavioral issues. I was a young man, and Yvonne was there, every day, in my face. And she was fun. She didn't mind if things got a bit rough, she didn't seem to care that I didn't gaze into her eyes and tell her I loved her afterwards. I suppose, looking back, most of the time she was drunk. But then we all were. And then there were the drugs, passed around like sherbet; this was the noughties after all.

I thought we understood each other. She was sleeping her way to the top—it was obvious. It didn't win her any fans among the women on the magazine, but they were in the minority anyway, and I quite admired her smarts, realising that keeping in with the boys was going to get her much further that any feminist agenda she might have entertained. And she was fearless. If someone questioned her rather louche behavior, she'd tell them she was behaving like the men who read the magazine. And what was wrong with that? She talked a good talk, had us all convinced.

How were we to know it was all an act?

Things came to a head at our annual editorial awards. Bertie had caught wind of her antics, suddenly noticed she existed. He was an old-school tabloid hack; cheeks red with self-induced coronary issues, breath that could turn milk sour. Every second word that came out of his mouth began with an F and rhymed with duck; my father would have been horrified to meet him. They were from different ends of the spectrum entirely. What women seem to forget is that we're only human, we men. We get swept along with the tide sometimes. And if they're not being honest with us from the outset, then what chance do we have?

But that night, there was a little sweepstake in the office among the features and news desks. Who would get to take Yvonne home? I was out of the picture; I had Camille staying over that night. I'll admit there were some stirrings of jealousy when I heard them all laughing about it. Was I falling for her? Fuck it, who knows. It's possible. I guess underneath the bluster and dropped knickers, I liked her. Is that a crime?

But that night, no one got to take her home. No one ever quite got to the bottom of what actually happened, but for some reason Bertie was seated next to her at our banqueting table. I guess he decided, despite being in his late 50s, that it was his turn. I remember what she was wearing: a tight, low-cut red dress that barely skimmed her backside.

The less chivalrous man would say she was asking for it, really.

I sat on the opposite side of the table, watching her flirting with Bertie throughout the dinner. Those same old tried-and-tested techniques.

At one point, she got up to go to the toilet, and he pulled her back down on to his lap. She giggled, struggling back to her feet and hitting him on the arm in mock recrimination. As she walked away, he slapped her on the arse. I downed the rest of my drink, an attempt to dull the feelings of confusion.

Our eyes met a few times over the course of the evening as I grew steadily drunker and I began to wonder—or was it hope?—if it was all for my benefit. I left early, in the end, unable to watch the sideshow any longer. Perhaps I knew, deep down, that there was more to it. On both our parts.

There's a movement all over social media at the moment. #MeToo, with women telling their stories of sexual harassment to the whole world. It's like they've stored them all up over the years, waiting for this moment. But we didn't see it like that, back then. She was using what she had in fair exchange. Bertie was only trying his luck. And he didn't need to bother; he was one of the most powerful men in our company, he must have had women throwing themselves at him all the time.

She came to my desk the next day, and she looked different, even then. There was a hardness in her eyes as she demanded we go to the canteen to talk.

"He attacked me," she said, over her cup of tea. Her expression was so fierce, I had to look away. It was the first time, really, that I saw her as a threat. "And I'm going to the police."

YVONNE

Ten days post ovulation.

Just a few more days left until I can take a test. Every other month I've taken tests earlier than recommended, and been disappointed. This month I am determined not to do the same. I will wait until the day my period is due, like a rational, sane woman in control of herself.

I can't sleep. Instead, I lie in the darkness, turning over Violet's message on her website in my mind. After reading it, I couldn't resist texting Henry, offering my support. He replied with just one sentence.

You've done enough.

I think back to that Saturday night, and the regret washes over me again. But I push it away. It wasn't my fault. None of it was my fault.

The fortune-teller was Katie's idea. She dragged me along—a bit of fun, something to tell the grandkids, she said, before hastily retracting that statement with an apologetic shoulder pat. I told her it didn't matter, because even though I was losing hope back then, I still had some faith that IVF would work for us. This was before our first three rounds, free on the NHS, all failed. I was still so naive back in the spring, thought we'd be one of the lucky twelve per cent of couples. The alternative didn't bear thinking about, and surely if we tried hard enough, in the end we'd be rewarded?

I was a little nervous though. For a start, who knew that fortune tellers lived in beautiful mews houses in Notting Hill?

"Fortune teller to the stars," Katie had corrected me when I asked. "That's why she can afford to live here."

Her name was Julianne. Slender, wearing a white shirt and dark blue jeans. No headscarf or gold hoop earrings. She looked like an interior designer.

We sat around her oak dining table and she offered us some herbal tea.

"Ladies," she said. "Both creative. Very good friends. Your friendship is important, a gift, something to treasure."

She was saying it more to herself than to us.

"Do you want your readings to be private or are you happy to hear each other's?" Julianne asked.

"Oh, I don't mind . . ." Katie said, looking at me. "What do you think, Von?"

I still wasn't convinced this woman was going to tell us anything we didn't already know, and I found myself shrugging.

"We'll only tell each other everything anyway," I said, and Katie nodded in agreement.

"You first," Julianne said as she turned to me, her voice suddenly sharp. She reached across the table and took hold of my hands. Hers were soft and warm. "Oh dear. So much loss."

Her eyes met mine. Beneath immaculately curled lashes, they were hard and searching, as though drilling into my soul.

"Issues with trust. Did your mother leave you, as a young child?"

"Aren't you supposed to tell me that?" I said.

"You're full of fire," Julianne said, sitting back slightly in her chair. I was finding her gaze uncomfortable now, and looked down at her hands as they covered mine. "Rebellious years as a young woman . . . inadequate parents. And a great sense of loss. A partner, or a baby?"

There was an awkward pause. Katie was staring at me. I never told her. I never imagined this woman would be able to guess, just from looking at me. But how else could she know? No one knew.

I snatched my hands away.

"I don't know what you're talking about," I said. Katie was silent beside me, Julianne's eyes still piercing my face. It was as though the whole room was waiting for me to speak.

143

"An unimaginable thing," Julianne said, her voice almost a whisper. "The hardest of times, and no one to support you. Because you weren't supported, were you? Afterwards? Things just got worse?"

The tension in the room was almost unbearable.

"I had a miscarriage. That's all. A long time ago." My voice came out more of a bark than anything else. "I thought you were supposed to be telling me my future, not my past?"

"I'm so sorry." I heard Katie's voice next to me. "You never told me."

"Honestly, it was years ago," I said. "I barely remember it myself."

"It's going to be all right though," Julianne said, grabbing my hands again. This time they felt sweaty, and I wanted to push her off. "Your husband. He's exactly who you need, and you'll be celebrating soon. Christmas. A new baby. That's what you want, isn't it?"

I frowned at her, doing the maths in my head.

"A new baby by Christmas? That's not possible."

"No, not by Christmas. At Christmas. That's when you'll find out. It won't be easy, but you'll get there. There will be sacrifices along the way." She paused. "But not yours."

Christmas is twelve days away. It had seemed a lifetime, that day in May, and now it's nearly here. I roll over in the bed and look at Simon.

He's a good man.

It's 3.42am. In just a few months I'll be awake every night at this time anyway, bleary-eyed and ragged, holding my baby to my chest. People say you don't sleep well when pregnant. I didn't notice it last time, but as it was a while before I realised I was pregnant, I wasn't really paying attention. And I didn't sleep that well back then anyway.

This time is going to be different. This time I will be ready, grateful, prepared.

"Not long now," I whisper, stroking Simon's hair. "I'll give you what you want. I promise."

LILY

"Everything all right, Lily?" Sylvia asks me when she comes to pick Archie up. I invited her in for a coffee, and now that she's perched on the edge of my tatty old sofa, cradling her mug, I notice the thick layer of dust on top of the DVD player, the crumbs under the sofa. When you live alone with a three-year-old who makes mess continually, it's hard to prioritise cleaning. As soon as it's done, it needs to be done again.

"Oh you know," I say, looking down at my chipped nail varnish, quickly hiding my hands underneath my legs. I painted my nails for my "date night" stalking Violet. I keep meaning to wipe it off and then forgetting. "This time of year is always hard."

The second I say it, I am filled with regret.

Sylvia looks down. "You could always come and stay with us for a bit?"

I smile at her. She means well, but she knows there's no chance I'll take her up on the offer.

"Thank you. You're very kind. But we're fine. It's just . . . Christmas." I try not to sound bitter. "It's always the hardest time."

"Of course," Sylvia replies.

There's an awkward pause and then Archie barrels in from his bedroom, holding his favorite toy, Bear.

"All packed, Archie?" she says, pulling him on to her lap. "Has Bear got his things together too?"

"Granny!" Archie says, his bottom lip jutting out. "Bear doesn't have anything. He's a bear! He has fur."

"Oh, of course," Sylvia says, grinning at me. "Silly Granny."

"Silly Granny." Archie gives a little titter of laughter and then wriggles off her lap, pounding his way back to his bedroom.

"Thanks for having him at such short notice," I say. "I really appreciate it."

"Any time, you know that," Sylvia replies. She glances at me, her eyes wide. "I just wish we could do more. You said you're looking for a new job?"

"Yes. They're desperate to keep me," I blurt. "They've loved everything I've done so far. They want to promote me, in fact, but I suppose I'm bored, and I'm hoping for something closer to home, so I can be around a bit more for Archie. Time for a new challenge, you know!"

Sylvia's eyebrows move together. She's of the generation that thinks a job is a job, that you should hold on to them no matter what.

"Well, that's a real shame," she says. "As you know, if we can help in any way . . . your dad's always keen. Financially, we mean. Not just with looking after Archie."

Your dad's always keen. Throwing money at the problem, his idea of parenting.

"You are so kind," I say, again.

Sylvia takes a sip of her coffee, and looks at me for a long time.

"You don't want to move closer to us? I'm sure you must have lots of friends in London, but . . ."

"Oh no, I couldn't . . ." I begin. *Couldn't think of anything worse*, I want to say. "Archie is so settled with the childminder; my life is here."

"Of course," Sylvia says, her eyes wrinkling as she smiles. As she does so, I remember her mentioning an operation to fix her cataracts last time we spoke. I have forgotten to ask her about it, and now it feels too late. "But you know we're always here for you."

I wave them off at the front door downstairs, my stomach turning over with guilt on so many fronts. Yes, I will be job hunting today, but Archie going to stay at Granny and Grandad's house wasn't strictly necessary at all. It's a treat to myself; a weekend of freedom, and the ability to meet Luke, as suggested, at Violet's panel talk this evening.

* * *

I spend the rest of the day speaking to recruitment agents on the phone—I booked today and Monday off work, and Ben sounded relieved when I told him it was to job hunt. He said he'd give me a glowing reference, even though we both know you can't do that anymore. It's for the best, even if it is terrifying.

I wonder what Violet would do in my situation. She complained of crippling postnatal depression, so bad she couldn't get out of bed, but at the end of the day she wasn't single and broke like me. So it can't have been that bad. She had Henry: handsome, successful, charismatic Henry and his painfully rich family. She lived in his beautiful Chelsea flat. She didn't need to do anything, if she didn't want to. She could have paid for a live-in nanny and focused entirely on her recovery. I didn't even have time to see the counsellor my doctor recommended. But then again, maybe too much time to think is a bad thing. Too much time to think fills the space around and inside you until you eventually drown in it. Keeping busy is the key to keeping sane.

It's been balanced on a razor-edge, though. It only takes one little shift before the whole stack comes tumbling down. I've barely a pound left in my bank account. It's got so desperate that I started researching food banks this week. It turns out you have to be referred by someone. I think I've got it hard, but that's proof there are so many people more needy than me.

I'm in my bedroom, trying to decide what to wear to this talk. I think back to the days when I had money to buy myself things—never much, I was never well off, but before Archie was born, things were comfortable enough. I still have some clothes from those days, but every time I try them on, it's as though they don't fit. They don't feel like "me" anymore. They're a relic from a previous life. So much color and pattern. Beautiful dresses in every shade under the sun, coated in designs ranging from small birds to dramatic zigzags. James used to buy them for me. He was big on presents, when we first got together.

I pull the dresses out, laying them on my bed. They seem shorter than I remembered. My figure hasn't changed much but I don't hold myself in the way I used to.

I so want to impress Luke.

I reach into my wardrobe again, just in case. Tucked into the far-right corner, one shoulder hanging limply from the hanger, is the shirt I wore on my first official date with James. Dark green, with black flecks and a wrap-over front. I had forgotten all about it.

I pull it over my head, tucking it into the waistband of my jeans and arranging it so that it drapes nicely. Then I sit at my dressing table and make my face up, in the way I used to.

I brush my hair through with dry shampoo and then tie it up in a bun, leaving a few strands to hang loosely around my face. In the mirror, I try out different expressions. When I'm not smiling, my face looks drawn and sad, but when I do manage a grin, I look pretty presentable.

My phone buzzes. It's Luke, saying he'll be there in twenty minutes. I text back a quick reply, and make my way to the Tube.

18 April 2017
From: gottheblues@hotmail.com
To: violet@violetisblue.com

Hi Violet,

I see you all had a great Easter. Mandy seemed really into it. Why was she even at your Sunday dinner? She's an assistant. Shouldn't she be with her own family? Or don't they get on? She seems the type to have fallen out with people over the years. Her laugh is enough to drive most people insane.

Did you notice the way she flirted with Henry when he carved the lamb? I did. I think you ought to be careful of that.

What do you see in him anyway? I know he's got a "cool" job, but I bought a copy of his magazine the other day and it was 90% adverts for aftershave and sunglasses. What little text there was seemed like complete drivel. And I didn't find a single piece by him. Does he actually do anything at work?

Don't you think you deserve better, Violet?

*   *   *

19 April 2017
From: gottheblues@hotmail.com
To: violet@violetisblue.com

You can reply to me, you know.

Just because I'm being honest with you, and sometimes the truth hurts, it doesn't mean you should just IGNORE ME.

At the end of the day, when you think about it, I actually pay your wages, by watching your content.

So I guess you could say I'm your boss.

Would you ignore your boss?

*   *   *

19 April 2017
From: gottheblues@hotmail.com
To: violet@violetisblue.com

Sorry. I've had a bad day. I shouldn't have been so snide about Mandy and Henry. But it's only because I worry about you, Violet.

Please reply.

YVONNE

I turn the shiny foil wrapper over in my hand, looking at the printed lettering, wondering about the person who designed it. Stupid, pointless, irrelevant thoughts, just here to distract me. I've never been a procrastinator. I'm a doer, proactive at every opportunity.

But this little plastic stick is the enemy. The thing that's crushed my hope, time and time again. Earlier this year, we had taken to testing together, with Simon politely turning his back while I did the deed, and then putting his arm around me as we waited for the result. But he doesn't know about this month, about its loaded significance or the fortune teller's promise. I know it's nonsense, of course, that her words were so generic they could fit anyone's life, like a horoscope, but I still can't help but hope there was something in it.

Simon thinks we're going to meet the consultant next week, is prepared to face the uphill struggle that is IVF all over again. Although I suppose all that's required of him is to flick through some magazines, deposit the goods in a pot, and then support me as I weep and wail.

I put the test down on top of the toilet and reach for my phone. A few taps and the GoMamas TTC forum loads. I scan through the latest posts. Several people are on almost the same cycle as me, and those who have tested have inevitably received BFNs—Big Fat Negatives. The rest are determined to wait, so it seems.

No point in testing until AF is due. I'm not wasting the money this month.

151

Nope, me neither. It's just heartache and disappointment, and it might all be for nothing. BFNs tell you nothing this early on, and BFPs are really unlikely this soon.

What a surprise. A BFN for me. I was so sure I felt different this month. I'm 12 DPO so I'm sure it would be showing up by now. Guess I'm out AGAIN for this month.

You're not out till the wicked witch arrives! Don't give up hope! Wait till your period is due and test again!

I know they're right, and as I read their posts, I feel myself relax a bit. Even if my tiny embryo implanted two days ago, the amount of pregnancy hormone in my urine is going to be minuscule. There's also that debate about whether it's best to test first thing in the morning or not.

This is insanity.

I'm about to quit the forum but notice I have a private message from Jade. I click to read it.

So??! Don't leave me in suspense! Why the silence? Tell me our secret plan has worked!

I don't reply. I'm ashamed that she knows the lengths I've gone to. It was her idea, but I should have told her she was mental.

I'm usually what the social media world calls a "lurker": someone who reads but doesn't engage. I've only ever posted on the Trying To Conceive threads, and that's only been out of desperation.

A lurker. I quite like that picture of myself. And it seems appropriate for this evening, when I'm going to be doing just that. Lurking in the shadows, in the hope of finding out how she is. Desperate times, desperate measures. Hopefully tonight I'll finally get the answers I need.

* * *

The event is held in the wrong part of London for me, but it doesn't surprise me she picked here. Shoreditch, mecca to the hipster mums, who pretend they're open and welcoming to outsiders but in reality are just as cliquey and mean as they were as teenagers. Just like all these influencers, who only engage with each other, largely ignoring their "fans." They certainly have no idea what life is like for a single mother living on the outskirts of Leeds, no matter how much they'd like to think they do.

As I approach Shoreditch Town Hall, I grow more impressed that Violet has pulled this off. It's so much bigger than I expected: more of a theatre or a church than a town hall, with an impressive columned façade and a sweeping flight of stone steps up to the entrance. I'm early, as intended, and I make my way up the steps thankful that there's no one else following me.

At the top, I pause, looking through the glass in the door. No sign of her. I'm safe. I go into the reception area. Three women are standing behind a table covered in name badges. They're chatting amongst themselves. I cough.

"Hello!" one of them says. She's wearing red lipstick and has bleached blonde hair like Violet's, scraped back into a high ponytail. She's wearing some kind of oversized pyjama top. "Can I just take your name?"

"Yvonne Foster," I say, remembering in time that I didn't give my real surname when I registered for the event.

Blonde bun woman frowns and runs her pen down a list she's holding.

"Let me see . . . There you are!" she says, drawing a very decisive line through my name. "Let me find you your name badge."

"It's there," I say, pointing at it.

"Yes!" she says. Her enthusiasm is a little wearing.

"Am I the first?" I say, as I clutch the badge in my hand. Not a chance I'm pinning it to my coat.

"No, there are a few people here already," she says. "Cloakroom is to your left, if you have anything you want to drop off, and toilets are just down the stairs. If you go inside the main hall, you'll find refreshments at the back, and the panel discussion begins at 6.30."

"Thanks," I say, blinking at her. I want to ask her if Violet is still hosting, but much like the pregnancy test, there's some delicious joy in the waiting, in the agony of not knowing. I guess it's called hope.

I make my way through to the main hall, heading for the refreshments table. It's been decorated with slogans from the event, and the drinks are themed. There are cocktails, named somewhat bizarrely after the influencers on the panel. Violet's drink is, of course, an unappealing blue and violet colored concoction, but I eschew it in favor of some water with peels of cucumber floating in it.

Slowly but surely, the room begins to fill up. Mostly with women just a little younger than me, mostly in groups. There are a few men, though, which surprises me. I never thought to invite Simon. I wonder what he would think, if I told him I was going to attend a panel discussion on the difficulty of progressing your career once you had a baby. He'd probably tell me I didn't have to worry. That's his main aim in life, stopping me from worrying.

At one point, a woman wearing a khaki jacket and ripped black jeans comes up to me, taking me by surprise. She has a razor-sharp bobbed haircut, complete with a thick fringe that finishes halfway down her forehead. It's a look my mother would have described as "severe."

"Hi," she says, "I'm Jules. Well, Julie, but who wants to be called Julie? Everyone calls me Jules."

"I know," I say and she frowns at my remark. "I mean, it's on your name badge. Nice to meet you. I'm Yvonne." I hold my name badge up so she can read it, then re-clutch it in my left palm.

She laughs, touching her badge lightly.

"Ah! Forgot I was wearing it."

"Easily done."

"Did you come here alone?" she asks, taking a sip of her drink, which I can see is the Big Momma cocktail, consisting of Bailey's and a lot of ice.

"Yes," I reply, but something makes me continue. "Well, sort of. I'm friends with one of the panel members."

"Oh amazing," Jules says, nodding. "Which one?"

"Violet Young," I say. I shouldn't have said anything. What if she knows her? What if she works for her?

"Cool," Jules says, seemingly unimpressed.

"'How about you?" I ask.

"Nope, never met them before. In fact, I hadn't heard of most of them, if I'm honest. But I saw an article about it in *Stylist* the other week on the Tube and though, fuck me, what a great idea. I mean, seriously, it's like we're in the dark ages over here when it comes to flexible working. My sister lives in Sweden and it's a whole other world . . ."

"Do you have kids?" I say. She doesn't look like a mother.

"Nope, not yet," she says. "I'm only twenty-eight. But it's important to get this shit sorted, isn't it? To show your support while you have the time. What about you?"

There's a beat where I consider it, but then I remember what the fortune teller said. That sometimes, believing things makes them happen.

"Not exactly," I smile, patting my stomach and raising my glass of water. It catches the light of the chandelier, twinkling in front of me, as if giving me its blessing. "I mean, not yet. But I'm pregnant."

LILY

Luke is waiting for me opposite the station, his record bag slung across his body. He gives a little wave and then ambles towards me. I feel myself flush as he approaches. I hope my eye make-up has stayed in place.

"Hello," he says. "Got here all right in the end then?"

"Yes, sorry," I say. "I had to suffer the slow crawl of the District all the way to Whitechapel. It's a long way from Acton."

He nods, smiling.

"I'm in Kentish Town," he says. "So not too bad."

I knew this already, of course. It was on his Twitter bio. But I don't want him to know I've found out everything there's possible to find out about him online, and he registers my carefully constructed blank expression.

"It's on the Northern line. Anyway, shall we go?"

"Great," I say. "You can fill me in on what you've discovered on the way."

"Well, first up, Amy is Henry's sister-in-law," Luke says, and I turn my face towards him, surprised.

"Oh!" I say, trying to work out exactly what that means.

"Married to his younger brother," he replies.

"How did you find that out? He's always been so private about his brother. There's nothing online about him. He's called Andrew, I think."

"Andrew was a bit of a tearaway in his late teens," Luke says, and the word tearaway sounds so incongruous coming from him that I have to stifle the urge to tease him. "Heavily into recreational drugs, that kind of thing. Believe it or not, Henry was the 'sensible' one. But Andrew lives on the family estate now, runs the place with his wife Amy. No kids yet."

"She seemed really young," I say, thinking back to our encounter on the doorstep, and how she said she didn't know London very well. "She was very pretty.'"

"Yeah, she's the daughter of a friend of the family. Posh too. I think they've known each other for years."

"So why would she have been at Violet and Henry's house? Babysitting while Henry was visiting Violet in hospital? It's a bit weird, isn't it?"

"Very," Luke nods, slowing his pace a little. I can see our destination—Shoreditch Town Hall—just ahead of us. "The family estate is in Somerset, so not exactly near London."

"Maybe one of Henry's parents died? Is that a possibility?"

"Henry's father died a few years ago, and his mother is still alive and kicking, very much the matriarch of the Blake estate. Maybe Andrew was there as well? Family visit?"

"I don't know. I only saw her."

"Let's see what happens tonight," Luke says, as we approach the steps up to the venue. "They haven't announced anything about Violet not appearing, so maybe she'll turn up and the mystery will be solved."

He turns to make his way up the stairs and I find myself pulling on his arm to stop him. He looks at me.

"Can I ask . . . can I ask you something?" I say, suddenly nervous.

"Sure." His eyes are wary.

"Why are you so interested? In Violet, I mean? I know it's your job—to interrogate the zeitgeist," I got that from his bio, and I pause for a few seconds, embarrassed that he'll now know I've looked him up, "but mummy bloggers? It's quite a random one, isn't it? For a young man to be interested in?"

He laughs, long and loud.

"Oh God, do you think I'm some kind of pervert?" He grins at me and his eyes are kind. "Fair enough. It is odd that I'm investigating this, rather than, what, compulsive gamers in their 40s?"

"It's just, you said you didn't have any kids. And before I had Archie, I knew nothing about the whole online mummy influencer thing. So it's just surprising . . . Sorry."

"Well, I could tell you that it was because my boss asked me to look into it, but that would only be half of the truth. You remember I mentioned my nephew? My sister had a really bad time after he was born. Postnatal depression. She knew about Violet, got a bit obsessed by her and her family. When Ellie pitched the idea to me, I told Ali—that's my sister—and she was really keen for me to look into it further. I guess I'm doing it a bit for her too."

"But . . ." I take a deep breath. "Why did you want to be in touch with me? Ellie could have told you everything I know, and more."

Not everything, I think to myself.

Luke's cheeks suddenly flush. He looks down at his feet.

"Um," he says. He looks back up at me, rubbing his chin, then giving a little shrug. "I don't know, I guess Ellie just thought we might, er, get on."

My eyes widen and I feel my heart begin to speed up. So she was setting us up, after all. Brilliant, Lily, just brilliant. Well done.

"Oh," I say. "Right."

Luke gives a strange sound—half cough, half laugh. We begin to climb the stone steps.

"How's your sister now?" I ask, glancing sideways at Luke. His cheeks are aflame now, the speckly blush spreading to his neck. Perhaps there's some hope after all. And he hasn't seen my blouse yet.

"She's fine," he says. "Actually, as soon as she went back to work, she was fine. She loved her job—she's an optician—and she missed all the interactions with people when she was on maternity leave. Guess she felt like she was failing as a mother by being desperate to go back to work. It was that obvious, sadly."

I give him what I hope is a sympathetic smile.

"One last question before we go in," I say, as we queue behind a bunch of women outside the front door. Somehow the answer seems vital, essential almost to my sense of hope for the future. For my . . . recovery. "Does she . . . does she still watch? Still care?"

Luke looks at me, and perhaps I'm imagining it, but it feels as though he understands how loaded my question is.

Of course, a little, he says, his gentle voice the balm my fear needs. "Like breaking any addiction, it's hard at first, but she's fine now."

I wish I could hug him. As we shuffle forward in the queue, I think of the word he's used, the word I've ignored for so long. I turn it around in my mind, trying to take ownership of it, to accept it of myself. *Addiction*. I have an addiction.

YVONNE

There's no escaping Jules. She's stuck to my side, as unwanted as a piece of chewing gum on my shoe, and I can't see any way of peeling her off. I told her I was going to the toilet, and she even said she'd come with me, that she needed it too.

We're sitting in the third row from the back, side by side, and she's flicking through the slim pamphlet that was left on our chairs, reading the biographies of the panel members, commenting from time to time. I'm fidgeting in my chair, barely listening to her ramblings, suddenly struck by nerves. Or is it excitement? On the last page of the pamphlet there are details of a JustGiving page, urging people to donate if they can, to support the flexible working appeal. When I read it, I feel a ripple of irritation run through me at the sheer blinded cheek of it. How much money has *she* donated, I wonder?

Then again, the event tonight was free. The refreshments were sponsored, but someone must have paid for the venue. Perhaps she does put her money where her mouth is, after all.

Violet's bio is in the leaflet, and so I read it idly. No one has mentioned her not turning up tonight. Only five minutes until curtain up. I pull my scarf up around my face, so it covers my chin.

"Blimey," Jules says, thrusting the leaflet under my nose. "One of them is an MP."

"Yes," I say. "She's the Minister for Women's Rights."

"Quite an event then," Jules says, taking a long sip of her second cocktail. "Your mate Violet must be very influential."

That word again. *Influential.* I don't know when this new description became popular, but over the past few years it's been *influencer this* and *influencer that.* A catch-all term for someone who has a large following across not just YouTube but Instagram, Twitter and Facebook as well. The thought that she is actively influencing people seems dangerous somehow. Especially given what happened.

"She is," I say, digging my nails into my jeans. The waistband is tighter than usual.

The chatter in the room dies down as bun-haired woman climbs the stage, holding a bundle of papers in her hand. Behind her is a long trestle table, set with chairs. She gives a brief smile to the audience and then turns her back to us, walking along the table, placing name cards in front of each seat. I strain my neck to see past her, to see what's written on the card in front of the middle chair.

She turns to face the audience in the centre of the stage, blocking my view. She's holding a microphone now, picked up from the table.

"Ladies and . . ." Her voice fills the hall, making everyone sit up straighter. She smiles over the microphone as the crowd falls silent. "Gentlemen! I'm so pleased to see that there are gentlemen here tonight! Thank you for coming out on such a cold night. I hope you didn't have to miss too many Christmas parties to be here. I'd just like to talk you through how this evening is going to work. First of all, we're going to have talks from each of our panel members, and then there will be a general Q&A session at the end. Afterwards, we'd love it if you would stay behind and enjoy a drink, and hopefully mingle a little with each other."

I glance at Jules. She's staring straight ahead.

"Now before I introduce you to our panel, I'm afraid I have a little bit of sad news. As you know, our panel host tonight was meant to be Violet Young, but I'm afraid due to personal reasons, she's unable to join us."

There's a collective groan.

"However," she says, her free hand floating upwards as if to quieten a bunch of unruly schoolchildren, "I am very excited to announce that taking her place is her husband, Henry Blake. We're so pleased to have a man on the panel—in fact, it was an oversight not to have included one—and Henry is an avid supporter of women's rights. So, first of all, please welcome Henry Blake!"

There's a ripple of applause that grows louder as it spreads. I shrink back in my seat as he climbs the steps and waves. This was not what I was expecting. Not what I was expecting at all.

* * *

The panel discussion is as predicted: women complaining about their lot while simultaneously showing off that they have managed to break the mould somehow, that they have overcome the odds by "making it work." There's some half-hearted chat about change, and how much better things are in Scandinavia, but no one seems to have a plan, or offer any advice on how we can improve things.

It's frustrating though. I was hoping for answers. I thought if Violet turned up she might explain her online disappearance and reassure me that all was OK, but her absence is just making me worry more.

Henry, to his credit, looks uncomfortable and out of place, pulling at his collar and making jokes into the microphone when the women ask him for a male's perspective. I trace his features with my eyes for signs of guilt, but there's nothing there. But then, I remember how easy it was for him to wash away any sense of responsibility, all those years ago. He's a master at it.

He does look tired though, and older than the last time I saw him. During the Q&A session at the end, I hoped someone would have the courage to ask him what's happened to Violet, but nobody did.

At the end of the talk the bun-haired lady gets back on the stage and thanks everyone a little too profusely for "giving up their precious time" and then makes a big show of thanking Henry for "saving the day." The four women on the panel sitting next to him turn down the corners of their mouths as they clap along with the audience. And rightly so, why he got the biggest fuss of them all is beyond me. People are such fools. He's not even that famous.

Throughout the talk, my eyes never left his face. I'm overwhelmed by how much I know about him. About how easy it would be to stand up and shout it all out to them all, to watch his face crumple with humiliation, their mouths fall open in disgust. I couldn't though, of course. My plan is at stake, and it matters more than him, or me.

Bun lady invites us to stay behind and "network," and with alarm I see the guest speakers stand and wander down the steps to the side of the stage, heading for the back of the hall. I expected them to slip off, but no. Henry is swept along, and I watch him, smiling awkwardly, patting a few people on the shoulder as he makes his way towards the crowd.

"Are you going to stay?" Jules says. My eyes meet hers.

"Um," I say. What's the easiest way to get out of here?

We are standing at the end of our row of chairs, my hand clutching the back of mine. Thankfully Henry and the women are across the other side of the room, in a huddle, holding their highball glasses and chatting.

"I'm sorry," I say, shrugging, resting a hand on my stomach. "Pregnancy. I'm exhausted. I'm afraid . . . I'm afraid I'm going to have to make a move before I turn into Cinderella."

"Of course," she says, with a faint smile of disappointment. "Lovely to meet you anyway. And good luck with the baby, and everything!"

I smile again, and pull my heavy winter coat over my shoulders, knotting my scarf around my neck and tucking my hair underneath it, and then I leave the room, slipping past Henry with my head down until I'm safely back on the street.

My footsteps land heavily as I pace my way back to the Underground. She must still be in hospital. I haven't learnt anything tonight, and my desperation is mounting.

HENRY

I'll remember that twenty minutes in the canteen with Yvonne for the rest of my life. The way she told me, very slowly, with that peculiar confidence I'd always seen in her, what she was planning.

"You'll lose your job," I said, but then, with horror, I noticed her eyes filling with tears.

I reached out across the table and took her hand in mine.

"He's an arsehole," I said. "You know that. I know that. But he's the boss. Just keep your head down and keep out of his way."

"How can you say that?" she hissed. "He pushed me against a wall, he had his hands . . ." She started crying properly then. I felt my blood pressure rise.

"Oh darling, I know, I know," I said, in as soothing a voice as I could summon. "But you know what he's like . . . he was drunk . . ."

She sniffed loudly. The dark look in her eyes returned. "I was frightened," she said. "Really frightened."

But she didn't look frightened. She looked vengeful.

"Find another job first," I said. "Trust me, you don't want to make an enemy of Bertie Letts."

"It'll be too late by then," she said. "No one would believe me."

"No one will believe you now," I said. I stroked her hand. It was true. "Darling, listen. People saw what you were wearing . . . they'll think you encouraged him."

She looked away.

"I'll help you find something else," I said, smiling. Henry the Hero, it was my most comfortable role. "I'll ask around. You're good at your job, I'm sure you'll be snapped up."

"Thank you, Henry," she said, but she didn't sound thankful at all. There was a beat, and I found myself holding my breath. "I appreciate it. But I might not need another job. There's something else you should know."

"What?"

"I'm pregnant," she said, and suddenly her face lifted, as though someone had pulled a camera out and asked her to smile. "I'm pregnant, and the baby's yours."

*   *   *

In hindsight, telling her I'd "sort it" wasn't the best reaction. But I honestly thought that was what she wanted to hear. I offered her the money to go private. I even found out the details of a clinic just off the King's Road. I tried to be sympathetic. I laid out all the ways in which it would ruin her life to have that baby. But she didn't listen.

She had these insane ideas. Of giving up work to live with me, us raising the child together.

I was backed into a corner. And there's no smoke without fire, as my mother would say. These women with reputations that lingered like bad smells, well, they brought it on themselves. *What did they expect?*

I made a mistake. It was *wrong*. And part of me knew it, even as the words slipped out. But don't forget, I was so young myself.

We were back at my flat that same evening, after work. Crisis talks. I'd had to feign a late-night meeting to put Camille off, and I could tell from the tone of her voice that she didn't believe me. It felt like the tide was creeping in closer, from all sides, ready to wash me out to sea. My carefully constructed life was beginning to disintegrate.

When reasoning with Yvonne didn't work, I tried pleading. When pleading didn't work, I became a cunt. Like I said, it was just panic. Immature, stupid panic. I wasn't equipped for this. No one at Harrow teaches you what to do when you accidentally knock up one of the skirts in your office. She told me she was taking contraceptives. It was just meant to be a bit of fun.

We were standing in the kitchen. I had been chopping cherry tomatoes, with the notion of cooking pasta, trying to make the evening "normal." She was glaring at me, leaning against the island unit, watching my every move. She blamed me for everything, so it seemed. For talking her out of reporting Bertie, for not using a condom—even though I'm sure I'd asked, and she'd said it would be fine. All my consoling had come to nothing; my reasoning had failed too. What did she want with a baby at her age anyway? I didn't know then what I know now. That she was so obsessed with me, that she thought we were *special*.

Eventually it was all too much. I put the knife down on the chopping board. One tomato rolled off the kitchen counter and on to the floor.

This couldn't be happening, not to me. My father was angry enough with me about my life choices as it was; this would tip him right over the edge.

"Look, Yvonne. You've slept with half the fucking ad team," I hissed in her face. "How do I know it's even mine?"

It only took a second. I saw the knife flash through the air, and then it was too late.

LILY

"I'm going to try to speak to him," Luke says, when the talk ends.

"Really?" I ask. I didn't expect him to be so brave. But then again, he's a journalist, I guess this is what they do: ask people questions they don't want to answer.

The talk was interesting but now it's over I feel frustrated and sad. There's something about hearing these powerful, clever women speak and share their insights that's reawakened my old ambitions. Made me remember who I used to be, before I was left alone, struggling to bring up a baby. All those dreams I'd had, washed away by my situation.

I remember those dark days shortly after Archie was born, when I'd imagine myself doing exactly what my mother had done. And then I'd found Violet, and Ben had offered me a nice safe office job, and slowly things started to look more hopeful.

A nice safe office job. But what was nice and safe about something that made you feel borderline suicidal, that drove you to drink more alcohol than you could rightly afford? And the irony of course is that now I'm at risk of redundancy.

These women, though, these women seem to have overcome all the odds. I suddenly see myself as an impartial outsider might do, and I look lost. Like a bottle thrown into a river, bobbing along wherever the current takes it, half drowning. No, not drowning. Sinking, slowly but surely.

"Want to join me?" Luke says, his eyes shining. He's smiling at me, and the image of his open, warm face is immensely comforting. He doesn't see me as lost. I don't know how he sees me, but it's not like that.

"Oh," I say, staring across at Henry. Most of the audience have left now, but there are still around fifty people left, bunched up across the back of the hall. Henry is in the middle of the biggest huddle, holding a bottle of beer and smiling at something one of the women is saying. He's not flirting, exactly, but he also doesn't look like someone who's recently suffered a tragedy. "What are you going to say?"

"I'm just going to be upfront," he says. "Ask him what's happened to Violet, tell him I'm writing a piece on influencers and the impact it has on their children."

I swallow. I think I'd be less nervous if he'd told me he was going to go over and start a fight with him.

"But . . . he's like a politician, he'll just squirm his way out of it . . . he's not going to admit to anything in front of all these women."

"Maybe not," Luke says, "but I think it'd be interesting to see him under pressure. You coming?"

I nod and follow him across the hall.

Instead of waiting for a natural break in conversation, Luke pushes through the cluster of people around Henry and addresses him directly.

"Sorry to interrupt," he says. He doesn't sound sorry at all. His voice is firm and commanding, and the women fall silent. Henry takes a step backwards, his eyes narrowing.

"Just wondered if I could have a word? Great speech, really enjoyed it. Glad to hear you're so passionate about women's employment rights. I'm a reporter with *The News and Mail*."

The women's eyebrows lift with interest. Henry's lips turn down at the edges, ever so slightly, and his jaw tightens.

"Is it about the flexible working campaign?" Henry says.

Luke twists his face, his head at an angle as he shakes it.

"Not exactly," he says. "But I'm sure we can add a plug to the cause if you'd be happy to talk to me for a few minutes."

There's a flash of something like anger in Henry's eyes, that quickly gives way to something else—a look of exhaustion. I've never been this close to him before, but from here I can see the purple rings under his eyes, that the lines on his forehead are actually deep grooves. He looks like an old man, and yet he's only forty-five. Despite all this, there's something ruggedly handsome about him. He doesn't look like a journalist, or a metrosexual—he looks strong, masculine, the kind who wouldn't blink at being asked to chop logs, or climb scaffolding. Only his clothes give him away; the chocolate velvet blazer, the shiny brogues.

The women all stare at Henry, suddenly aware of the tension. But Luke is a disarming opponent: scruffy but determined.

"Mate," Henry says, giving a deep sigh. "I'm here to talk about the issues that really matter. Namely, ensuring that women who give birth don't lose their careers as payment for doing so. I'm afraid I don't have time for anything else."

There's a murmur of assent among the women. They all gaze at Henry as though he's said something profound. I feel a sudden certainty that I don't like him, that all my suspicions were right. He's too smooth for his own good. Then there's an uncomfortable realisation; in some ways he reminds me of James.

"Your wife was sad not to make it tonight, I presume," Luke says, ignoring everything. His eyes are locked on Henry's, as though they are the only two people in the room. "What's the difficult personal matter she's been dealing with?'"

"Personal," Henry spits. "That's what it is."

"But she's well?" Luke continues, and my heart starts to pound. "Not been ill?"

"She's fine," Henry says, but the second the words are out he looks regretful. "Now if you don't mind . . ."

"So she's not in hospital?" Luke says, his voice loud now. People across the other side of the hall stop talking, and suddenly the air is thick with silence.

"What?"

"Hospital? She's not ill? Only you were seen at . . . now, let me get this right, The Royal London Hospital, I believe? Last weekend?"

My mouth falls open a little. There's a sting of hurt that Luke never mentioned the name of the hospital to me before, that he hasn't confided in me.

"That is really none of your business," Henry says, pulling his blazer together. He looks at the huddle of mothers around him. "Quite frankly I'm amazed you have this much time on your hands. Bit of a tip, mate, if you want to do genuine investigative stuff, maybe try investigating something that actually matters. You know, like child poverty in the north, something that has some significance." There's a sneer to his voice that fills the cavernous space. It pollutes what had been a hopeful atmosphere.

"You don't think your wife being injured has any significance?"

"Who said anything about my wife being injured?"

"It's just a hunch," Luke says, and he sounds like a prosecution lawyer, holding court. Everyone is listening, everyone is spellbound. "Seeing as she's gone missing, suddenly abandoned a job that she loved and that paid her pretty well; you've had to have your sister-in-law come and stay to help out with the children . . ."

Henry turns away from Luke again. "I'm sorry, ladies, but I really ought to be getting back to my family." He tries to stride past us towards the exit, but the gaggle of women fences him in. There's something in the way he said the word "ladies"—a hint of condescension that he hasn't managed to hide. We are all staring at him, waiting for him to explain.

"And of course," Luke says, raising his voice even further. "There's the other matter . . ." He gives a dramatic pause, and I find myself smiling with pride. My hero. I stand a little closer to him, so that everyone knows he's with me.

Henry turns his head, frowning.

"Your previous form . . ." Luke says. "Your previous form for violence."

Henry seems to collapse inwards.

"Now listen," he says, his voice soft but tinged with panic. "I don't know what you're talking about, but . . ." He pauses, gathering his thoughts. "You ought to be ashamed." There's new menace in his tone now, as though he's remembered that attack is the best form of defence. "This is a really important event, and you've come here to try to overshadow everything with your pathetic tabloid attempts to find a story, no matter that there isn't one."

"So you weren't once arrested for assault then? You didn't attack an ex-girlfriend?"

"Get out of my way, man!" Henry shouts, and the crowd shrinks away from him. His eyes bulge from his face, suddenly dark and wide.

He pushes past everyone, breathing heavily, brushing my coat with the chocolate velvet as he makes his way to the exit. But just before he gets there, he stops. The whole room watches, hands to mouths, as he straightens himself up, and turns back towards us.

"I'm sorry," he says, looking past me and Luke and back at the crowd. For the first time this evening, he sounds sincere. "The last thing Violet wanted was this kind of drama at an event that meant so much to her. I thought me coming tonight would make her happy, would show her that I support her. But I shouldn't . . . I shouldn't have come."

YVONNE

My punishment for this evening greets me as I wander on to the concourse at Waterloo station. There are crowds of people filling it, so unusual at this time in the evening, more akin to rush hour than 10pm. I look up and my fears are confirmed. There's been a fatality just outside Vauxhall, leaving the entire system in chaos. There are no trains, as suspected, going anywhere near my home.

A middle-aged woman standing to the right of me is shouting at a customer service representative, who's shrugging his shoulders at her.

"I'm sorry," he says, sounding anything but. "I can't tell you how long it'll be. We need the police to reopen the line. Like I said, it's a *fatality*."

He says the last word with scorn, and she shrinks back, finally ashamed. She notices me listening.

"Sure it's tragic and all that, but why these people choose to do it this way . . ." Her voice has a hint of Irish lilt about it.

"I'm sure they weren't thinking straight," I say. "If they were depressed enough to do something like that, I expect they weren't able to think through the consequences."

"Pfft," the woman says. "We've all been stranded when some idiot has done this before. We all know what an inconvenience it is for everyone else."

I turn away from her, unwilling to absorb any more of her bitterness. But despite my sympathy, I find myself sighing deeply, pulling my phone out from my bag. It *is* really inconvenient. Not least because I'm not even where I'm meant to be. I told Simon I was having dinner with Katie in Clapham Junction. Thank God that he's not the kind of man to check these things.

My phone rings twice before he answers.

"Hi babe," he says, sounding sleepy.

"Are you in bed?" I ask, surprised. I picture him lying there in his vest and boxer shorts, and I feel a surge of longing. I wish there was a way I could magic myself there, right now, into Simon's warm arms. What a frustrating waste of time this whole evening has been.

"Yeah," he says, the sound muffled. "Bit of a headache. Don't think I drank enough today. Long day."

"I'm afraid it's going to get even longer, my love," I say. "Because the trains are messed up. Someone's thrown themselves under a train at Vauxhall . . ."

"Shit."

I look up at the timetable board, my eyes flicking along the word "Delayed" flashing over and over in aggressive digital lettering.

"It just says delayed at the moment. What are the chances? I hardly ever go into London and it's late . . ."

"Don't worry," he says. "You won't wake me."

"It's not just that. I'm tired too." I want to add that my body is busy building a new baby, but I'm not about to jinx anything yet.

"You could get a taxi?"

I remember again: he thinks I'm only in Clapham.

"Oh, I looked," I say. "But Uber have put on surge pricing, and anyway, it'll be twenty minutes before anything can get to me."

"Rubbish," Simon says. "Sorry, babe."

"I miss you," I say.

"Miss you too."

"I won't text you when I'm on a train," I say. "You try to get some sleep, and hopefully I won't wake you when I get in."

"You can wake me," Simon says, yawning. "I like it when you wake me."

We finish the call with our usual declarations of love and I try to decide what to do next.

I need the toilet: too much sparkling water gulped down in an effort to hide my face from Henry during the talk. I glance around the station. In the middle is a giant Christmas tree, decorated with huge pink baubles. It reaches almost to the roof. Behind me, I spot something else. Boots.

I weave my way through all the tired and frustrated travellers and wince as I step into the harshly strip-lit shop. The front few aisles are all beauty products, razors, deodorants and anaemic-looking sandwiches. But further back, tucked away among the sanitary products and condoms as though somehow secretly shameful, I find them.

Clearblue Digital is the one I have at home, the one all the women on the forum use. A whole life-changing experience is just minutes away. If I buy one of these and pay my 30p to go to the toilet, then I'll know my fate. What would happen if I found out that I was pregnant here, on a freezing night when I'm stranded at Waterloo station?

Tonight I see my future laid out, Sliding Doors style, two distinct paths. I think of the woman who threw herself under a train at Vauxhall earlier, and I wonder if she was here, and she'd lost the love of her life. Perhaps she'd spent the best part of seventeen years trying to recover from losing a baby enough to conceive another one, and she'd found out her last chance was gone, snatched away. And perhaps then, understandably, her life lost all meaning, or more importantly, hope, and the only sensible thing to do was to end it. Perhaps she stood here, at Waterloo, under that Christmas tree, surrounded by people who had places to go and people to love, and the whole thing felt pointless.

Seventeen years ago, I was that woman. I had lost everything in the space of three months, and I had no idea how I was going to rebuild myself

But I managed it.

I turn and walk away from the pregnancy tests. All this muddled thinking, it's all because I still don't know if she's all right. Cause and effect. Every action has a consequence, and I need to know, for sure, what mine has been. I need to see him, one last time, to find out. I can't take the test. Not until I know.

LILY

"What was that about?" I say to Luke once we are secreted in a corner booth of the nearest pub we could find. My fingers are twitching in my lap. Is this a date? It must be a date, surely. There was no need for us to come here, but Luke wandered towards the pub unquestioning, and I was happy to follow.

It's pathetic, but even if it's *not* a date, it's such a treat to be out, post 10pm, under no pressure to get home to take over from whoever's babysitting Archie.

"The man's a dick," Luke says. He gulps his pint. Guinness, the only thing he drinks.

I asked for a gin and tonic so that I wouldn't be tempted to order more than one. I hate it, so I have to sip it slowly.

"But you don't seriously think . . ." I say, finding it hard to form the words. "That he'd do anything to Violet? Not anything serious?"

"Who knows."

"So," I say, sitting back against the upholstered seat. There's a fire on in the corner and it's gently warming the left-hand side of me, like I'm being enveloped in a hug. "What was the story with his ex? What did he do?"

"It was years ago now," he says. "I had to do some serious digging. It wasn't a serious offence, but an ex-girlfriend accused him of assault. The police dropped the case though when she refused to testify against him. Pretty common outcome by all accounts."

"Were there any details?"

"No, just that there was a domestic."

"Gosh."

"Yeah," he says. "There are rumors too, that he's been playing away. That he's always had other women on the go, throughout his marriage."

"But . . ." I say, the thoughts clumping together in my mind. "I don't get it. Violet wouldn't put up with that. Surely she would know if he was cheating on her?"

"People can be blind as bats when they want to be," Luke says. "It's called love. Or so I've heard." He gives me a little wink and then grins, and I feel my face grow hot again.

I'm suddenly desperate to check my appearance, and so I make my excuses and push my way through the crowds to the toilets. The ladies is unexpectedly empty, and I stand by the basin for a few minutes, trying to examine myself impartially. By some miracle, my eye make-up is still mostly intact, but the blusher I hastily swiped across each cheek has long gone, and the shadows under my eyes are starting to reappear.

I reach into my handbag and pull out my make-up bag, applying what little I have to make the best of things. At the bottom of the bag I see an unfamiliar lipstick. Susie gave it to me last week, telling me that it didn't suit her olive skin tone. It's a kind of bluey-red, far more dramatic than I'd usually wear, but I put it on anyway.

Back in the pub, Luke has nearly finished his pint. He smiles up at me as I wander over and take my seat beside him.

"Oh," he says. "You look nice."

My hand flies to my face.

"Oh, er, thanks," I say.

There's a pause and the two of us stare at our drinks. What is he thinking, and how can I get him to open up? I used to be good at flirting, a long time ago.

"Have you got to get back?" he says, after a while. "Relieve the babysitter?"

"Oh," I say. "No, I mean. No, he's gone to stay with his grandparents for a few days."

"Your parents? Do they live near?"

"Yes and no. My . . ." I pause, swallowing. "My mother died when I was a baby, and my father lives in Dover with his new wife. We're not that close."

"I'm sorry."

"No, it's OK. He's older . . . a bit set in his ways." I think of the way Dad snapped at Archie last Christmas for swinging on the living room door handle. His lack of tolerance for any sort of mess. Five minutes after the Christmas presents were opened, Archie's were sitting in a pile on the bottom of the stairs, ready to be taken to our room. How I had wished I belonged to Violet's family, where Christmas meant non-stop giggles and chaos. "I find him quite suffocating, if I'm honest. My stepmum is fine but we've never really been that involved with each other."

"It must have been terrible to lose your mother so young. And . . . Ellie told me about your husband," he says, gently. "That he'd died, too."

"Oh. Did she?" I say, surprised. I can't remember telling her about it, but I guess I must have done. Or I put something on the bloody forum.

"Must have been terrible," Luke says, and I can see he's doing the same thing he did with Henry. Probing, scratching about under the surface, trying to see what's hidden and coax it out.

I nod, my cheeks burning. "It was . . . very sudden."

Luke waits for me to continue. I pause. I could do it—I could tell him everything, the whole story I've shared before, so many times. It would be easy, like reciting my full name and date of birth. The details of James's "death" have been recounted so often that they're imprinted on my memory, as real as anything else that ever happened to me.

I could do it.

Or I could tell him the truth.

But if I do that, there's no going back.

"Do you mind if we don't talk about it?" I say, looking down at my lap. "It's . . . very difficult."

Of course not," Luke says, and his neck flushes. "I'm sorry, I didn't want to pry."

"It's fine," I say. "I did wonder if Ellie might have told you." I scan my brain, trying to remember what *I* told her.

"Losing your husband . . . And you had a baby to look after. Jesus, Lily. I can't imagine."

"That was the hardest thing, I think," I say, swallowing. I want to use the present tense, because it still is. "The loneliness. I just had to get on with it, but when Archie was asleep at night, I felt like the only person in the world. I'm an only child . . . All I wanted was a family of my own; I thought Archie would have a brother or sister at some point . . . I was determined that he wouldn't have the same sort of childhood as me, but . . ." I shake my head. The tears are falling freely now, because this part is true. "Anyway. I was alone, and grieving. That's how I first discovered Violet . . ."

I think of the two Violets I know. The one who saved me, and the one who has let me down, by disappearing on us all. My tears dry up.

"I completely understand," Luke says. At some point during my speech he's put his hand on top of mine. He squeezes it gently. Despite my sadness, there's that familiar kick of adrenalin. It's working. He's falling for it. He's falling for *me*. Men just can't help but want to rescue a damsel in distress. It's cynical but it's true.

"Sylvia and my dad have been very helpful," I say. "They wanted me to go and stay with them but I knew I'd be even more isolated if I did . . ." I sniff back the tears. "So I sorted out childcare, found a job. But that was the other thing . . . the thing that made it so hard . . ."

Luke looks up at me, confused, and I can't resist.

After all, what I'm about to say isn't a total lie.

"James," I say. I rub my hand against one side of my face. "It wasn't only that he left us . . ."

The mess of emotions washes over me: guilt, anger, misery, excitement, all mixed together, making me nauseous.

I think about James, alive and well right now in Wimbledon. If he's still in Wimbledon—which, of course, he might not be. After we split up, he deleted all his social media accounts, and blocked my phone number and email address, making it impossible for me to stalk him.

Luke's eyes widen in curiosity.

"It wasn't only that he left us, you see," I say, wiping away a tear; "it was that he left us with nothing."

YVONNE

I push my way through the thick lines of people at Waterloo and go back underground. Simon will be fast asleep now anyway. He won't care if I get home at 2am. I'll get a night bus if I have to. So long as I get home before the morning, it'll be fine.

I wait on the Jubilee line platform. I'm sure Henry will be there, tonight, alone. He'll slam the door in my face when he sees it's me, but he'll open it again, eventually. I'll stand on the doorstep, shouting of the cold, of the risk of being attacked, and he won't want to look like the bad guy. Not again.

The train arrives and it's busier than I expected it to be, full of drunk Christmas revellers incongruously singing Auld Lang Syne at the tops of their voices. I sit back, wrapping my coat around me, grateful for my baby-on-board badge and the man who offered me his seat, a half-hearted smile on his face at his Christmas gesture.

We pull into London Bridge and as the train lurches to a halt, the girl who had been leading the singing leans over and vomits in between her feet. Some of it splashes on her boots, and she looks up, groggy, catching my eye.

She's me, in a former life. I give her a look of pity that she doesn't acknowledge. I want to tell her that she doesn't need to do this, that she's worth more than she thinks, but she's too drunk to care, so I leave the train, making my way over to the Northern line. From here I'm about twenty minutes away. I should get there before 11pm, with any luck.

Everything runs smoothly, as though the universe is on my side. When I arrive at my destination, I stand on the long escalator, looking upwards, and start to get second thoughts. I'm so far from home. So far from Isleworth. If this goes wrong again, I've got no one close by to help me, to come to my rescue. I shake the thoughts away. Now's the time for courage.

I exit the Tube and walk along the fashionable main shopping street of her neighborhood. This is where she belongs. And she never appreciated it. Even now, I'm still irritated with her for that. She just thought it was the norm, to pop down to the local florist for a hand-tied bunch of hydrangeas encased in thick brown paper, to stop on the way back at the deli to pick up some cheese no one has ever heard of for her dinner party that evening.

I'm nearly there now, and the streets are quieter. The houses all loom large above me, watching me, marking me out as an outsider. They're fortresses, protecting their spoilt and ungrateful occupants. But fortresses can be overcome.

Finally, I arrive at his street. Their street. I feel a pang for Kensington, for the short time we spent there, wrapped in each other's arms. Our youth, the promises he made me, that were written in dust, blown away by a whisper.

I make my way along the street. And then I am there, outside his house. Number 36 Acacia Avenue.

I climb the steps, my legs steady and strong now, and I press the brass bell, hoping that behind this door I'll find the answers—the reassurance—that I need.

HENRY

The ironic thing is, I respected Yvonne a bit more after she had sliced open my arm. As I watched the suspicious nurse stick Steri-Strips across it—it was only a flesh wound, thankfully; *"I shouldn't be allowed in the kitchen!"* I'd winked—I found myself admiring Yvonne's balls. They were certainly bigger than mine. I know it had been an accident, her hand had slipped as I pushed her away from me, but she hadn't even felt the need to come to the hospital with me. Instead, she just dropped the knife in my kitchen and ran.

The police came later that evening, but they weren't very interested in my side of things. She'd twisted it all. She'd got in there first, claiming self-defence. She'd actually accused *me* of assault. When I saw her at work the next week, she ignored me. Didn't bother to ask me how I was. Didn't seem to care that she might have left me about to collapse on the floor, bleeding profusely from a major vein. That I might have been blue-lighted to hospital, spent time in intensive care, but still made it back in time for the weekly covers meeting. Maybe she could tell she'd only nicked the skin. Maybe she'd done it before to other men. But still, cutting someone with a knife—you ought to feel some guilt about that, surely?

Understandably, she stopped coming to the pub with us all after that. I lived in fear she would tell everyone about her pregnancy—after my initial irritation that she hadn't enquired after my health died away, more than anything I just wanted her gone. Gone from the magazine completely. And I was in luck. One evening, I ran into a bunch of other Bennet Media journos down at the club and I heard them talking about a new launch. A woman's fashion weekly. Mix of reportage and work-to-bar outfits, aimed at young commuting professionals. Glossy cover, but cheap paper stock inside. They were recruiting, and yes, they needed a whole picture desk. I sang her praises, told them she deserved a little promotion, that she was the best-dressed in the office by miles, that she was wasted on *King*. And just like that, my little problem went away. Or at least, got moved to the eleventh floor.

I carried on with my life, trying to push to the back of my mind what she might or might not have decided to do about the baby. Her salary barely broke five figures, so I knew she couldn't afford to keep it. I hoped she'd come to realise that, in time. And I'd done my bit, hadn't I? I'd wanted to give her the money to go private, but after she refused my offer and then stabbed me when I was trying to talk it all through *like a grown-up*, well, I changed my mind.

But the guilt remained. Especially when she sent me that email, later, telling me how things turned out. It's always there, lingering at the back of my mind. It didn't help that it was a boy, and I only have my three girls. I think about him sometimes. What he would have been like. But that doesn't mean I don't think it was for the best—for her, for me, and for the baby. *Incompatible with life*, that's the phrase she said they used.

If I'm honest, I managed to push it to the back of my mind quite well. The past was in the past. But then my wedding day came, and like a wound that never truly healed, the whole thing was split open again.

A few weeks ago, when I was travelling home on the Underground, an inebriated lady younger than me called across the carriage. "Oi you! Instagram husband!" I looked up, only because my Bluetooth headphones had run out of battery and so I wasn't listening to music as I usually am. I asked her to repeat herself, and she took it upon herself to come and sit next to me and tell me how much she loves my wife.

Everyone loves my wife. People joke about their better halves, but in this case there's no doubting that my wife is the better of us two.

And up until last week, I'd somehow managed to stop her from realising it.

LILY

The gin and tonic didn't work. After our uncomfortable conversation about James, I need something stronger. Luke is only too happy to oblige, and heads back to the bar.

I should have told him the truth. Dangerous, Lily, dangerous, I say to myself, but I don't care. I deserve a night off, don't I? Maybe a little fun, even. I have cried myself to sleep most nights, ever since James left me. It's been so long since I've done this, sat in a pub with a man. A man who's attractive, and interesting, and more importantly seems to like me. I'm *allowed* to do this. I'm only twenty-seven.

An hour later, we are both drunk. I escape to the toilet, sitting down. It feels as though the cubicle is closing in and opening out on me, my head fuzzy. In front of the basins, I strike up a conversation with a stranger about my eye make-up, soliciting her opinion. She tells me I'd look better with wings, and I shut my eyes and allow her to draw them on for me with her own pencil. As she chats to me, telling me I look gorgeous, I half-heartedly think about how Violet once did a video about make-up hygiene and I feel like laughing out loud at her, telling her how stupid her content is. How stupid we all are for watching.

The girl gives me a hug, and kisses me on the cheek.

"Good luck, sweetie," she says. "I've been watching you—you can tell he's smitten."

"You're so nice," I say, as I wash my hands. "Not like my friend Violet. She's let us all down again. She doesn't care. We're all idiots for watching, you see. She doesn't care."

The girl frowns, looking confused, and turns away before she hears me mutter the word *bitch* under my breath. But I don't care if she's heard or not, it feels good to say it out loud. Violet is a bitch.

Back in the pub, I concentrate very hard on walking to the table without bumping into anything. I'm used to this feeling, of course. But only at home, where the carpet pathway from my sofa to my bed is trampled flat, familiar and reliable.

"Mustn't fall over," I whisper to myself as I push through the people. The lights flash on and off and a bell rings, and then I remember what it means. *Time, please, ladies and gentlemen.* That's the end of my fun, the end of the night. I'll be turfed out now, spat out into the cold street, the joy of this evening souring into regret as I trudge to the Tube. My head will throb in response to the buzzing strip lighting on the platform. The train will throw me up and down, sloshing the contents of my stomach up into my throat. I will crawl into bed, without removing my make-up, and feel ashamed for the rest of the week.

"Hey," Luke says, as I collapse on to the booth seat next to him. "You were ages. Was going to send out a search party."

I stare at him. He's drunk too. His eyes are bloodshot, a little too wide.

"Shall we make a move?"

I groan inwardly. I want to hang on to the last few minutes of what's been an enjoyable evening, but of course he's desperate to get out of here, winged eyeliner or not.

"I suppose so," I say, heaving my coat on over my shoulders.

We walk to the Tube together. He's so close to me; my hand keeps brushing the outside of his jacket. I'm wallowing in a new self-pity now, thinking what might have been and what I've ruined.

We reach the mouth of the station and he pauses.

"Hey," he says. He looks down at the escalator as it sucks people under. "I don't really like the idea of you trying to get home on your own."

"I'll be fine," I say, shrugging my shoulders and pushing him away. I feel my balance shift and narrowly avoid falling over. Great, now he feels responsible for me. "Big girl."

"Nah but . . ." He shifts slightly, linking his arm through mine. "I wouldn't feel happy about it. I'll come with you."

"Suit yourself," I say, eyes wide. "How will you get back?"

"It's fine, I'll get an Uber."

I think of the way he spoke about his sister, the genuine concern in his eyes.

"Are you sure?"

"Yes. Come on," he says, and he tugs me on to the escalator.

He turns to face me as we descend. He's on the step below me. If he were a stranger this would be an invasion of personal space. But he's not a stranger. I bring my hand to my forehead. My thoughts begin to muddle.

"I feel like such an idiot," I say. "I shouldn't have drunk so much."

"Don't be daft," he says. "You didn't drink that much." He winks at me, and then, a split-second before he does it, I know what's going to happen. He winds his arms around my waist, and pulls me towards him. Our faces are almost touching as he gazes at me.

"You're adorable," he says. "You do know that, don't you?"

I look away, embarrassed. Then I look back, and I feel myself leaning in towards him. I want him to kiss me.

But he doesn't. The escalator ends, and he stumbles backwards, unaware. I nearly fall on top of him, but grab the handrail just in time to steady myself.

"Shit!" he says, in a heap at my feet. People wander past us, stepping over him, tutting. I haul him up. His hands are warm.

"Serves me right for trying to snog you on an escalator," he says, and takes my hand, leading me towards the southbound platform. "Come on. Let's get you home."

YVONNE

There's no answer, so I ring again. I might wake the children, but then again, they sleep on the top floor, tucked away like some Victorian kids in a nursery. A room each. A whole suite of children's rooms, in fact, with a bathroom painted in blue, a *Finding Nemo* mural splashed across one wall. I remember the vlog when Violet unveiled it to them: *Kids Get The Surprise Of Their Lives!*

The lights are off in the house, the whole thing covered in darkness. I peer through the stained-glass panels on either side of the door to see if the light is on in the kitchen at the back of the house, but it isn't.

He's still up, I know it. He never goes to bed before midnight, no matter how sleep-deprived he is. It accounts for how much he's aged since he had the children, but he's stubborn like that, refuses to let anyone else change his routines, his ways of living.

I walk back down the stone steps and to the side of the house. I know where he'll be, if he's not in the living room. His little oasis, his hideaway, where we met once before. The vast black gate looms before me. I tap in the security code—2015, the year they moved in—and wait for it to unlock. As it clicks open, I think of the way he told me what the code was, with the casual manner of someone who's never lost anything that mattered.

I walk through the gate and shut it behind me. I'm in their garden. Their huge-for-London, perfectly manicured garden. A neat lawn, edged by smooth grey paving slabs, some well-tended flowerbeds and not a lot else. Just a black-painted shed in one corner, and then his man

188

cave at the end. Clad in cedar, like something out of *Grand Designs*, entirely at odds with the architecture of the house itself.

I walk down the side path and the garden is suddenly flooded with light. Security lights, activated by motion. They must go off all the time when the foxes are prowling. There's only one door at the front of his man cave. It has an integral blind, which is pulled down, but slithers of light are escaping from the edges, and I know he's in there.

It's been nearly two weeks since I last saw him.

I tiptoe up to the door. What will he be doing in there? Probably smoking, listening to blues and feeling sorry for himself. He was always so good at that. I'd pander to it, of course. I was so in love back then, so in awe. I was a human ego-booster, a pathetic puppy dog wanting nothing but for my master to acknowledge me.

I pause outside the door to the cabin, turning around to look at the house. She's not there, of course. She'll be at the hospital. But someone must be inside, looking after the kids. Perhaps Henry's mother is there. I remember the way she looked at me when we bumped into her outside the Bluebird Cafe. Like I was something she had stepped in. The way he called her *Mother*, before introducing me, dismissing our relationship, referring to me as a work colleague and a friend. I had to excuse myself and rush to the toilet, locking myself in and giving in to a few brief sobs, before pulling myself together, telling myself it was only a matter of time before I got what I wanted.

If only I'd known back then that it would take me seventeen years.

I knock on the door. Softly at first, then with more force. The glass in the door is thick, triple-glazed probably, and even if I put my ear right up close to it, I can't hear any sounds from inside. Maybe he's asleep. But no, not with the light on. I could try the handle, it'd probably be unlocked, but I'm too scared of what I might find to enter uninvited.

I knock again. Still nothing.

Eventually I pull my phone out of my pocket and dial his number, my heart pounding in my chest as it rings.

The call connects, but he doesn't say anything. He hasn't forgiven me yet.

"I'm outside," I say, my voice edged with that new-found power. "Let me in."

I hear a sigh, and then he hangs up. Seconds later there's some movement behind the door, and then it opens.

He stands in the doorway, staring down at me. His lip curls upwards as he takes me in. In one hand, he's holding a crystal glass, filled with amber liquid.

"What the fuck," he says, and immediately I know he's drunk, from the hoarseness of his voice. The bags under his eyes that were evident on stage just hours beforehand have suddenly increased tenfold, huge dark welts that give his face a skull-like appearance. One corner of his shirt is hanging out from underneath his jumper. His hair is tousled and greasy, and his nose is shiny with sweat.

It is like a liberation. All those years of agony, and finally, I have won. I don't need to be here. I don't need to be here at all. There is nothing in this washed-up, forty-five-year-old man that I want. Or need. I have Simon.

It is like a spell has been broken, and I am finally free.

"Is she OK?" I say, my voice tight, precise. "That's all I want to know. Just tell me she's OK and then I'll leave you alone."

I stare hard into his eyes.

"You," he spits, the whisky glass rising in his hand. The other points towards me, finger jabbing mid-air, as though he's trying to poke me in the face. "Always . . . *you*. Turning up where you're not welcome. So tell me, Yvonne, why are you *here* tonight?"

He stumbles slightly, leaning on the doorframe.

"Please, Henry, just tell me if she's OK . . ."

"No!" he roars, cutting me off. "She's NOT OK and she never will be again. There, are you happy now?"

And I know then that coming here was a stupid idea, that he wants me dead.

Briefly, I raise my eyes to the dark sky. I turn and leave just in time, hearing the crack of his whisky glass as it hits the patio behind me, smashing into pieces that jump across the ground, spinning where they land.

HENRY

Look, I'm prepared to take the blame for most of it. For a start, it was my fault, I suppose, for being so hands-off with the wedding. For never checking, for never asking, for never showing an interest. I'd feigned busyness, made jokes about my crude taste, thrown out platitudes like "whatever makes you happy will make me happy, darling" as though they were get-out-of-jail-free cards. Served me right, my father would have said.

I first saw her from one of the front bedrooms of my parents' house. It wasn't my bedroom; it was one of the spares. Larger, with an en suite and sunbleached floral wallpaper that Violet said would work well in the pictures, fitting our theme of "faded English country glamor" perfectly. I never imagined that on the morning of my wedding I would wake up in that room. It will forever be my great aunt's bedroom, because it's the one she always insisted on at Christmas. She said she liked the fact it overlooked the driveway, that you could see people approaching.

And so I was in there, the muted scent of mothballs possibly a figment of my imagination, when I first saw her. But before I saw her, I heard her. Not just her, but the other one too. Crunching up the gravel driveway, laughing a little. He was more serious, issuing instructions. She was teasing him, making comments about the morning mist. I leant out of the window. Andrew was with me, pressed up against the freestanding mirror, muttering about his buttonhole. But his chatter faded into the background as I stared out and strained my neck to confirm what I believed to be true.

It took a few seconds for me to understand what she was doing there, but then I realised. And as I realised, I realised something else. She wouldn't be here just that morning, but all day. She would be there, even as I said my vows. If not literally in my face, then in the background, staring, watching, recording. Which was worse?

I felt my throat constrict, tugged at the collar of my shirt.

"All right, sir?" Andrew asked me, as I looked up at him. "Not too late to change your mind!"

"Fine," I said, but I pushed past him and closed the door of the en suite.

"Not being sick in there, are you?" he joked, tapping on the heavy mahogany door. "I've got some Scotch out here if it'll help . . ."

I stood at the basin, leaning on the sides, staring at my face in the mirror. The color had drained from it, my skin almost as white as the single rose that sat against my lapel. A bead of sweat formed on one side of my forehead, glinting in the light from the window above the toilet behind me.

I wasn't hot, though. It was December. The house was old. On the coldest mornings, the insides of the windows were covered in slivers of ice. Violet thought it was romantic, but she'd never had to live there.

The doorbell sounded out. I heard my mother downstairs, welcoming them in. It was only a matter of time before she would be making her way up the huge curving staircase, before she knocked on the door.

It was only a matter of time before we were face to face.

I had spent so many years trying to forget her. Atoning for my sins. But I should have known I never could.

* * *

Everywhere I looked, all day, she was there. Or rather, her camera was, her face hidden behind it. I had no idea what she was thinking, what she was doing.

After the ceremony passed by in a blur, I took myself off to the toilets. So many people, in my face, congratulating me. Making jokes about how Violet had finally tamed me. Telling me she must be special.

"What can I say!" I said to them all. "A man's got to admit defeat at some point." And Violet had rolled her eyes, and everyone had laughed, and then I'd gone over and kissed her on the forehead, as if to rub out the idiocy of my previous statement. What did she even see in me?

In the gents, I locked myself in a cubicle and sat on the toilet lid. Tried to convince myself that it was a mistake, some kind of weird accident. But I knew it wasn't. No way. This was Yvonne. Nothing about her was accidental. It was all meticulously constructed, her carefree façade, when in truth she was in control of everything the whole time. If you peeled off her skin, underneath you'd probably find a mass of cables and electronics. Robotic. Single-minded.

After the wedding breakfast, I went outside for a fag. I needed to escape the hordes of guests, many of whom I barely recognised, although they all seemed to know me. I crept round the back of the catering tent, where there was just enough light from the kitchen for me to light my cigarette, and I stood there, watching the smoke hang in the air as I exhaled.

The day had gone to plan, apart from that one thing. Violet had grabbed me at the end of the photography session, pulled me into the cloakroom. Someone had finally taken Lula from her, and it was the first time we'd been alone all day. She kissed me hard, pushing me against the wall, and I could taste the champagne on her breath, mixed in with tobacco. She never smoked. I smiled at her, told her how beautiful she was, and she lifted her wedding dress to reveal her legs underneath, pushing her hips against my trousers. I was grateful then, for my primeval instinct, for the fact that I'm a man and my brain doesn't interfere with anything below my waistline. She was eight years younger than me and sexy as hell. My new wife.

Afterwards, we held each other for a while, slumped against the wall. She told me how much she loved me and I murmured the same back. We were sweaty, stuck together, her silk wedding dress almost indecently thin against her skin. I stroked the back of her thigh underneath the fabric, my head resting on her shoulder. I wanted to stay in that cloakroom forever.

* * *

By the end of the night, I was very drunk. Violet had disappeared to bed with the baby, telling me to stay and enjoy myself. Someone had brought out shots, and my head was spinning.

I went outside again to get some fresh air, wandering down the lawn-lined walkways, looking at the moon. Alcohol had pushed Yvonne back to the past where she belonged. I assumed she had left, but as I strolled further I reached the car park, and saw something I recognised.

She was leaning over the car boot, loading it with equipment. I stared at her for quite a while, taking in her shape underneath her clothes. I stopped walking, but it was too late. She turned and saw me.

"Congratulations," she said. She'd already said it to me earlier in the day, but her tone was entirely different now. Vicious. "She's . . . impressive. So much for your bachelor blood."

I was drunk, arrogant, thought it would be OK now Violet was safely tucked away in our room.

"Yvonne Adams," I said, throwing my hands up into the air. I laughed, long and loud, like an idiot. "Well well well. What the fuck are you doing at my wedding?"

She glared at me then. There was a silence that hung in the air, leaving me feeling stupid, suddenly. And then she narrowed her eyes, slamming her car boot shut.

"Go to hell," she said, calmly, before climbing into her car and driving off.

22 May 2017
From: gottheblues@hotmail.com
To: violet@violetisblue.com

Hi Violet,

Long time, no see. You're pregnant again. Congratulations! How many children are you going to have with that man?! No, but seriously, I'm THRILLED FOR YOU.

We'd all guessed ages ago, but you probably know that. It's always quite obvious. Your face bloats up when you're pregnant. It's just the water retention—don't take it the wrong way. Just part of that magical pregnancy glow.

Three kids. You'll have your hands full, for sure. I didn't think much of Skye's reaction when you cut into your gender reveal cake and she saw the inside was pink. She was so desperate for a baby brother, wasn't she? Is it the first time she's realised that life doesn't always go to plan? That there are some things you just can't control? Guess it's tough when you're used to getting everything you want all the time. Not that I'm saying your kids are spoilt, but . . .

You know what, Violet? I'd be the same. I'd buy my kids all the crap under the sun if I could afford it. That's what mothers do, isn't it?

Still, Skye's getting older now. Not sure it's really right to film her sobbing her heart out because she's getting another little sister when she wanted a brother. Bit intrusive, don't you think?

Did you notice the way Mandy laughed at her when she ran off crying and flopped herself down on the sofa?

I've told you before, Violet, and I'll tell you again. I don't like her, and I don't trust her.

LILY

I open my eyes slowly. They feel dry, even though they've been firmly wedged shut. Something's not right. And then I realise; I'm on the wrong side of the bed.

I'm on James's side of the bed.

Memories float into my mind like blurry clouds. James, lying next to me as I fall asleep. James, gone when I wake up.

I'm sorry, Lily. I never meant to lead you on.

And then the worst thing of all, all that time later.

I've met someone else. She doesn't want us to be in touch.

That hollow feeling in my stomach as I lurched out of bed, ready to face another day staring at my phone, hoping for a text that would never come.

I'm facing the curtains, which have been pulled together but not properly, the middle gaping open like a wound, spilling light into the room. I glance around, not wanting to lift my head. I can hear something; someone. In my flat.

I roll over in the bed and sit up. My bedroom door is open, and from here I have a straight view to my kitchen. Luke is standing, with his back to me, whistling and doing something with my toaster.

He hasn't gone. He hasn't left me.

I smile, despite my thumping head, and look around for my phone, finding it dumped on my dressing table. It's nearly out of battery, but it tells me that it is 9.15am. 9.15am!

Of course, after we left the pub and came back to mine, the rest of the evening is a blur. I know I insisted he come in, and I have a vague recollection of opening the bottle of red Sylvia brought me yesterday—a special one from their last booze cruise to Calais. I was meant to be saving it for Christmas.

But what happened after that? Did we just chat and fall asleep?

I look down. I'm in my pyjamas. My clothes are dumped, as they always are, on the chair by my dressing table. The room looks the same as usual for first thing in the morning—messy, but no sign of any gay abandon having taken place. Perhaps Luke slept on the sofa. Or in Archie's room? But if so, why is my bedroom door open?

I look back towards the kitchen, still half hidden under my duvet. Luke turns and sees me, smiling broadly.

"Morning, sleeping beauty," he says, waving. "Breakfast is nearly served."

I rub my eyes with my fists, suddenly aware of my appearance. In the mornings I usually look like an absolute troll. I smile at him and pull my hair around my face as much as possible. He turns back to the toaster and starts buttering fiercely, and I seize the opportunity to run to the bathroom.

It's clear I didn't take my make-up off before going to bed last night, as the winged eyeliner that girl put on me in the pub toilets is still there, smeared across my eyelids. My lips are dry and stained from lipstick.

I can't believe he's still here—better than that, he's in the kitchen, making me breakfast. I set about making myself presentable. I wash my face thoroughly, the hot flannel like a balm against my skin. I smother it in moisturiser. There's not much I can do with my bird's nest of hair, but I run my fingers through it, giving it a little lift, and try to convince myself that the bedhead look is still in.

I pull my dressing gown on over my pyjamas, wincing as I spot the splodge of Archie's porridge that's been dried on one arm for about a month. And then I go through to the kitchen, perching on the one bar stool.

"Perfect timing," Luke says, grinning. He's so nice. How can he be so nice? It doesn't seem possible. "Hope you like bagels."

"Where did you . . ." I begin, confused. I'm not the sort of person to have bagels in my house. And then I see something else: smoked salmon and a fresh box of eggs with only three eggs in it.

"I nipped out to Sainsbury's Local while you were still asleep," he says. "You left your keys on the side. Coffee?"

He's done all this—just for me.

"Oh my God," I say.

"Steady on, it's only breakfast," he says, but he's grinning again, as he tips perfectly fluffy scrambled eggs on to my bagel, and lays strips of smoked salmon on top. "I put the heating on too, hope that's OK. Hope you like eggs. And salmon."

"I do," I reply, pulling the plate towards me.

"Wait!" he says, pulling an expression of mild horror. "You need the pièce de résistance!"

I frown, but then he turns back to the chopping board by the sink and picks up half a lemon, squeezing it over the salmon.

"Pepper?" he says.

"Yes, please."

We sit—me on the bar stool, him on the tiny patch of kitchen counter—and eat our eggs. I'm ravenous, and I try to remember the last time I ate breakfast properly, like this. Usually I just finish off whatever Archie's left, or grab a banana and eat it on the way to the Tube.

"So," I say, when I've finished. "About last night . . ."

"Yes," he replies. He's still grinning at me. "Didn't quite turn out how I expected either."

I think back to our original reason for meeting—to watch Violet host a panel talk on women's employment rights, and can barely remember it. The whole thing—the whole crusade—seems to have lost all importance. Susie always teases me about my obsession with Violet, telling me if I had my own life I wouldn't care so much about hers. She was right, of course she was right. It was that obvious.

"I can't . . ." I say, sipping the strong coffee he handed me. "If I'm honest, the details are a little fuzzy . . ."

"Don't worry, we didn't do anything . . ." he says, and there's a kindness in his eyes. "Nothing non-PG anyway. I slept on the sofa."

"Oh," I say.

"Not that I didn't want to . . ." he adds, suddenly looking uncomfortable for the first time. He sighs, puts down his plate. "I really like you, Lily. But I understand that . . . well, you've been through a lot. I don't want to take advantage."

"Oh," I say, again. I smile half-heartedly, as I feel something edging over me. A sense of regret. No, not regret. Guilt. For not telling him the truth about James. Why oh why did I tell everyone on the forum that he'd died? It was so stupid, so unbelievably stupid to make up nonsense like that just so a load of strangers would feel sorry for me. I never imagined it leading to *this*. I think of Archie, at my dad and Sylvia's, playing happily and thinking his mother is at home applying for jobs, working her hardest to get them out of the massive hole they're in. Not standing around in her dressing gown eating eggs with a man she barely knows.

I look back at Luke. He's frowning slightly now.

"Sorry, I . . ." I say, giving a useless shrug. "I'm just not very good at this stuff. Out of practice, I guess."

"No pressure," he says. "I was going to leave you to it, actually. Just thought it would be good to get something inside you before I did . . ." I start to giggle. "Oh God." He hits himself on the forehead and rolls his eyes.

"Sorry. You know what I mean," he adds.

"Thank you," I say, trying to pull myself together. "For everything— for last night, for this morning. For letting me sleep. I haven't slept like that in years."

"Glad you had a good rest," he says. "You seemed a little worse for wear last night. At one point, you were rather furious with life."

My face flushes.

"I don't remember much of it," I say. "I'm sorry."

"Don't be daft," he says, taking our plates and soaking them in the sink.

"What are you doing today?" I ask, suddenly desperate to keep him here. The thought of a day alone, sitting at my geriatric laptop, filling in job application after job application for jobs I don't really want fills me with gloom.

"I'm meeting a source," he says, tapping his nose and smiling. "Someone who knows Violet pretty well. Or used to, at least. A friend of Ellie's."

"Oh," I say. Violet again. Where is she now? "Is that all you can tell me?"

"Afraid so," he says. "I just don't know if it'll lead to anything concrete yet."

"What about the hospital lead? Now we know it's The Royal London?"

"It's not really my style," Luke says, padding towards the living room and lifting his jacket from the arm of my sofa. Fragments of memory filter back to me—the two of us, tangled up together uncomfortably. The ferocity of the way I kissed him. "And he could have been visiting for any number of reasons. It might mean nothing at all."

"If he'd done something to her," I say, the coffee starting to kick in, "then surely the police wouldn't let him near her?"

"Not if she hasn't pressed charges," he replies. "Domestic abuse cases are notoriously hard to see through. If she forgave him, then there's nothing anyone could do."

I sigh, suddenly wishing I'd never heard of Violet, or Henry, or her children. All the hours I've wasted on her, when I should have been living my own life.

"Now, listen you," Luke says, leaning down to kiss me on the forehead. "Good luck with the job applications. I'll call you later."

YVONNE

12 DPO.

The sun streams through our bedroom window. It's a rounded bay as befits the thirties architecture of our house, and the windows are uPVC, with anachronous leading that chops the panes into little squares, cutting out much of the light. But this morning, they look beautiful, I think, as I lurch reluctantly out of sleep. Simon is already up, playing a game on his phone. It's his day off. But more than that. It's D-day. The day everything has been leading up to.

Finally.

"Morning, m'lady," he says, putting his phone away. "What time did you get home in the end?"

"It was really late," I say, and he reaches down to kiss me briefly. "You don't want to know. Took so long for them to sort out the trains. Glad I didn't wake you." I shake my head. I don't want to think about last night, the way Henry looked at me. He won't give me the answers I'm looking for, but on the journey home last night I saw on GoMamas that he'd apparently been spotted coming out of The Royal London Hospital, which means she must still be alive, at the very least.

And tomorrow I'm going back into the police station to go over my statement.

It's all going to be OK. The past will soon be dead and buried.

Today is a day to look forward. It's all about the future, what the fortune teller predicted, the closure, the curative reward for all my suffering. I should be tired—I've barely slept—but I'm the opposite. I'm completely wired, as excited as a child on their birthday.

"Cup of tea?" I look up at him, teasingly.

"Sure," he says, and he bounds out of bed. He pulls on his dressing gown and heads for the door.

"Herbal!" I call after him as he leaves. "I don't mind what, but herbal, please!"

I settle back down underneath the duvet and lift my phone from the bedside table. It's 10am now. I imagine Henry, lying in a drunken stupor on the floor of his stupid man cabin. Full of regrets. Good.

Several minutes later, Simon strolls back into the room, holding a tray.

"Chocolate croissants," he says. "Your favorite. Seeing as it's my day off."

He's right, they are my favorite, but I don't usually allow myself to have them. Everyone knows the old "eat for two" rule is a myth. It's only in the last trimester that you should really pile on the maternal fat stores, in order to prepare your body for breastfeeding. But still. Today's a day of celebration.

"Hold that thought," I say to him, as he places the tray on the bed. I slide my legs out and stand up. I'm wearing my long silk nightdress, a Christmas present from him last year and his eyes rove across my body appreciatively. "Back in a sec."

I walk slowly across the carpeted hallway towards our bathroom. It's the only room we could afford to do up when we moved in, and I love it. All calming spa-like colors, with a huge stone bowl for a basin, and built-in oak cupboards. The floor is warm under my feet—an indulgence but one that was well worth the money.

It's a stunning bathroom. Similar to Violet's en suite—I'm not denying that I took inspiration from her house tour vlog. Nothing wrong with that. It's not like she will ever see it.

I reach into one of the cupboards and take a test from the pile I neatly lined up at the back of the top shelf yesterday. I open the wrapper but there's no hesitation this time.

Afterwards, I lay it on the side of the basin as I wash my hands, not allowing my eyes to wander near until the three minutes are up. Once they are, I pick it up and look at it. In my excitement my eyes take a few seconds to focus.

I walk back to the bedroom, clutching the test. I should have thought of better ways of doing this, but now the moment's here I've run out of ideas. My head is filled with white noise, buzzing and diluting any rational thought. Before I know what I'm doing, I've thrust the test into Simon's hand, and am staring at his confused face.

"I know I should have waited," I say. "But I knew. I just knew . . ." The tears come from nowhere, cascading down my face.

"What?" Simon says, looking down at the little white stick with its clear blue letters. *Pregnant 2 weeks*. "What? I don't understand!"

"I told you!" I say, climbing on to the bed, disrupting Pushka, who seems to have snuck in and made herself at home while I was on the toilet. "I knew this month it was going to work! I just knew it!"

"But . . ." Simon says, still staring at the test. His hand begins to shake, just a little. "I thought it was so unlikely . . . my sperm . . . they said . . ."

"I told you—all the vitamins and antioxidants! There was a ninety per cent improvement in sperm morphology in some of those tests—it's *worked*!" I squeak into Simon's ear as I wrap my arms around his neck. The sleeve of my nightdress falls into the bowl of cereal in his lap, soaking it with milk, but I don't even care. "So much of infertility is a mystery—you hear all the time about couples getting pregnant just before they start their first round of IVF. I knew it! It's all the healthy eating . . . the timing . . . Having sex every day. Everything we've done. We tried so hard this month . . . it all paid off."

"Yvonne," Simon says, finally looking me in the eyes. His own begin to fill up. Just a little, but enough for me to notice. "I'm going to be a dad."

"Yes, babe, you are," I say. I climb back across the duvet and take my place beside him in the bed again, reaching for the tray with my breakfast on. The croissant smells delicious. I wonder when I'll start to go off things like this, when the nausea will kick in. I try to think back to last time, but then blink the thoughts away. I mustn't compare. This is a new experience. A new pregnancy. A new baby.

I look over at Simon. His bowl of cereal is still lying in his lap, but he's staring ahead, at the wall opposite our bed. Staring ahead and grinning, his eyes unfocused.

I take a big bite of my croissant and shift back a little, resting my back against our buttoned headboard. Something hard jabs at my thigh, and I reach down to see what it is. My phone. I've finally taken back control, and I want to cry tears of joy.

I don't care about you anymore, Henry, I think. I don't care. She's alive. I'm pregnant again.

It's over. It's finally over.

HENRY

I know it's a cliché, but it was like an itch that needed scratching. It had been a more than a year since I'd last seen her, when she'd gatecrashed my wedding. I suppose, deep down, some part of me still felt guilty about how it had all turned out. Guilty enough to Google her one afternoon, when I was bored at work. I'm a journalist. Naturally curious. And Vi would never know. I wasn't hurting anyone.

A couple of keystrokes, a couple of clicks and there she was, looming large on my screen. That face. Seeing it so close up, in such high definition, brought back a confusing mix of emotions. Guilt, relief, lust. Pity. All mixed up in one big fuck-up ball of mess that lodged itself at the pit of my stomach as a reminder of all that I'd done wrong.

After she left Bennet Media—after the whole, awful business— she disappeared for a while. She had only lasted a couple of months on the women's magazine. I heard rumors from friends of friends that she'd gone to stay with her dad in Bedford. It seemed plausible enough, although she'd never talked about him much. Not sure she really liked him. I never asked anyone outright how she was. I didn't want it to get back to her, didn't want to give her any ammunition. If I'm honest, it was a relief to have her off the scene, and she fell to the back of my mind.

But then, when I Googled her, there she was again. Back online, fronting a slick new website, offering her services as a wedding photographer. I nodded approvingly at the huge image on the homepage. A couple entwined in a cornfield. It looked more like a magazine photo-shoot than a real wedding, but there was no denying her talent.

I scrolled through the images, suddenly panicked, wondering if there were photos of my and Violet's wedding on there. But then I remembered the way the other chap had introduced her, as his "second shooter." Made some joke about her bringing up the rear, claimed she was brilliant at capturing the "reportage" moments, whatever the fuck they were. Her shots of the day were the best though. When the finals had come through, Vi and I sat at the kitchen table and clicked on them one by one on my laptop. Vi had tears in her eyes, and there were moments where I thought I might go that way too. She had a talent, Yvonne. For capturing you at your most vulnerable.

I clicked back on her biography page, reading the bland, colorless summary of her life, which mostly amounted to "loved art at school, then after an ill-advised foray into the world of magazine art direction"– *ouch*—"found my passion in capturing the raw emotions felt on the most important day of many people's lives." She claimed to be based in Middlesex but "willing to travel!" No word of a husband, or life partner.

My leg began to twitch up and down under my desk as I read. Like I said, it was an itch that needed scratching.

I justified it to myself, as I so easily do. I wanted to see if she was OK. What happened was awful for me, but worse for her, no doubt about that.

I had never told Violet about the baby. The stupid thing was, if I had, she probably would have been sympathetic. A little jealous, perhaps, a little hurt that I'd not shared it before. But she would have held her arms out, and hugged me, and told me how terrible it must have been. And she would have asked after Yvonne. Probably would have wanted to meet her.

At the wedding, I'd been drunk and I was so rude to Yvonne. It was the shock of seeing your past right in your face like that. At your wedding, of all places! But I shouldn't have laughed at her like that.

It was an apology. That's all. She probably wouldn't reply. She probably never wanted to hear from me again.

I clicked on her Contact page. There was just a form there, no direct email, and I started to type into the tiny box.

Hi Yvonne,

Nice site! Glad to see you are doing so well. I feel bad, about the wedding. I was drunk, being a prick, as usual. I don't know, I guess it was just the shock of seeing you again, after all that time. But you looked gorgeous, so well . . .

I paused, deleted the last sentence. It sounded like a come-on.

You looked great. Glad to see you've made a success of yourself—not that I'm surprised.

I tried to ignore the itch, but I couldn't. In for a penny, in for a pound.

Are you married? Seeing anyone? Hope you've settled down and are happy. Would be great to have a catch-up drink sometime, if you fancied it. No pressure, of course. Tell me to fuck off if you like. I probably would.

Take care of yourself, H x

I clicked Submit without reading it over, and leant back in my chair. The itch was scratched, but I didn't feel better. How could I? I wouldn't ever feel better.

Not until she told me, face to face, that she forgave me.

LILY

I'm sitting in a cafe opposite the office, trying to pray. Well, not pray exactly—I've never been religious. But I'm asking the universe very, very nicely, if it might consider letting me get the job I just interviewed for. Because for the first time since January, I feel excited about work again.

It's a relatively junior position—press assistant for a small charity helping single parents—but it's the first job I've actually felt passionate about since I gave up my career. And although it's not conservation work, saving parents rather than saving animals somehow feels a bit more appropriate given my situation. I understand these people; I'm one of them.

Even more excitingly, the salary is slightly higher than my current one, and they've just taken in a massive amount of funding, so there's room for progression. I'm hoping the PR manager who interviewed me could see my enthusiasm was genuine. There was lots of talk of working with influencers, partnering up so that they could support the charity's work. I can't think of a more perfect job for me.

The interviewer was really impressed when I said I was friends with Violet.

I sip my Christmas-themed coffee and stare out the window at the crowds wandering down Ealing Broadway. That's another massive bonus—the office is so close to home. Maybe the universe is aligning, giving me a break for once. I take my phone out, re-read Luke's message, asking me how it went. I type a reply.

Really well, I think! She said she'd let me know before the end of the week. Fingers crossed. How's your day going? X

I lay my phone down on the table in front of me, my finger running over the cracks in the screen.

It's so easy to talk to Luke. Effortless. In the same way it was with James at the beginning. Until it all went wrong, of course.

James is an arsehole. But Luke and me. It's working. No awkward pauses, or struggles to think of what to say. The conversation just flows. But it's making me nervous, how easy it all is and how well things seem to be going.

He texts back immediately.

Where you at? I'm at a loose end in Hammersmith—could come and meet you? X

It's the first time he's put a kiss at the end of a message.

I spend the next twenty minutes scrolling through Instagram, waiting for him to join me. Henry hasn't updated his page since before the talk, unsurprisingly. He hasn't tweeted either. Violet is still AWOL. I search Henry's name as a hashtag, just to see if anyone has said anything online about him. There are a few sycophantic tweets and pictures of him at the event, leaning forward into his microphone, his arms raised and gesturing.

I scroll to read the comments underneath the pictures, looking for anything revealing. But there's nothing. I open the GoMamas app on my phone, navigating to the "Violet is Missing" thread on the forum. Someone has added what Luke revealed at the event, that Henry was seen coming out of The Royal London Hospital, but no one has really bothered to comment on it. How can these people call themselves true fans?

I open my private messages. The one Ellie sent yesterday is still there.

Hi Lily, hope you're well. Do you have time for lunch again this week? There's something I need to talk to you about . . . bit awkward over messaging. Drop me a line when you're free. Ex

I swallow. I'll have to reply to her at some point, but right now, I don't know what to say. It's clear she's surprised about how things have developed with me and Luke but there's something else about the tone of her message that makes me feel uncomfortable. Like my clothes are suddenly itchy.

I wish I could remember everything I've shared on GoMamas. That's the problem with spilling your guts out on Internet forums. You think you're anonymous, hiding behind your username, and that nothing you've said can be traced back to you, but it's simply not true. I certainly never imagined I'd end up dating someone I met through a forum friend. What might I have said in the past to have put her off me? Or to make her think Luke deserves better? I dread to imagine what rubbish I've spouted on there after the best part of a bottle of wine.

I feel a pang of nostalgia for the uncomplicated way I met James, six years ago. It was in a bar. At the end of a long night, I was in the cloakroom queue, raffle ticket in hand, waiting to collect my jacket. He walked past and caught my eye before joining behind me. He pushed in front of the people behind me in the queue to introduce himself, and I was impressed by his confidence and his charm. The woman behind the cloakroom counter rolled her eyes at our flirting and I felt like a film star, lit up by the attention.

I know I was too keen, that at twenty-four he was too young to settle down, that he still wanted his freedom. But it was my first proper relationship, and I was so sure we were meant to be. I suppose I got a little carried away. It's still so hard to believe how badly it all turned out.

Luke interrupts my trip down memory lane by leaning down and patting me on the shoulder. I jump slightly in my seat.

"Oh! Sorry!" I say, smiling up at him. "I was miles away."

"Hope you were somewhere nice," he says, unwrapping his scarf and laying it over the back of the chair next to me. He turns to look at the menu behind the cafe counter. "Freezing out there. What do you fancy? My treat."

"Is it lunchtime already?" I say, stupidly. I've been sat in the cafe for over an hour. It's been so nice to just be sitting still, just existing.

"It's twelve," Luke says, pointing at the huge clock on the wall opposite. "I'm starving. I'm going to get avocado on toast. You?"

I smile.

"Same," I say. "Let me . . ." I reach into my handbag and pretend to fumble for my purse, but he puts his hand on my arm, gently.

"On me," he says.

"Thank you."

The food arrives and it's only then that I realise I'm actually hungry. I've been so distracted thinking about the job, a new future.

"This is amazing," I say as I slice into my toast, and Luke laughs at me.

"You know you're far too easily pleased," he says, his eyes twinkling. "I need to broaden your culinary horizons. So tell me more about the job?"

"Oh it's just . . . it's perfect! I don't know why I didn't have the courage to apply for things like this before. And the commute would be so much better—I'd save a fortune. In the summer I could probably even walk; it's only about twenty-five minutes by foot. Or get a bike . . . ha!"

"It sounds great," Luke says. "I've got everything crossed for you."

"Thanks," I say. I pause. "So what's the latest with the article?"

"Yeah, bad news," Luke says, looking genuinely cross for a second. It's the first time I've ever seen him look anything other than cheerful. "The paper has pulled it. Decided it's too aggressive to mention Violet and Henry, as Henry is such a powerful figure 'in the industry.' But without them as a case study, the whole thing falls apart. My commissioning editor was as gutted as me, but her boss had the final say."

"But all your work!" I squeak, trying to imagine spending all those hours on something, only to be told no one wants it anymore. "Will you still get paid?"

"Nope," he says, spearing at the salad on the side of his plate. "I've spoken to the commissioning editor, should be able to get a kill fee. But I might just try to hawk it elsewhere. Someone will pick it up. I've got some friends. I'll ask around."

"It's not finished yet though, is it?" I say. "I mean, we hadn't got to the bottom of what actually happened to Violet."

Violet. Like an unhealthy relationship that drags on and on until one day one of you finally snaps and there's no going back. In the past week, I feel like I've broken free of her spell. I don't really care what's happened to her. No, that's not completely true. Of course I care. I'll never not care about Violet. But this time, it won't affect me. It doesn't affect my life.

"It'll come out eventually. So what's next?" Luke's voice cuts through my thoughts and I look back up at him.

"Sorry?" I say.

"What's next for you today? I've got to get back home; I've got an exciting film review to write—400 words on the latest Marvel franchise."

"Ha! I look forward to reading it. As for me . . . Sylvia is bringing Archie back at four," I say, looking at my watch. It's nearly half past one. "So I've got a few hours to get some Christmas shopping done."

I think of the comforting bundle of ten-pound notes zipped into the inner pocket of my handbag. I've saved ten pounds a month since the beginning of the year, to make sure I had enough to give Archie a decently filled stocking. It's taken all my willpower not to dip into it before now, and I'm so relieved I haven't.

"Oh God, I haven't even started mine yet," Luke says. "What a cliché, right? I'll be the man on Christmas Eve tearing round Westfield, spending twice as much as he budgeted out of sheer desperation. Then again, wouldn't be Christmas if I didn't."

I laugh. And that's when I realise. This is the man I've been waiting for all my life. Not unfaithful, deceitful, horrible James. But kind, decent, loving Luke.

Luke and Lily. It even *sounds* right.

I love you, I suddenly think. *I love you for not thinking I'm a weirdo for my YouTube habit, for not being put off that I have a child. I love you for seeing me, despite all of that.*

"Thanks for lunch," I say. "I really appreciate it."

"Pleasure," he says. "Good luck with your Christmas shopping. Make sure you get me something nice."

YVONNE

I've taken a test every morning and evening since I found out, and I now have a clutch of them, which I'm keeping in a shoebox. I don't know if it's the kind of thing the baby will want to see when they're older, but you never know. It'd be nice to be able to show them how vigilant I was, right from the beginning. Checking they were all right every day. More than that though, keeping them means I can look back at them when I'm feeling insecure. Seeing the pink lines grow stronger each morning fills me with a strange combination of elation and fear. Because I know at any time, it could all be snatched away again, and this time the stakes are so much higher.

I've got no symptoms yet, other than slightly swollen breasts. Nothing else. No cramping—a sign that my uterus is stretching. No nausea. No metallic taste in the mouth. A little bit of bloating, but that's it. I'm not eating more than normal. I'm very determined this time to stay in shape. Last time, I got carried away, thought I could eat all the carbs I wanted, and I was a stone heavier when I gave birth. Considering Nathan was only 1.2kg, very little of that was from him.

The most noticeable difference in my life since finding out is Simon. He's like my little shadow now, following me around the house, checking that I'm well at every opportunity.

"Can I get you anything?" he says, popping his head around the living room door. He's been in the kitchen, cooking my favorite—chicken stir-fry with quinoa.

I smile up at him from my spot on the sofa.

213

"No, thank you," I say. "I'm fine."

"Five more minutes." He grins back at me. "Bet you're starving."

I'm not, particularly, but I nod and grin back at him anyway.

After we've finished eating, we sit in the kitchen and Pushka joins us on the table, sniffing around for scraps.

"All right, Push," Simon says, scratching her on the head as he stands and clears the plates away. He hated her when we first got together. He wasn't a fan of cats. But she was a deal-breaker—she came with me; we were a team. I couldn't explain how important she was to me. She had been my only comfort for years. A replacement for Nathan, but of course, she never quite lived up to him.

Simon doesn't know about Nathan. He doesn't know I've been to the police, either. I swallow, reaching for my glass of water, my mouth suddenly dry.

"There's some stuff I need to tell you, Si," I say, as he boils the kettle to make me my nightly cup of peppermint tea. "Could you sit down a minute?"

His eyebrows rise but he joins me back at the table. Pushka stares at him as he sits down, licking her back and curling up into a croissant. I wouldn't normally let her sit on the table like this, but I can't bring myself to push her off.

"Everything OK?" he says, a note of panic in his voice. "You haven't started bleeding?"

I shake my head.

"No, nothing like that."

"What's the matter?"

"Do you remember what I told you when we were on honeymoon?" I begin. "About the man who attacked me when I was in my first job?"

He swallows, nodding.

"Well, he was arrested a few weeks ago. On historic sexual abuse charges." I pause, allowing the information to sink in. Simon's eyes darken.

"Did you . . ."

"No," I reply. "Not then. The police wouldn't tell me much, but the accusations date from before I met him. A long time before." I give a bitter laugh. "I suppose he's been doing things like that his whole life."

"So you've spoken to the police?" he says, frowning. "Why didn't you tell me?"

I take a deep breath.

"I don't know . . ." I say. "I just wanted to see what they would say if I shared my story. I suppose I thought it might come to nothing, but they took me seriously. They took a statement, in fact. They're building a case. It might take months but . . . I said I'd be happy to testify against him, if it came to that. It's a long time ago now, so there's every possibility it'll come to nothing, but at least I've finally said my piece. After all this time . . . It feels like a huge burden has been lifted."

"Oh Von," he says. "I wish I had known . . ."

"All the pregnancy stuff has been a good distraction. I'm sorry I didn't share it with you, but part of me hates talking about it, raking up the past like that . . ." I tail off, thinking about Henry, how inextricably linked he is to what happened with Bertie, how I hate even mentioning his name in Simon's presence. "I want to be rid of all the memories of that time. It wasn't a happy period in my life."

"I know," Simon says, stroking my hair away from my cheek. "But it's over now. You're so brave, Von. The bravest woman I know. It's why I've always loved you so much. Your strength."

I smile. I don't feel strong. Most of the time I feel on the edge of sanity; my determination to become a mother at any cost the perfect way of avoiding dealing with things. Just give me a baby, I've always thought. Give me a baby to love and then I won't need to worry about myself anymore—I'll have something far more important to worry about. It was a bit simplistic, but surely there was some logic to my reasoning?

"There's something else I need to tell you. I've booked a doctor's appointment for tomorrow," I say, speaking slowly, choosing my words with care. "Just to get myself registered on the system."

Want me to come with you?" he says, immediately.

"No, no, it's fine," I say. "I don't think much interesting happens. But there will be other appointments in the future . . ."

215

"Just let me know when they are and I'll make sure I don't have any sessions booked," he says, reaching over and squeezing my hand. I think of Henry, the way he stared at me in the canteen.

Pregnant? You cannot be serious!

"The thing is, I was pregnant once before," I say. I can't bring myself to look Simon in the eye. I should have told him before.

"I know," he says, and my head lifts in surprise. I stare at him.

"How . . ."

"I read the forms, the ones we had to fill in for the consultant when we did IVF last time," he replies. "You left them out on the kitchen table. Sorry. I wondered when you were going to tell me, but then I thought it probably wasn't a big deal. It said you had a termination. I guess I thought you didn't want to talk about it, so I never mentioned it."

"Oh," I say, overwhelmed with conflicting emotions. Amazement that he'd bothered to read the forms, embarrassment that I had under-estimated him. Relief that he wasn't angry with me.

Dread that I was going to have to tell him everything now. That I was going to have to explain it all.

"They're not . . . a big deal, are they?" Simon asks, taking my hand. The kettle starts bubbling away in the corner of the room, steam rising steadily. "I mean, lots of women have them. It said you were twenty-three, I guessed you just weren't ready to become a mum."

"Yes, they're common, I suppose," I say, nodding. "But the thing is . . . it was, it was a bit different in my case."

Simon's eyes are wide, waiting for me to continue.

"It was a late termination," I say. I take a deep breath. "At twenty-two weeks. I had a late termination."

"Right," Simon says, nodding. Twenty-two weeks won't mean any-thing to him. He won't understand that at twenty-two weeks a baby is fully formed, that they look just like a full-term baby, only smaller. He doesn't know that if a baby is born at twenty-two weeks, they have a ten per cent chance of surviving, that they're just a few weeks short of the age at which they're considered truly viable. Worth saving.

He won't understand that when I held my baby, even though he was only twenty-two weeks old, he looked absolutely perfect.

I can't speak. Instead, I am back there. Sitting outside the hospital in the fierce winter sunshine after they had injected my poor baby's heart to make it stop beating, waiting for them to tell me there was a bed free so I could deliver him. They had told me to go home, to wait until they phoned me, but I couldn't bear the idea of trudging back to my bedroom, of pretending everything was all right when my flatmates asked why I wasn't at work. How long could you carry a dead baby around inside you? It seemed inhuman, what they were asking of me. But I wasn't a priority; the priorities were the women who were going to give birth to babies that would scream and kick and, most importantly of all, breathe.

I stood in the bright sunlight, putting my hand on my stomach, knowing that he was already gone. They said I should have someone with me, but no one wanted to know. So I sat there alone, and I rang his phone number, again and again, and he didn't pick up. Not the first time, not the seventieth time. He never picked up.

"It was years ago," I say, the words tumbling out. "It was for medical reasons . . . I didn't have a choice. I didn't want to do it—my God, I didn't want to do it—but the doctors told me I had to, because there was no hope. It wouldn't have worked; I could have carried him to term but he would have died. There was no hope. It was the only option."

"What was wrong with him?" Simon asks.

"He had something called Potter's syndrome." I try to slow my breathing, to say each word carefully and clearly, so that I never have to say them again. I remember the way I felt when they told me; the flash of illogical paranoia that made me think perhaps he'd planned it all, somehow. "It's a complicated . . . condition." The consultant sucked her cheeks in as she broke the news, before telling me I was young, that there was no reason to think I wouldn't be able to have another, healthy baby. A proper one. One that was meant to be.

They only found out at my twenty-week scan. The baby didn't have enough amniotic fluid . . . they need it to swallow and then expel as

217

urine, and then swallow again. It helps the baby's kidneys develop, as well as the lungs. Without it, they don't develop normally. The baby is fine when it's still in the womb, receiving everything it needs from the mother, but once it's born, it will die. They said there was nothing they could do. No way to save him." I pause before forcing out the three words that circled endlessly in my mind in the months after the termination. "They all die. Some babies live for a few days after birth but they told me they all die eventually."

My voice has been relatively calm up until now but suddenly grief overcomes me and I start choking on my own sobs, fighting to catch my breath. Seventeen years of pain, boxed up and fenced in, released in a moment. I scrape my chair back, lurching forward in my seat, digging my hands into my knees as I try to contain myself. The tips of my fingers start to tingle and my chest feels as though it might explode. I throw my head forward between my legs, knowing I'm going to faint if I don't get more oxygen to my brain.

"I'm sorry," I sob, as my tears soak the terracotta floor underneath me. My ears are ringing, and in the background I'm vaguely aware of the sound of the kettle as it reaches a furious boil. "I'm sorry, I'm sorry, I'm sorry."

HENRY

A week after I sent Yvonne that message, we were sitting in a bar, around the corner from the office. Not one of our old haunts—that would have been far too risky. Somewhere that served fifty different types of gin. I thought she would like that. She used to like gin. But clearly times had changed, and so had she. Apparently, she wasn't drinking.

As soon as she turned up, I regretted it. It was unnerving, the whole evening. The only way to get through it was alcohol. My old friend. For the first twenty minutes I questioned what I had been thinking. She was enjoyable to look at, as ever, but the conversation was awkward, too polite. None of the carefree cattiness that used to flow between us. She didn't want to talk about what had happened at all. She was confident: too confident. Like an actress playing a role.

She would have made a bloody good actress.

"I'm sorry about the wedding," I said, after my second pint.

She sat back in her chair, regarding me with an expression that reminded me, somewhat disturbingly, of my father.

"What are you sorry about?" she said.

"I swore at you, or something, didn't I?" I ran my fingers through my hair. I felt flustered, as though I was suddenly losing my composure. That was how she always made me feel. She stripped away my confidence, left me feeling on edge the whole time. There was something catlike about her. Something evil.

"I can't remember," she said. "It doesn't matter."

"Why did you come?" I said, reaching forward and leaning my elbows on the table. I felt the familiar stirrings of desire as she looked at me coolly over the top of her glass. Her almond eyes were ringed in thick brown eyeliner and they were suddenly the only things I could see.

"I don't know," she said, shrugging slightly. "Old time's sake."

"Well. You look beautiful," I said, the words tumbling out carelessly. I met her eyes again, my hand making its way under the table towards her knee. Her fucking knee! But it was all I could find, and I rested it there, looking up at her.

She didn't say anything. That was the thing about her. So cool, calm and collected all the time. What went on in her head? I knew she had wanted me once, but now, it was impossible to tell. She looked down at my hand, and simply and quietly picked it up and laid it back on my own leg, as though brushing off a fly.

"I better go," she said.

"I still want you," I said, my voice thick now. I knew how I sounded: like an old, drunken lech, but I didn't care. "I never didn't want you . . . but you were so needy; we were so young."

"Henry . . ." she said, standing up. So controlled, so fucking controlled. "Don't."

She pulled on her jacket and made her way to the entrance of the bar. It was June, and still light outside, even though it was 9pm. I followed her, draining the last of my pint as I left and flinging it back down on the table, where it skidded to an awkward stop.

Out on the street, she looked back briefly to see whether I was behind her, but then started marching ahead, as though I was a stalker she needed to shake off.

"Hey," I shouted across the Mayfair crowds. People stared at me.

I broke out into a half-hearted jog, pushing my way through the people until I caught up with her. I grabbed her arm, yanking her to a stop, and twisted her round to face me.

"What?" she said, pulling her arm away.

"Why are you running away?" I asked. I leant in a little too close to her, and I felt her body soften in response, even though her jaw was clenched. She still wanted me. "I thought we were having a nice evening."

She breathed out, raising her eyes to the sky.

"We were," she said, speaking so slowly she was practically spitting each word out. "But now I'm going home."

"Yvonne," I said, releasing my grasp on her arm. Some of her thick brown hair had blown in front of one of her eyes, caught on her long eyelashes, and I swept it away with my fingers. She looked past me, but her eyes were glistening.

"I was an arse to you," I said, my arms going round her back now, pulling her towards me. "We were young, weren't we? Young idiots. God, it must be more than ten years ago now . . ."

"Sixteen years ago," she spat. "It was nearly sixteen years ago."

"OK, sixteen. I was a tosser, I admit. I still am. But you know . . . you certainly got your own back."

I pulled up my sleeve, grateful for the personal trainer sessions Violet insisted on. I would always be soft around the edges, but there was at least some shape there now.

Yvonne looked down at my arm, the silvery scar still just about visible. She sniffed, turned her head away, looking into the crowds.

"Hey hey," I said, gently easing her face back and tilting it towards mine. "I deserved it. I know I deserved it."

"For fuck's sake, it was an accident! And it was nothing in comparison with what I went through," she hissed, and I could see then that she wasn't even sorry. "You broke me."

"I know," I said. "I'm sorry."

"Go back to your wife," she said, those dark brown eyes like pits again, strong and unblinking.

I looked down at the pavement. Of course that's what I should do. Of course it was.

"I don't want to," I said, and I couldn't be sure if it was the alcohol, the lust, or my guilt talking. The problem was, she was too good for me. Violet. But Yvonne. Yvonne was on my level. Fucked up, narcissistic, entirely self-absorbed. We were perfect for each other.

I suppose I should have been prepared for it, but it still took me by surprise. The noise first, that distinctive clap, then the sting spreading as my hand rushed to my cheek.

I stared at her, in shock, but she was already striding away again. And this time she didn't look back.

LILY

Despite being weighed down with shopping bags, there's a new-found lightness in my step as I push my way through my front door. I have twenty minutes before Sylvia turns up with Archie and I'm determined that the flat be presentable. I don't want her thinking I can't cope. I hide all Archie's presents at the back of my wardrobe and then push the hoover around the patches of carpet that aren't obscured by furniture or boxes of toys. There isn't much of it, so it doesn't take long.

Then I rummage about under the sink until I find an ancient can of Pledge and a duster, and I spray everything—the television, the coffee table, the base of our Christmas tree. Next, I deal with the teetering pile of ancient catalogues shoved under the coffee table, also covered in dust. I sort them into piles and take the recycling pile outside and dump it in the green bin, along with last week's wine bottles. Finally, when I'm back in the flat, I slice the cake I bought especially for Sylvia (Battenberg, her favorite) and make a pot of tea. She's very particular about her tea, likes it strong.

They're on time, and I feel that familiar tingle of joy at seeing Archie again as I push the buzzer and tell them to come up. My little man.

"Mummy, Mummy!" he calls from the stairwell as I open my front door. "Look!"

He's waving something in my face. As he draws nearer, I see it's a new plastic truck. Bright yellow.

"It has batteries!" he squeaks, shoving it at me.

"Don't I get a hug?" I say, taking it from him and laughing as I fold him in my arms.

"No, Mummy," he says, wriggling from my grip. "Get off." He pushes me away, then stares at me for a split second, frowning at me in irritation. He's not a cuddly child, never has been. I blink, turning away, and Archie rushes towards the fish bowl.

"Spike!" he says, reaching for the pot of food next to it.

"Not too much!" I say, as he opens the lid.

After giving Spike a three-course meal, he turns back to me, grinning.

"Granny said there might be cake."

"Granny might be right," I say, smiling at Sylvia. "He remembers everything."

"Oh yes, he does," she agrees, nodding. "Come on then, young man, let's hope it's Battenberg."

*　*　*

There's a deep scratch on one side of Archie's face. I only notice when he's in the bath, and his hair, sodden from splashing, is stuck to the side of his ear.

"How did you do this, Arch?" I say, fingering the angry red line that runs from his temple almost to his chin. Sylvia has been telling me to cut his hair for ages, saying he looks girly with it hanging down by his shoulders, and I suddenly wonder if she's right. I would have noticed this sooner if it was shorter.

"Dunno," he says, lifting up his plastic rocket and splashing us both again.

"Is it sore?"

He stops, rocket mid-air, regards me thoughtfully. A finger lifts to his cheek in exploration.

"No!" he says, smiling.

Children get injured all the time, Lily. I think of Anna, the bumps and bruises that she records for me almost weekly in her accident book. He's got a boisterous personality.

"I'll put some magic spray on it before bed," I say, rummaging around in the bathroom cabinet for the Dettol. "You'll be right as rain in no time." But I realise I'm reassuring myself, not him. He doesn't care.

Later, as I'm tucking him into bed and turning to leave his room, Archie pulls on my arm.

"You did it, Mummy," he says.

"Did what?"

He shifts himself on to his little elbows, looking up at me with huge eyes, and pulls his hair to one side.

"The scratch," he says, as his chubby fingers fumble to find the mark.

I stand back.

"Archie," I say, horrified. "No, I didn't."

He gives a small sigh, and lies back down, rolling over and grabbing his toy dog.

"Yes, Mummy, the other day, before I go to Granny's," he says, softly. "It's OK, you didn't mean it."

"Archie," I say, firmly. "I would never hurt you."

"It was when I was naughty. I should have been in bed." He pauses, considering. "Sorry, Mummy."

I swallow, leaning down beside his bed, and stroke his hair away from his head.

"Darling, you're confused," I say, the words sticking in my throat. "Mummy would never hurt you. It's time for sleep now."

I kiss his head and stand up, watching as his eyes gently flicker shut.

*   *   *

Later, I lie on the sofa, my laptop on my lap. I Google all my usual comforts, but of course, Violet has abandoned me, and I can't find anything to distract me. I watch a few vlogs from other YouTubers but they're boring, inane. If Violet is in hospital, what exactly has happened to her?

I wish she knew how important she was to me, the sense of hope she had brought into my life.

That night when I realised James had blocked me across everything was the turning point. It had been months since I'd got in touch with him, but I was feeling particularly low that evening. January blues, I guess. Up until then he had tolerated my attempts to contact him over the years. He'd even replied a few times, although he never took me up on my suggestions to meet up, saying he couldn't give me what I wanted. Just before Christmas, he'd told me he'd met someone else, and that she wasn't happy about us "being in touch." That evening, I called him fifty-eight times in the space of an hour, and it went straight to voicemail each time. He was a salesman, he never switched his phone off. Then I tried texting him, but my messages weren't delivered. That's how I knew for sure he had blocked me. I went out the next day and bought a pay-as-you-go phone but as soon as he worked out that number was also mine, he blocked that too. His new girlfriend had won. And there was nothing I could do.

It was the worst week of my life, but then I saw a job advertised as Violet's assistant, and it was like a small crack of light flooded into my pitch-black existence. I spent hours carefully crafting my application, detailing all the reasons why I would be the perfect candidate.

As I sent the email, I made a vow to put James behind me. I thought it was all going to be OK. I was going to get a job with Violet, and everything was going to work out.

But it didn't. And six months later, when the hopelessness of my situation threatened to engulf me completely, I made the worst mistake of my life.

Archie had climbed out of bed after his lunchtime nap, somehow managing to open our front door and walk down the stairs. I suppose I must have forgotten to deadlock it. I'd always cursed the fact I'd rented a flat on the first floor. The stairs didn't seem to matter when I was young and carefree, but as soon as I found out I was pregnant, I knew they were going to be the bane of my life. And they were.

After making his way down the stairs alone, Archie tripped on the bottom step and toppled face-first on to the filthy stone floor of the communal hallway.

There was only an egg on his forehead, in the end, but I fell to pieces when I found him, my sobs mingling with his. His cries were so loud that our neighbor upstairs had come out to see what was going on. She drove us to hospital, all the while staring at me out of the corner of her eye. Judging me. Wondering how I could have let such a thing happen.

Archie was fine. My nerves, however, were not.

The nurse looked at me as I sat in the cubicle, clutching him as though somehow I wanted to meld him to me permanently.

"Sorry, we have to ask this," she said, her voice neutral. "Has anyone in the family ever had any contact with social services?"

It was like she'd struck me with a whip.

"No, no," I'd stuttered. "Nothing like that."

"It's OK," she said, patting me on the leg. "We just have to ask." But then she wrote something down on his notes, and wouldn't let me see.

I made a promise then. To never let it happen again. I went straight home and ordered a stair gate to put in front of the door to his bedroom.

Archie was fine, but I never quite recovered.

YVONNE

I didn't expect the guilt about Violet to return this quickly. I didn't expect it to return ever, if I'm honest. But there's something about getting what you want—getting everything that you want, even after all this time, and all this pain—that makes you reassess.

I'm driving back from my latest family shoot—three kids between the ages of two and eight, and I'm sure that hasn't helped. It's a beautiful winter's day, the trees covered in a delicate layer of frost that makes them look as though they've been dusted with icing sugar. The setting for the photoshoot couldn't have been better: a blissfully empty patch of the south downs. The children were in matching knitted hats, made for them by their grandmother. The parents were getting on. The dad was especially enthusiastic about the pictures. But the whole thing was overshadowed by that familiar feeling that I couldn't ignore.

Guilt. Responsibility.

It's so unfair. Nothing that has happened to me has been my fault, and yet I am the one who suffers.

I pull into our driveway, looking at the miniature Christmas tree in the bay window of our living room. It's wonky, the branches on the left pulling it to the side. It looks naff, on reflection. Like a poor woman's attempt to do Christmas with style. I don't have the right-sized bay window for this kind of thing. I don't live in Violet and Henry's house. Their bay is the same size as my entire living room.

Christmas. Why did it have to happen just before Christmas? I didn't plan it that way, I really didn't. It was just the way the dice fell. It was never my intention that anyone—least of all her—get hurt.

I pull my phone out from my handbag and scroll to find Katie's number. I want to tell her everything. My finger hovers over the Call button but I can't bring myself to do it. She's too good, Katie is. She'll try to talk me into telling Simon. She won't make me feel better, no matter how much I want her to. She'll make me feel worse.

There's only one way out of this mess. I have to know what's happened to her. Ignoring my rumbling stomach, I type the hospital address into the satnav on my phone and rest it on the dashboard. Then I put the car into reverse, and I leave.

*　*　*

There's a queue to get into the hospital car park. I wait in the car, my engine idling, and ignore my usual lunchtime phone call from Simon. Instead I text him that the shoot over-ran, and that I'll call him later. He replies with a heart, tells me to look after us both, and signs off with a kiss.

Look after you both. My hand flies to my flat, firm stomach. I haven't thought about the baby today at all. I used to think that was all it took to keep them safe. I thought so long as I was thinking about them, then everything would be all right. But it didn't work with Nathan. I never stopped thinking about him, from the second I found out I was expecting him, but my thoughts couldn't save him. Nothing could.

I do four laps of the tiny hospital car park before giving up and stalking an elderly couple who are shuffling slowly back to their car, waiting for them to leave. Then I look up at the hospital, wondering what kind of reception I'll get.

I take my phone again and Google the details of the intensive care unit, committing them to memory. Then I straighten myself up and climb out of the car. I wish Henry had just told me how she was when I asked him outside his cabin, but I should have known I wouldn't get a straight answer. Even if he had been willing to talk to me, he would have exaggerated for effect, played it up, made it sound worse than it was. He'd have done anything to hurt me.

As I walk towards the hospital entrance, I find myself saying a little prayer that when I get there, they'll tell me that she's been discharged. Or that she's been moved on to a standard ward. So I can make some silly laugh about being confused, plaster some relief on my face, and head off, conscience clear.

But somehow, I don't think that's the news I'll be getting. The image of the last time I saw her flashes through my mind. It has been haunting me for seventeen days now.

I take a deep breath. I'm ready to see her again. She's going to be fine. Once I see her, and I know it for sure, I'll be able to move on. We'll all be able to move on once and for all.

* * *

I had expected it to be more difficult, but the nurse at the little desk at the front of the ward smiles at me as I ask where to find her, claiming I'm Violet's cousin, Caroline. Her mother had commented that we looked alike at her wedding.

"Of course," she says. "She's in bed seven on the left."

She's speaking softly, as though preparing me for what I'm about to see.

"I haven't seen her since . . ." I say, my voice low. "Since the accident. Will it be very upsetting?"

She frowns a little and I kick myself. People don't ask these kinds of questions, Yvonne. Genuine people don't say things like that.

"I'm a bit phobic of hospitals," I say, smiling and giving an embarrassed shrug. "I know that's pathetic."

"She's sedated but peaceful," the nurse replies. "Talk to her, though—we always encourage talking to patients, and don't mind all the machines."

I smile and shudder slightly at the thought of her lying there, all wired up, breathing through a ventilator.

"Is there anyone else with her? I don't want to disturb anyone."

"Mr. Blake is with her at the moment," she says and a dagger of panic plunges into my chest. But it's too late to back out now. "I wouldn't be able to let you in otherwise. Security . . . And they're a particularly cautious family, as I'm sure you understand."

I nod. She turns back to her computer.

"Thanks for your help," I say, and she smiles briefly. "Appreciate it."

Could I be arrested for this? Am I breaking the law? I make my way down the hospital corridor, the scent of disinfectant burning my nostrils. I seize on it—a symptom of my pregnancy, or just an inherent sensitivity of mine? Some people say music is the most powerful thing for bringing back memories, but for me it's always been smells. The smell of my father's pipe first thing in the morning, telling me he was awake, that my day of disappointing him was about to start. The smell of Henry, the sweat underneath his armpits as I buried my face against him . . . And then this smell, the smell of the hospital the day after I gave birth to a sleeping baby.

The ward is decorated with murals, which seems a shame when most of the patients here are unconscious, and unaware. My hand settles on my stomach and I stroke it, trying to communicate with the tiny embryo within. The size of a chia seed, the type that Simon sprinkles over his breakfast. We laughed about that this morning, held one in each of our hands, trying to imagine how something so tiny could be something so huge at the same time.

As I walk, I wonder what kind of reaction I'll get from Henry when he sees me. Whatever he does to me, it will be worth it for the peace of mind.

I keep walking, knowing that the next patient I see will be her. But before I see her, I spot something else: her name in colorful letters, hung above her bed.

I know without being told that this is Skye's handiwork, that she will have sat there determinedly after school, making it for her beloved little sister.

To help make her better.

*   *   *

Henry is not by her bed. He's nowhere to be seen. There's a nurse close by, but she's staring at the machines, writing something on a sheet of paper. I shut my eyes, breathing deeply for several seconds before truly looking. Lula's bed is covered in teddies, forming a little circle around her impossibly still body. She's lying on the bed, a nappy on, even though she was potty-trained months ago. Her head is positioned on one side; there's a tube coming out of her nose, taped to her face with plasters. One of her hands is a mass of wires, while the other is draped limply over her favorite teddy bear. Andrew. A present from her uncle, named after him. I remember the video, the way Violet laughed about how attached she was to him.

Other than all the wires and tubes, she looks utterly perfect. Not a mark on her. Not a scratch. Her crazy curly hair is spilling out across her pillow, matted in places. Her eyes are closed.

My hand goes to my mouth as I edge a little closer to the bed. I want to say it was all her mother's fault. She should never have invited me round. But I know that's unfair. That's twisting the truth to suit me.

I think of Nathan, when I held him. My tiny, imperfect baby. And then I look back at Lula.

"I'm sorry," I whisper, the tears falling on to the linoleum floor in fat splashes. The words are inadequate, but they're all I have. "I'm so, so sorry."

Seconds later, I feel a hand grip my shoulder and my body freezes in fright.

"Get out," Henry's voice hisses in my ear. "Get out and leave my family alone."

HENRY

Violet and I had had a row. She's strong, Violet, but she has a temper too. We screamed at each other and she threw a plate at my head, collapsing in angry sobs as it broke against the wall behind me.

I stormed off to work that day, telling Violet that I'd had enough of it all, that she should damn well give up the whole bloody vlogging business. That we didn't need the free fucking holidays and the endless deliveries of gender-neutral baby leggings. That we didn't need strangers who thought that the way we cut up grapes for the kids was wrong leaving us shitty comments criticising our parenting, and approaching our kids for long chats in playgrounds.

What we needed was privacy. But she told me I had no idea what it was like for her, that the positives far outweighed the negatives, that she wanted to *make a change* to the way mothers with PND were treated, and that this was the best way to get people's attention.

So when I got into work, and opened my email, and saw one from Yvonne, I was in the right frame of mind. The subject line said simply *Lunch?*. I read it straight away.

Hey, I'm working in town today, wondered if you were free for lunch? No worries if not. Yx

It had been well over a year since I'd last seen or heard from her. I occasionally wondered if the crazy emails Violet had been receiving had come from Yvonne, but she had seemed so together when we'd last met, that it felt unlikely. But then again, you never knew what was going on under the surface with Yvonne—there was always a chance. After all, I'd hardly expected her to turn up to my wedding, had I?

If I'm honest, there was a sick part of me who wanted the emails to be from her. Violet was annoying me, our relationship fracturing further each day. I had always been drawn to Yvonne's craziness, liked the fact she didn't care what people thought. And a lot of what was said in the emails was right, after all. I mean, that Mandy *was* a moron.

Seeing her name in my inbox that day brought back all the memories again: all the things I liked about her. Her unpredictability. The way she once left me notes on my desk at work, dragged me into empty meeting rooms. It was all such good *fun*, until it wasn't anymore.

I replied straight away.

Hello, stranger. Why not? Don't do a runner on me this time. 12 at Mayfair House? Hx

It wasn't cheating. I justified it to myself. My wife was having lunch with people all the time. Not just women, but men, husbands of her female entourage who were involved in her campaigns. I admired them on the one hand, but couldn't help wondering why they weren't busier. Doing a proper job, providing for the family.

I was my father's son, after all.

The email from Yvonne lifted my spirits and I was uncharacteristically cheerful all morning. So much so that my PA, Pippa, asked if I'd got lucky last night. I'd made some joke about having two kids and a newborn, what did she think? She smiled and made some sarcastic comment about how hard it must be for me.

Sometimes it felt like women were starting to hate men a little bit more every day. And my wife was at the fucking forefront of it all.

I got to Mayfair House early and found my favorite table free. Yvonne came in a few minutes later. She must be forty now, but she doesn't seem to age, that woman. Her hair was slightly shorter than before. Even though it was October, and cold outside, she was wearing a tight black dress, with black tights and a black leather jacket. There was a silk scarf in her hair, like a kind of hairband. I thought back to

Violet that morning as I'd left her, in her grey t-shirt and those godaw-ful dungarees, and then told myself I was an arsehole.

"Hi," Yvonne said, and she was different this time. Smiley.

"You slapped me," I said. "Last time we met."

"Yes," she said, her eyes wide. "But you deserved it."

I shrugged. Couldn't argue with that.

"What are you drinking?" I asked, handing her a menu. "Still teetotal?"

"Yes," she replied, but she was relaxed this time. As she sat down I noticed something else too, on her left hand. A square diamond in a platinum band, exactly the same as the one I bought Violet, just smaller. And underneath it, a wedding ring.

"I see congratulations are in order," I said, the words like a reflex. I pointed at her hand. "Who's the lucky guy?"

"He's called Simon," she said, holding her hand up to her face, let-ting the ring sparkle in the light. "He's a personal trainer."

I pulled myself more upright in my seat.

"Well done," I said. "Bet conversations around the dinner table are thrilling." As soon as I said the words I regretted them. The transpar-ency of it all. My petty jealousy. The thought of some other man, prob-ably younger and most definitely fitter than me, having what I once had. What I once threw away.

"He's head of the PT team at Peter Daunt, actually," Yvonne said, smiling up at the waiter who arrived to take our drinks orders. "I'll have a Perrier, thanks."

"Glass of house red," I said, barely looking at the waiter. "No, fuck it. I'll have the same. Just some fizzy water."

The waiter nodded and wandered off.

"Well," I said, trying to recover myself. "That's great. Congrats. Sounds like you've got yourself a good one."

"Do you want to see a picture?" she said, but before I had the chance to reply, she was pulling out her phone and waving it in my face. I squinted, not wanting to admit that my long-distance vision was going.

He was handsome, in a very bland way, but as I looked more closely, I realised he looked familiar.

"Which Peter Daunt?"

"Chiswick," Yvonne replied, her voice sharp.

"Very happy for you," I said, eventually, handing the phone back. But something was making me uneasy. If she had a plan, she wasn't letting me in on it.

We ordered lunch, making small talk over it like two polite strangers. She asked me about the magazine, her face remaining impressively impassive as I talked about my promotion earlier this year.

I never plucked up the courage to ask about the emails.

I regretted not ordering the wine. As the plates were cleared away, I wondered what the purpose of this lunch was. Her way of showing me she'd moved on? That she'd found someone literally bigger and better?

We left the bar—I paid, and she didn't object—and headed for the stairs. It was busy now, the lunchtime media crowd pushing past us to get to their "meetings." We were halfway down the stairs when a fat man barged through, and pushed Yvonne slightly. She stumbled against me, the weight of her body falling against mine. I caught her by the arm, and our eyes met. Time seemed to stand still for a second. I wanted to lunge at her, but then I remembered last time.

Seconds later, she was leading me to the toilets. She didn't speak, and I didn't either. Once we were locked in a cubicle, her mouth was on mine, and her hands were everywhere, and within seconds I had hoisted her up against the wall, and I was fucking her with everything I had, thinking even though this was how the trouble started in the first place, how inevitable it had all been, how inevitable it always was, and how somehow, that made it OK.

Unfinished business, a voice in my head said. *That's all it is.*

LILY

After dropping Archie at Anna's, I walk to the Tube station, wishing I had enough data left to check my emails, even though it's far too early in the day for there to be anything of interest in my inbox. Waiting to hear back after a job application is absolute agony.

I remember the last time I was in this position, earlier this year.

I had spent ages perfecting my application for Violet's assistant position, feeling sure I'd get an email the next day. But the email never came. No matter how many times I refreshed my emails, nothing ever came. It was a week later, one Saturday afternoon when I was idly scrolling while pushing Archie on the swings, that I first saw Mandy's smiling face on Violet's Instagram feed.

I read the caption, trying hard not to throw up.

Meet my new assistant! Mandy, 22, social media grad, karaoke queen and bright as a button. The children love her, I love her and I'm only slightly concerned how much my husband will love her too . . . Hands off @henryblake she's mine. You're far too old for her anyway. HAHA. So happy to have this fresh face joining the VIB gang. Lots of fun in store. We're headed off to Regent's Park this afternoon for a proper inauguration. Please welcome her with open arms, peeps! Xxx

Even remembering it now makes me feel sick.

What was wrong with me? Why did no one I loved ever love me back? First my own mother, then James, now Violet.

Why did I misread all the signs every time?

I was so angry. I left the playground in a rage, pushing Archie like a woman possessed to the Underground. I got on the next train that arrived, and headed to Regent's Park. It took me a while to find them all but there they were: Violet, Skye, Lula and Mandy. Laughing in the winter sun. Lula was pushing her dolly in a pram. Skye was on her scooter. Mandy and Violet were arm in arm, trailing behind the children. One big happy group.

A group I had so desperately wanted to join, but one it would appear I wasn't welcome in.

I had never felt so alone.

* * *

Susie and I are in the office kitchen when my mobile rings. It's so rare for anyone to call me that I half jump-back in surprise, worried it's Anna telling me something's wrong with Archie. But it's a number I don't recognise. My heart lifts a little, daring to hope.

Five minutes later, I'm squealing in Susie's ear like a four-year-old.

"I got it!" I say. "I got the job. The charity one. She said they were overwhelmed by my clear passion for the charity's work. I can't believe it!"

"Oh, that's amazing. Congratulations!" Susie hugs me, then stands back, turning her mouth down at the corners. "Although selfishly, I have to say that it's utterly rubbish for me. I can't believe you're going to leave me here. So, tell me more, when do you start?"

"January, but it depends if Ben will let me off my notice period. Hopefully he'll be thrilled to see the back of me."

"When are you going to tell him?" Susie says.

"Right now," I say. Susie squeezes me again and pats me on the shoulder. I feel a pang of sadness at the thought of not working with her anymore. She's the first person I've met since it all went wrong who's felt like a true friend. She needs me. I must remember to stay in touch with her.

The door to Ben's office is open, and he's frowning at his laptop. He looks up as I approach, a split second of stress passing across his face before he smiles awkwardly and gestures for me to come in.

"Hi," I say, "sorry to disturb you."

"It's fine," he says. His voice is thick, almost as though he's a bit drunk. "Just finalising the marketing budget for Q1. You're a welcome distraction."

I smile, sitting in the chair opposite him.

"Hopefully I will be," I say, sipping my tea. "I just wanted to let you know that I've accepted another job." I pause, waiting for his reaction.

His head shakes momentarily, his eyebrows rising.

"Oh, congratulations," he says. "I hope you didn't . . . I mean, I don't want you to think I pushed you out."

"It was for the best," I say. "You did push me, but in a good way. I was treading water here, we both know; the new job is something I feel so excited about. It's a small company, but they've just had some amazing funding, so there's plenty to get my teeth stuck in to." At the end of this little speech I'm slightly out of breath.

"That's great," Ben says. "I'm really pleased for you."

"There's just one thing . . ." I say, suddenly panicked that he'll be annoyed, or say no. "They want me to start in January. The first week back after New Year. Which means that if I resign today, I'm only giving you two weeks' notice . . . and the office is closed for Christmas from Friday, which means tomorrow would be my last day . . ."

"It's not a problem," Ben says, waving his hand in the air as though I'm a fly that's hovering over his lunch. "You don't need to work your notice. Congratulations, Lily."

I stand up, pressing my fingers around my mug.

"Thank you," I say. There are deep grooves under Ben's eyes, tinged with purple. I think of Susie, of his wife Abigail, the mess his business is in.

"Thank you for helping me out," I say. "You really helped me get back on my feet. I don't know what I would have done. I know we didn't always see eye to eye but . . . I will always be grateful for that."

Ben's mouth twitches into an embarrassed smile as our eyes lock together. He gives a little shrug and I turn to leave the room.

* * *

239

It's 6.30pm and I'm trying to get Archie into the bath. He's running round the flat, giggling with glee as I chase him and tackle him to the ground for tickles. We're both laughing like crazy when the doorbell rings.

"Oh who's that now!" I say, but my usual irritation at our routine being interrupted is a million miles away. Since I found out I got the job it's like I've been painted again, in brighter colors. Everything feels easier, lighter than before. I don't even want a drink.

I grab the intercom phone by the door.

"Hello?"

"It's me," Luke says. "Er . . . surprise?!"

I press the button to release the front door, then turn my attention back to Archie, who is peering at me from round the corner of my bedroom door.

"Archie, I can see you!" I say, and he dissolves into giggles again.

I open the front door and Luke comes in, shopping bag in hand with a very obvious bottle of champagne poking out of the top of it. My hair has been wrenched from my bun, half of it hanging in strands in front of my face.

He's here. He's come to celebrate with me. I can't stop my face from grinning.

"What was that noise I could hear halfway down the stairs?" Luke says, handing me the bottle of champagne.

Archie starts giggling hysterically again.

"It was Mummy!" he squeaks, pointing a small finger at me. "Mummy was a great big monster! She was chasing me!"

"Was she indeed?" Luke says, taking off his coat and hanging it on the handle of my living room door. "What a naughty mummy."

"OK, Arch," I say, still panting slightly. "You win. But now it's time for your bath."

"Ohhh," he says, his tiny forehead wrinkling into a frown. "But I want to show Luke my dinosaurs."

"Next time," I say, firmly.

"How about I read you a story after your bath, mate?" Luke says, bending down to Archie's level. "Would that be any good?"

Archie nods, slowly, thinking about it.

"Lucky you, Arch," I say. "I hear Luke is very good at voices."

"Oh yes!" Archie says, punching the air with the utter over-the-top enthusiasm only a three-year-old can have. The perfection of this evening is overwhelming. A huge weight has been lifted financially, I have a cosy night in with a man I adore, a new, exciting job on the horizon and a son who loves my new boyfriend.

Who needs Violet after all?

3 June 2017
From: gottheblues@hotmail.com
To: violet@violetisblue.com

I have to tell you something about today, Violet. It's important.

I knew that Mandy would be taking Skye and Lula to the park, because she has no imagination, and that's what she does when you have a meeting to go to.

I found her straight away. She was sat on a bench right across the other side of the playground, Skye was all over the climbing frame, Lula was doing repeated trips down the slide. Mandy was smoking a cigarette and chatting to one of the other mums or au pairs or nannies or whatevers. She wasn't even watching them. Skye had a stone in her shoe, was struggling to get it out, so I went over to help her. She was so sweet. I offered to push her on the swings, and we had a lovely chat. She told me all about her mum's job as a YouTuber, how she was expecting another baby sister soon. How she didn't mind having another baby in the house, so long as it didn't wake her or her daddy up with its crying. Apparently her daddy gets "really" grumpy when Lula wakes him up.

Nice man, that Henry of yours.

She told me all about Lula's nightmares, and the fact she was seeing a special doctor to help her with them. A child psychologist at such a young age, Violet? Really?

Skye was so trusting, bless her. It would have been SO easy to have slipped her little hand in mine, and taken her home with me.

We chatted for fifteen minutes in total. Mandy didn't look up once. Anything could have happened.

242

How could you leave her with that woman?

I'm telling you this as a warning, Violet. Because I care.

*   *   *

5 June 2017
From: gottheblues@hotmail.com
To: violet@violetisblue.com

Well done, Violet! You got rid of her. I KNEW she wouldn't have told you what had happened at the park. You made the right decision. You could never trust her now—I could have been anyone, with any kind of horrible agenda. How could she put Skye at risk like that? I'm so happy you took me seriously. Thank you.

*   *   *

5 June 2017
From: violet@violetisblue.com
To: gottheblues@hotmail.com

If you ever approach my family again, or send me another email, I will call the police.

YVONNE

I wake drenched in sweat. Which, given that it's only two degrees out-side, and the heating is off, is impressive. Next to me, Simon is breath-ing slowly and steadily. Deeply. The sleep of a child, of the innocent.

I try to remember what the dream was about, but it's all patchy and muddled, like a film I have half slept through. Violet was in it though, of course. Those big eyes, staring at me, raw with tears. Asking me how I could have done it, as though it was entirely my fault, as though none of the blame lay with him. I push the memories away. Tell myself I have done nothing wrong. Not really.

It wasn't my fault.

It wasn't even my idea. I would never have thought of it if it wasn't for Jade, my "friend" from the forum. Both our partners had poor sperm counts, and we started chatting privately about it. Neither of us could afford more than one round of private IVF. My odds of success were eleven per cent, hers only marginally better at thirteen per cent. She made a flippant comment suggesting we both have a one-night stand with someone random instead.

They'd never know, she wrote. *Cheaper than a sperm donor, and at least you'd get to see who the bloke was.*

I have an ex, I replied, *I never really got over him. And a year ago he randomly got back in touch, we met up for a drink and he made a pass at me . . .*

Is he fertile?

And the seed had been sown. Quite literally.

It was more than that though. It was the chance to take back some power. It's taken this long to realise that one of the reasons I pined after Henry for all those stupid, pointless years was because he had ended things with me, not the other way round. That, and the fact that his chosen life partner paraded herself and their angelic children in front of cameras for everyone to see. It was cruel, so unbelievably painful, given how I'd lost Nathan.

There wasn't anything that special about Henry, not in the cold light of day. I just couldn't stand the thought that he'd thrown us away.

I creep out of bed and pad downstairs, filling Pushka's bowl with cat biscuits and opening the fridge. It's 7.08am. Simon will be up soon: he has the day off, and we're meant to be going Christmas shopping. I put the heating on, make a cup of chamomile tea and take it through to the living room, curling up on the sofa underneath my faux-fur throw. I sip my tea, staring into space. Our Christmas tree—now moved to the hearth—still looks small and insignificant.

Today, the guilt is not just about Violet and Lula. It's about Simon. Simon, who loves me in an entirely simple and wholesome way.

I try to imagine the sort of woman he'd be truly happy with. She'd be a hairdresser, or a nail technician. Naturally maternal. A keen baker. The sort to have a gang of loyal female friends that she went to school with and never lost touch. They would all stay in the same area, settling down round the corner from their parents. She'd be called Lizzie, with immaculately curled blonde hair. Hair extensions, of course. She'd get them for cheap from the salon where she worked. She'd have a tan, year-round.

Perhaps this is why Simon's mum has never liked me. She knows I'm not a Lizzie. She doesn't trust me, and quite rightly. A mother's instinct, after all. My tan is natural—the result of a Spanish mother who succumbed to cancer when I was in my teens. That worries her: bad genes. But the most important concern is my age. I'm only sixteen years younger than her and she hates it.

Pushka comes into the living room, gives a wide yawn and jumps up neatly on to the sofa, settling down beside me. I stroke her head, trying to imagine what the future will hold. I never expected to feel this way. I thought I'd be able to do it: to take back what I was owed, without anyone getting hurt. But I was so naive.

* * *

The shopping is fine: a distraction that I almost enjoy. We bicker over what to buy my father, making jokes about how miserable he is, how perhaps a ticket to the euthanasia clinic in Switzerland is the only thing that would make him truly happy. It's tasteless, as jokes go, but I don't care. I appreciate Simon's rough humor, his lack of concern about being polite or appropriate. It shows how honest he is: what you see is what you get. Unlike with others, whose charming persona hides a rotten core.

Anyway, the little sympathy I had for my dad disappeared in the days after Nathan's death. He refused even to go to the funeral with me, despite the fact I'd organised it to take place in a church, to please him. There was no explaining to him, no chance of him understanding that the alternative to the medical termination might have killed us both.

I am tired though, more tired than usual from traipsing around the shopping centre in Kingston, and everywhere I go I see children. From teeny tiny babies strapped to their mothers' chests to gangly teenagers sprawled on the floor outside McDonald's, Topshop bags scattered around them like oversized confetti. After three hours, we have nearly everything on our list, and I am exhausted.

At one point we pass Mothercare, and Simon drags me inside, thrusting tiny outfit after tiny outfit under my nose, asking for my opinion. I tell him it's too early to buy anything. Even though I have a wardrobe full of outfits for this baby, now that I'm finally pregnant, I am newly terrified of jinxing the whole thing. I tell him that I want to wait till after the viability scan I booked, even though Nathan would have passed that with flying colors, and I know it's no guarantee that everything will be all right. That's the thing with pregnancy. There are no guarantees at all that in nine months I'll be holding a healthy baby.

"Just one thing?" he says, and it's so unlike him not to back down that I find myself nodding and taking the tiny babygrow in the softest fleecy cotton to the counter, refusing a gift receipt and acknowledging the shop assistant's eyebrows as they lift upwards knowingly.

We're silent in the car as we drive back home. It's dark, even though it's only 4pm, and I'm wishing the winter away. I want it to be spring, when I'll be nearly twenty weeks, when we'll be able to know whether the baby's kidneys have formed properly.

"You're quiet," Simon says, laying a hand on my knee. He's driving more carefully than he used to. "Not feeling sick or anything?"

"Just tired," I say, laying my hand over his and squeezing it. "I'm fine."

"Hard work growing a whole new human being," he says, and I glance at him in the dull light of the car. The shine in his eyes is reflected in the headlights that pass us. I've made him so happy—there's that at least.

"Hmm," I say, giving a slight nod. "Sorry."

He waves his hand in the air as if to reassure me, and I feel a sudden, rushing urge to burst into tears. What have I done?

What I have done has been done now. There is no going back. It's my burden to carry, just like the other one. There's no relief in coming clean, not for anybody. I just have to deal with it.

"I love you," I say to Simon, and then it's too late. The tears don't care about my resolve, about the fact it's not fair on him. That poor little girl, Lula. They tumble out of me, dripping on his hand, and he twists his head towards me in surprise.

"Hey," he says, trying to look at the road and my face at the same time. "What's the matter? Von? What's happened?"

"I'm sorry," I say, and my fists are balled up against my eyes, rubbing at them, trying to make it stop. "I'm sorry, I love you, I'm sorry."

"Baby," Simon says, and in his voice I can hear that he can't cope with this, and I know I'm being selfish again. I need to pull myself together, because he doesn't deserve this. "Please. We're nearly home . . . Do you want me to pull over?"

We're nearly home. My sorrow turns to anger, anger at myself. The tears dry up and I thump my fists on my legs in frustration.

"I'm sorry," I say, the words sticking in my mouth. "I'm just tired. Ignore me. Let's get home and . . . a cup of tea, that will help. Proper tea."

Simon's shoulders drop with relief.

"Pregnancy hormones," I offer, and he smiles. "Just so overwhelming, after all this time . . ."

He nods, but doesn't say a thing. We round the corner into our road, and I feel myself relax again. Perhaps I just needed to cry a little, to let it out. It's Christmas. Lula is in the best place possible, with round-the-clock care. The nurse I spoke to afterwards was optimistic about her recovery, although she wouldn't tell me anything specific.

It's all going to be all right.

I stare out the window at the houses along our street; the tastelessness of the Christmas decorations smothering them all. But then I see something else, a little further up the street, outside our house, and my hand flies to my mouth in shock.

A Range Rover. Cream leather seats, a panoramic sunroof.

Henry's Range Rover.

I remember the video of them going to pick it up: Violet stuck in a supermarket car park the next day with the alarm going off and no idea how to stop it.

He's here, outside my house.

It shouldn't be a surprise, really. He's come to find me, to ruin my life, the way I ruined his.

HENRY

It put me in a better mood than anything had done for years. If I sat down and tried to examine it—to examine myself—I came to the conclusion that I was a predictable old man, as bad as my father. That the thought of her with her buff personal trainer, all waxed torsos and six packs, brought out something entirely natural in me: a predatory, competitive instinct. I should have fought it, but I wouldn't be the first not to.

And anyway, Violet didn't seem to care. We were barely speaking, by then. Her great "career" sat between us, like an unwanted houseguest, filling our private spaces and stopping us from communicating. I was sick of it all. The constant criticism online, the lucrative sponsorship deals that required me to grin like a loon over a bowl of cereal. But worse than that was the fact that Violet was often too busy having her photograph taken to actually look after our children, and instead left them in the care of a teenager who didn't know the first thing about child safety. I was sure it was Yvonne who had approached Skye in the park, and asked her all those questions about us, but it could so easily have been someone more sinister.

But Violet didn't listen. She didn't fucking listen.

Sometimes, I watched her with the children from the corner of the room, feeling like if I suddenly self-combusted, she might not notice for days. What was my purpose in this family? Just to pay the bills, to read the kids a story every now and then. To stay out of Violet's way when she was filming.

I still wanted her though. I woke nearly every morning full of lust for my beautiful wife. But if I approached her, she would push me away with a groan—or worse, smile at me sympathetically, asking if we could "do it later" as though it was some awful chore she needed to work up the energy for.

The thing with Yvonne only lasted six weeks. As transgressions go, it wasn't the worst. Just a blip on the long horizon of marriage.

But for those six weeks, I was a dishonest shit. I would smile at my wife, and tell her not to worry about me. Then I would go into work, text Yvonne, and sit like a lovesick idiot staring at my phone, waiting for a reply.

She didn't always reply straight away. Not like the early days, when she was always there—literally, out there in the open-plan office—to be summoned at any opportunity. We didn't talk about those days. We didn't talk much at all. We mostly rented hotel rooms in Mayfair—I got a good deal through my membership. I would tell the team I was working from home, tuck my laptop under my arm and head right three times out of the office. She was usually already there, sitting at the dressing table, fiddling with her phone. There were always a few minutes of awkward small talk, before the inevitable happened again. And again. It made me feel young.

The only serious conversation we had was about contraception. She told me she had had a coil fitted. We never talked about the baby, but sometimes afterwards, I'd lie next to Yvonne, looking at the shape of her nose, and imagine what he would have looked like. He didn't feel real, though. He felt like an idea, or a thought I once had. Not an actual person. Not like Skye, Lula and Goldie.

Anything we did say was just small talk; chat about new restaurants we both wanted to try, what we'd order from room service, the decor of the hotel. It was short and sweet, and it felt entirely different from my other, proper life: the exhausting rollercoaster I shared at home with Vi and the kids.

Of course I knew it was wrong. It felt like a treat to myself, but something indulgent and naughty, that I'd have to pay for in the long run.

It doesn't make it OK, but I always knew I would pay.

LILY

Ben lets me leave work early on my last day. It's almost as though he can't wait to see the back of me. Susie takes me for coffee and cake at the French patisserie around the corner from the office. She pays, insisting, and I realise how generous she's been to me over the past year—all these little gestures that really add up. I will miss her.

"I'm so proud of you," Susie says, forking her cake. "I've got good feelings about 2018 for you! A new year, a new job, a new man."

I laugh and finish her sentence. "A new me."

"Exactly."

We hug goodbye outside the cafe, but as I turn to leave, she calls me back.

"Lily . . ." she says. "Can I . . ." But then she stops, her mouth twisting and her delicate eyebrows meeting in a frown.

"What?" I ask, smiling at her, but inside my chest my heart begins to pound.

"It's just . . . something that's been bothering me. Ever since I babysat Archie."

I nod, swallowing.

"I know it's none of my business, but I noticed that you didn't have any photos of Archie's dad anywhere in your flat. I thought there'd be one of your wedding, at least."

My eyes widen. I knew I should never have let her in. I knew she wouldn't be able to resist a good old nose about. The thought of her poking around my things!

"Oh. I don't like to be reminded of him. It's still very painful."

"That's what I thought," she says. "Only . . . I asked Archie. I know I shouldn't have done, but I wondered if he had any pics. And he said something really strange."

"What did you ask him?" I say. It feels as though the ground has suddenly shifted beneath me. I lean on the lamppost next to me for support.

"I just asked if he knew a lot about his daddy . . . you've always been so secretive about him . . . and he looked at me, like I was an idiot, and he told me very plainly that he didn't have a daddy."

"Did he?" I say, giving a choked laugh. "Well, that's three-year-olds for you."

Her frown intensifies.

"You must have been very young when you met James. You said it was eighteen months before he left his wife, but he died three years ago. How old were you when you got married?"

I hold her stare.

"You know if . . ." she says. "You can always talk to . . ."

"It's freezing," I interrupt, pulling my coat around myself. "You better get back to the office."

Her frown morphs into a confused smile, and she lingers for several more seconds, as though waiting for me to speak.

"Take care of yourself, Lily," she says, her voice clipped. And then she turns and walks off.

I stay a while on the pavement, watching her as she walks back to the office. Trying not to feel sad. She would have forgotten me by next week anyway, like most people do.

I push my way through the Oxford Street crowds towards the Underground, my brain firing on all cylinders. I start my new job just after New Year. A fresh start. I need to put the past behind me.

Anyone who knows what I have been through is bound to understand why I've made mistakes. After all, what did I do to deserve James, being a single parent, everything bad that's ever happened to me? I did well enough at school and was no trouble for my father, even though he patently resented every second he had to spend with me and blamed me for my mother leaving.

I've spent my life determined not to be like her, but of course it's inevitable that I should fall into the groove left by her footprints from time to time.

Except I haven't left Archie, and I never will.

I think back to the fibs I told the interviewer at my new job, the way I casually but deliberately threw into conversation that I was good friends with Violet's sister-in-law, Amy. "Good friends" is definitely pushing it, but at least I've met her. She'd remember me, surely? The damsel without data. As for Violet, they seemed very excited when I said we were close.

As I walk to the station, I think of all the emails I sent her, the comments I left on her feed. Late at night, when I was so drunk I didn't really know who I was anymore, or how I felt about anything. They started off patronising—*don't think this is a great idea, encouraging your kids to throw snowballs is kind of violent, no? but love your channel!*—but as the weeks wore on, and she never once responded, my thoughts and feedback turned darker. Who did she think she was? Everything in her life was just handed to her on a plate—the unfairness of it all made me want to vomit.

I had loved and looked up to her so much but then she turned out to be just like all the other people I cared about. Pushing me aside, pretending I didn't exist. It was difficult to swallow, and I needed a way of letting out my feelings. I thought if I put them down in emails and sent them over, then I'd get them out of my system. I just wanted her to *acknowledge* me.

But I took it too far, with what I did to Skye.

It was the anniversary of James's and my first date, and I'd been drinking. I left Archie in bed, napping, and went off to the park to find Mandy and the kids. It was ages before Mandy finished her fag and realised that Skye wasn't on the climbing frame anymore.

We had such a lovely chat, Skye and me. Part of me wanted to take her home. I thought what a wonderful big sister she would make for Archie.

But then I heard the shouts. We were right at the other end of the playground on the big swings, out of sight.

I wouldn't have hurt Skye. I told her she had better get back to Mandy, then slipped away. I watched from behind a tree. Saw the way that Mandy screamed at Skye for running off, and it broke my heart. It wasn't her fault. She hadn't run off; Mandy just hadn't been watching.

I shouldn't have asked her all the questions about Violet and Henry, but I didn't hurt her. And then I got home, and found Archie at the foot of the stairs, screaming for me, being cradled by my neighbor.

"Where the hell were you?" she hissed. "He's been crying for ten minutes!" I had never felt so ashamed, stammering out some excuse about nipping to the postbox, explaining that he was such a sound sleeper I thought it was safe to leave him.

I had sobered up by then, and the irony of the situation was not lost on me. My obsession with Violet's children had nearly lost me my own.

I'm suddenly breathless. I stop short outside a coffee shop, pulling out my phone to check the time. And that's when I notice the screen of my phone is illuminated. I have a new message from Ellie, and I open it.

Hi Lily. I saw Luke for lunch today. I understand you've had a shit time of things and I wanted to talk to you face to face about this, but as you never got back to me, I didn't get the chance. Thing is, I know it was you that trolled Violet. After we met in the cafe, I thought your face seemed familiar. It took me a week or so to work out why. Then I went on to Instagram and looked at some of the old comments on Henry's feed. Some of them were really weird. Really . . . intense. I thought you were Violet's fan, not a troll? Listen, I don't know you, not really, but Luke's a decent guy. I had to tell him. I don't want him to get hurt. Hopefully you can explain your behavior better than I could. Maybe you should think about getting some help? Ellie

I stare at my phone, my heart back to that same sickening thudding in my chest.

She's told Luke. How could she? Why, why, why? Why would she do that to me?

Yet again, it feels like the universe is endlessly punishing me for my mistakes.

For leaving Archie alone when he napped, for all those stupid emails I sent Violet, for talking to Skye at the park . . . for pushing James away with my jealousy and neediness, for that stupid mistake one night a few weeks later.

For not getting that random bloke's number, because it meant that no matter how hard I tried, Archie would never, ever know who his real father was.

And now, for thinking I could just meet someone new, get a new job and live my life as though none of this Violet business ever happened.

Of course I wasn't going to get my happy ending. How hilariously stupid that I ever thought I might.

I look across the road at the off-licence. Unthinking, I march towards it, not even caring about the money as I thrust a ten-pound note across the counter in exchange for the first bottle of vodka I see.

YVONNE

I am sitting in the car, frozen with fear, as Simon pulls into our driveway. The Range Rover is looming large out of the corner of my eye, blocking in next door's battered Toyota.

Just a few more seconds until we have to get out, and then it's game over.

It's pitch dark outside, and I turn my head slightly, squinting to see if I can spot Henry in the driver's seat. Wondering if there's a way I can get a message to him not to do it, to leave us in peace. But there's no way he'd be able to see my expression from here. And no way that he'd care, either.

My brain races, trying desperately to think of a reason—something I've forgotten, perhaps, that we need to go back for—any reason not to go in the house. But it's pointless. He knows where we live now, and he'd just come back. He'd sit outside until he caught us. There's nothing I can do.

I'm gripping the sides of the passenger seat and then my ears are filled with the shrill ringing of Simon's mobile phone. It makes me jump, and he picks it up from the cubby by the handbrake.

"Sorry, babe, it's Jamal."

I nod. "No worries."

Simon turns off the engine and leans on the door. I listen to him answer the phone, and as he drones on about shift schedules between Christmas and New Year, I run through that night again in my mind.

Wondering if there's any way out. Anything I can do or say to escape the inevitable.

*　*　*

I remember it so well. Henry's text had come out of the blue. I had only been home for an hour and was lying on the sofa, my throw over my legs. I admit, I was feeling smug about it all, even considering telling Jade that our plan had worked. Simon was enjoying one of his football-and-pub sessions, and wouldn't be back until midnight at the earliest.

Need to see you. Urgently. Can you come back?

I tried calling three times but he didn't pick up. I sat back down on the sofa, deciding to ignore him. I didn't need anything more from him.

But then my phone pinged again.

Please. Can't talk. Just come.

It didn't sound like him. It was my curiosity that compelled me to get back in the car and return to Islington. It was 7pm when I arrived. I remember because I checked whether I needed a parking ticket or not.

Violet was away at her parents' for the weekend, with the kids. It was Henry's idea to meet at their house earlier on—for lunch, he said. Simon had been at work as usual. I didn't mind. The timing was per-fect—the day before I was due to ovulate—and I was beginning to get desperate. So we ate lunch, and I just about coped with being perched on a bar stool surrounded by huge canvas photographs of the five of them. After all, I knew the inside of the house well—I had been there so many times before through Violet's blog. It was smaller than it looked on camera.

There was a massive vase of lilies on the island unit in the kitchen. I wondered if she always had flowers like that in her kitchen, and how much it cost her, but other than that, I felt nothing about being there, in their space. Perhaps I should have felt more shame.

After a lunch ordered in from a deli round the corner—little pots of sundried tomatoes and artichokes and lumps of cheese, followed by chunks of chewy sourdough—we inevitably went upstairs. Not to their room—I insisted—but one of the spares. It was brief and to the point, any nostalgic passion I'd felt for him long worn off. He seemed to enjoy it, and the timing was critical. I lay in bed afterwards for as long as I could manage without it looking suspicious.

"Not getting up?" he said, after coming back from the bathroom. He'd had a shower, was rubbing his hair with a towel, and the words circled my brain, a description I'd read in a novel once. *Washing me off. He was washing me off.*

I smiled—sticking to my tactic of only speaking when absolutely necessary—and scrabbled around for my knickers, which were hanging from one corner of the bed.

"I hope you're going to wash the sheets," I found myself saying as I redressed. The afternoon light was beginning to fade and the huge shutters were open at the window, but as we overlooked the back of the house, there wasn't much chance of us being seen. Violet and Henry seemed to have the biggest garden in London.

"Well . . ." Henry said, grinning. "I suppose I was hoping there might be a repeat performance tomorrow. If madam was up for it?"

"I can't tomorrow, we're having lunch at Simon's parents." Saying his name aloud in that room, in that company, pricked me with guilt.

Henry nodded.

"She'll be back mid-afternoon anyway," he said. "Next time."

Next time. Would there be a next time? It was hard to tell. Last month had been a failure; the timings were off, which was why I was here now. It all depended on how long it took for my plan to actually work.

I pulled up at the house, after turning the day's events over in my mind throughout the journey. Part of me was worried that he'd decided he was now in love with me, or something equally ridiculous and inconvenient. But part of me was also worried that I didn't completely hate the idea. It was a huge weakness, a massive Achilles heel. I had spent so many years recovering from what he did to me, making sure there was nothing but contempt left, but the line between love and hate is so finely drawn, and it's so easy to find yourself standing on the wrong side.

I ran up the stone steps quickly, clueless to what awaited me. The lights were on inside, the hallway ablaze. I stared down at the umbrella stand in the porch for a few seconds as I waited for Henry to open the door. It was solid brass, and I found myself wondering how often it had to be cleaned, and who did it.

In fact, I was looking down at it when the door opened, and when I looked up, expecting to see Henry, there was Violet. Eyes blazing, nostrils flaring, like an angry horse waiting to trample an opponent.

* * *

We stood there, staring at each other, for several seconds.

"Hi," I said, eventually. It was worth a shot. Why would he text me when she was in? It didn't make sense. "Sorry, I think I might have the wrong house . . ."

She didn't speak. Instead her features shifted, from anger to confusion then back to anger again.

"You?" she said. "You're . . . you did our wedding photographs . . ." Her frown deepened. The downlight above her head cast unflattering shadows across her face. She looked older than me. That's what children do to you. Drain the life from you, like tiny little vampires.

"Jesus Christ!" she shouted, and then she started to cry. She was shaking as the realisation dawned on her. "Our fucking wedding! Did you meet at our fucking wedding?!"

I froze, like a deer caught on a country road by the glare of headlights. Then there was a sound from behind her, footsteps lumbering down the stairs, followed by a shout.

"Vi!" the voice called. "Who is it?"

Henry stopped on the bottom step and our eyes met briefly. The look he gave me urged me to deny everything. There was anger there, as well as fear. As though it was all my fault.

After all this time, he still wouldn't take responsibility for anything. "You texted me," I said, looking over Violet's head straight at him.

He frowned at me, shook his head, looking at me as though I was an idiot.

"It was me. I texted you," she hissed, and I looked back at her. "We came home early to find Daddy hanging the spare room sheets out to dry. That was suspicious enough. I've known there was something going on for a while now, but I thought it was just me being paranoid. But then I saw your messages on his phone . . ."

"Vi! You've totally got the wrong idea . . ." Henry shouted from his position on the stairs.

"I'm sorry, Violet," I said, ignoring him. "Henry and I have known each other for a long time. Nearly twenty years."

In that second, I didn't think about Simon, or the repercussions. I didn't think about anything at all. There was nothing but hot white fury that he was going to dismiss me again, just like he did last time. Like I was nothing but a piece of rubbish he'd had the misfortune to come across.

"I suppose we just never got over losing our baby," I said, and as she fell to the floor, sobbing on the doormat at my feet, I found myself smiling. Just a little.

HENRY

I tried to deny it, but even though she kept sobbing, over and over, Violet wasn't a fool.

"Her," she spat at me, pointing at Yvonne, who was standing tall in the doorway of our home. "Our fucking wedding photographer!"

"She's crazy, Vi," I said, trying to pull her towards me. She shoved me backwards. "She's been obsessed with me since the wedding. I've been trying to tell her it's not happening, but she's so persistent. I felt sorry for her . . . I only invited her round earlier today to tell her that she has to leave me alone for good. That all this stalking has to stop."

I glanced briefly at Yvonne. Her mouth was set in a tight line, but her eyes were wild.

"What's she talking about?" Violet shouted. "She knew you before! What baby?"

"I told you," I roared. It was always the easiest way to shut women up, and with satisfaction I noticed Violet shrinking back from me. "She's a fucking mentalist. She's obsessed with me! Been stalking me for months! It's your fucking fault, all this filming, putting our whole fucking lives out there online for all the mental people in the world to find out where we live! I bet she's the one who sent you those crazy emails!" I paused, lowering my voice. Enough of the anger. "Please. Shut the door, let's talk this through."

Violet pulled herself upright, turning to face me.

"I want to hear what she has to say," she said. She took a step back from me, towards Yvonne. "I don't believe you. If this has been going

261

on for ages, why didn't you tell me about it? And why didn't you let me call the police when I wanted to?"

She turned and pulled Yvonne into the hallway.

"You," Violet said, spitting again, "are you going to tell me exactly what's going on. Now."

For a few seconds the three of us stood there, frozen like stupid characters in a play wondering whose line was next. Eventually Yvonne spoke. I tried to catch her eye, but she wouldn't look at me.

"We met years ago," Yvonne said. "When we both worked on *King* magazine. I was the picture assistant; he was one of the commissioning editors. We had a . . . relationship. I got pregnant. But the baby died at twenty-two weeks."

She didn't flinch as she said the words. Violet's face was a mask now, her eyes red and streaming. I knew she believed her, believed every word that was coming out of her mouth.

"Henry dumped me when I got pregnant. Said he was too young to be tied down, told me he wasn't the marrying kind. He had a girlfriend, too, it turned out. A proper one, from the right social background, not like me. I was too common for him, apparently. *Mother* didn't approve. He's nice like that, your husband. But we . . ."

"Daddy! I really need you to see this!!"

I turned to the voice. Skye was standing at the top of the stairs, in her pyjamas. She stared down at us all, a wrinkle of confusion on her smooth forehead as she spotted Yvonne.

"Skye," I said, angrily, but my voice was hoarse from shouting. "Mummy and Daddy are busy. Go back upstairs!"

"No, you have to come now, Daddy! It's so funny!" she said. "It's Lula! She's fallen asleep in the bath."

And after that I don't remember any more. Just the panic as I tore up the stairs.

The blind panic and the horrific realisation that this was how I was going to pay for what I had done. That what I thought was already bad was about to get so much worse. Worse than I could ever have imagined.

YVONNE

In the water, her hair billowed out behind her like candy floss. She was face down. Unmoving.

The time it took for us to register what was happening seemed to last for hours. But surely it could only have been a few seconds before we were hauling her out, and everyone was screaming.

Amid all the noise, a voice in my head piped up, repeating the same thing.

I didn't want this. I didn't want this.

* * *

We are still in the car. There's a thump from the boot: some of the Christmas shopping giving up and tumbling over.

"Cheers, dude," Simon says, ending the call to Jamal and turning back to me. "Sorry about that, babe. Let's get inside."

I put my hand to the door and find that I'm shaking uncontrollably.

"I . . ." I say, but no words come. Simon looks at me, confused. But he doesn't speak, he just stares into my eyes.

"I love you," I say, grabbing his left hand with mine. It's taken all this time to realise it, to properly appreciate it. "Just remember that. I love you."

He gives me a puzzled smile and kisses me.

"I love you, too," he says, his eyes wandering to my stomach. "And that little one in there."

He opens the door, and before I have the chance to say anything else, he's out of the car and collecting the shopping from the boot. I fumble at the handle of the passenger side, desperate to get out, as though I might throw myself in front of him like some kind of human shield, blocking whatever it is Henry is about to tell him.

I stand up, and there he is. Henry. Standing in front of his stupidly large car, staring directly at me. He takes a step towards us. I open my mouth to speak, but before I have the chance to say anything, Simon does.

"You all right, mate?" he calls over at Henry. He's standing directly under a streetlight, and the light is as harsh on him as it was on Violet that night.

Henry continues walking towards us, and I grab Simon by the hand.

"Don't," I say. The only thought thundering through my brain now is that he mustn't find out that the baby might not be his. He must never find out. "Let's . . ."

Henry reaches the edge of our driveway and stops, his eyes never leaving us.

"Let's go inside," I whisper, tugging on Simon's sleeve. For a second, I meet Henry's eyes, and instead of being filled with rage as I'd expected, they are full of a melancholy I haven't seen since the day of the funeral, when he turned up unexpectedly. I'd emailed him the details, not expecting him to show up, but then he did, and I wished he hadn't come at all. He refused to speak to me. He refused to even look at me. He blamed me, in the same way my father did. He's just like my father. A misogynist through and through. That was always the problem, I just couldn't see it at the time.

"Please," I say, my voice pitiful. I'm not sure if I'm speaking directly to Henry or Simon, or even to myself. There are a few tense seconds when time seems to stand still. My hand is resting on my stomach and as Henry's eyes flicker across my body there's a shift, like a light going on. I don't know if he knows, if he can tell.

"Sorry, mate," Henry says, looking past me at Simon. I realise Simon is clutching the Mothercare bag, that Henry is staring straight at it. "I think I've made a mistake."

And with that, he presses a button on the remote in his hand. The car's indicators flash and then the headlights come on, and before I can bear to breathe out, he's climbing back into his car, and driving away.

GoMamas

Topics>Mummy Vloggers>Violet is Blue>Violet's Whereabouts
22 December 2017

Horsesforcourses
Is there anyone still out there? If so, you might want to know that there's finally been an update. And it's not a good one, I'm afraid. Take a look at Violet's blog—her management have released a statement.

Coldteafordays
Oooh! Back in a sec!

Coldteafordays
Oh my god, that poor child. That's terrible.

Bluevelvet
So, so upsetting.

Horsesforcourses
The poor family. I feel absolutely awful for all the speculating we did. It makes sense now—the ambulance, the screaming, everything. I can't believe we thought Henry had beaten her up. And all this time . . . poor Violet, what must she have been going through?

Coldteafordays
Hangsheadinshame

Bluevelvet
I'm off to have a good, long hard look at myself.

Horsesforcourses

Me too.

Bluevelvet

Does anyone know which hospital she's in? Not for sinister reasons I promise! I was thinking we could send her some flowers . . .

LILY

I wake with a pounding head and a stomach that feels like it's full of gravel. There are unexpected sounds coming from my living room, and I frown in confusion. Luke's voice, higher and more enthusiastic than I've heard it before, and Archie's familiar appreciative squawks as the two of them play some unidentifiable game.

I shut my eyes again. I want to hide in here forever. My memories of yesterday post-6pm are fuzzy and indistinct. A vague recollection of a teary phone call to Luke, begging for his forgiveness, then nothing more. I don't even remember picking Archie up from Anna's.

But the fact Luke is here is a good sign, isn't it? Whatever Ellie told him can't have been that bad.

Reluctantly, I swing my legs out of the bed, feeling for the carpet under my toes. I pull on my dressing gown. My whole body aches as I tiptoe towards the living room. Luke looks up as he hears me approach.

"Ah," he says, and in my hungover state I can't interpret the look on his face. "Feeling better?"

"I . . ." I say, but can't find the words.

"We made you a card, Mummy," Archie says, hauling himself to his feet and tottering over to the coffee table to pick it up. "To make you get well soon."

"His idea," Luke says, as I take it from Archie. "I told him you weren't feeling very well, that you needed some more sleep."

"Are you better now, Mummy?" Archie says, hugging my legs as he looks up at me.

I bite my lip.

"Getting there," I reply. "Thank you for the card. It's lovely."

"Why don't you get a shower?" Luke says. His eyes are cold, pragmatic. "And Archie and I can finish the Shopping List Game, which he's royally beating me at so far. I'll put some coffee on."

"Thank you," I say, under my breath as I stroke Archie's hair, but Luke just nods.

* * *

Luke stays with us all day. He is the perfect gentleman—the perfect friend—but with Archie taking all the attention we don't have a chance to speak about the previous day, or what Ellie told him. I drink a lot of coffee, and take multiple paracetamol, and by the afternoon, once we've been for a bracing walk in the park on Archie's insistence, I feel a little bit more human.

Luke is quieter with me than usual, but at least he's here. That has to count for something. After lunch, when Archie is doing quiet time in his room with his books, I try to apologise, but Luke brushes me away, changing the subject.

"Let's talk later," he says. "I thought you might want to see this. Statement from Violet's manager. Finally." He hands me a piece of paper, and I take it from him and read.

My client Violet Young is aware that there has been some speculation in the media as to why she has recently closed her social media channels. Unfortunately, her second daughter, Lula, is in hospital recovering from a serious accident. She does not wish to comment further on the matter, and asks the media to respect her privacy and leave her family in peace at this difficult time.

"A serious accident?" I say, looking up at Luke. I think back to the time when I stalked Henry as he walked Skye to school. It hadn't occurred to me that Lula should have been with them, that she started nursery there in September. I can't believe I hadn't noticed her absence. But suddenly, things start to make sense. It's Lula that's been in hospital all this time. Not Violet.

"I wonder what happened," I say. "God, poor Lula. She's only three."

"Apparently Violet's been at the hospital almost constantly since it happened. Understandably."

"But why . . ." I begin, the thoughts scrambling in my mind. "Why would she delete her social media accounts? Bit of a random thing to do? Wouldn't you just leave them? Not update them?"

"That's what I thought too," Luke says. "I've gone back to her manager, asked for more details. Doubt I'll get any, though."

"But Luke . . ." I say, reaching out to touch his arm. "It's none of our business. A child has been injured. We should do as they say and leave it alone."

I hand the piece of paper back to him. Luke nods, his nose wrinkling at me, then folds it and puts it in his pocket.

*   *   *

Archie is in bed, and finally Luke and I sit on the sofa together. Side by side, not snuggled up against each other as we usually are.

"Thank you for today . . . for looking after us both. I know Ellie told you some things about me . . ."

Luke takes a deep breath.

"Perhaps it would help," he says. "If you could explain it to me a bit. I don't think you . . . I always thought I was a good judge of character. I just need to understand, I think. What motivated you. When you've got so much going for you. Why were you so worried about what some random woman was up to? To the extent that you would leave those kinds of comments?"

I sniff.

"It hasn't been easy for me, you know," I say, and even though I feel like crying, there are no tears there. "I've had . . . some issues. Growing up. You know I told you my mother died? That wasn't strictly true."

Luke's eyes widen.

"She walked out on me and my dad, when I was six months old. Never came back. He was too angry to look for her, and by the time he realised she wasn't coming back, it was too late. We never found her. So she might be dead. But I don't know for sure."

Luke blinks slowly.

"And then your husband died?" he says, shaking his head. "I'm sorry, that's a lot for someone to deal with."

I shift away from him, staring past his shoulder at the pathetic Christmas tree behind him.

"Archie's father isn't dead," I say, my voice small. "I don't know who his father is. It was a one-night stand. I'd been . . . in a difficult relationship for some time. The man had just ended it." I pause, glancing back at Luke, but he's staring at me blankly. Have I already lost him?

I let out a deep sigh. Luke is frowning now, his eyes a mixture of upset and shock.

I rub my face with my hands.

"The night I knew he had ended it for good, I went out and got blind drunk, brought some bloke home. I don't even remember what he looked like, not really. When I woke up in the morning he was gone. Didn't leave me a number. I don't even remember his name. That's the hardest thing of all. I'll never be able to tell Archie who his father is."

"God, Lily. Why did you say he was dead?" Luke says, his voice tight. "You could have told me the truth."

"I don't know. I guess I was ashamed. It was the easiest way to get people to truly feel sorry for me. Everyone thinks they know that a single mum's life is hard, but they have *no* idea just how hard. It just slipped out once, when the health visitor came round to weigh Archie. Even though she was trying to be kind, the flat was a mess, I was a mess, Archie hadn't slept and I was barely holding it together . . . I could tell she was judging me for being a single mother. To have got myself in that position in the first place. So I told her my husband had died. You should have seen the way she changed when I said it. It was like she suddenly saw me completely differently—she was *so* much more sympathetic. And I needed that sympathy. I needed that support. Am I any less deserving of it because Archie's father is some arsehole who used me for a night of fun then did a runner when I was still asleep? Does that make me a worse person than if he had died?"

"No, of course not. But to lie about that . . ."

He stands up and I grab his arm and pull him back down on to the sofa, my fingers digging into his skin.

"No!" I say. "Don't leave. Please, just listen . . . Let me explain. Let me explain everything."

He doesn't say anything. But to my relief he sits back down, staring at me.

"It was just a little fib at first, to the health visitor, but it didn't feel like one. After all, I *was* grieving. I was grieving for the end of my relationship; I was grieving that my son didn't have a father. At first when I started watching Violet, I found it comforting. To see someone else with a young baby who was suffering like I was. But then . . . her life started to get better. And mine didn't . . ."

Luke stares at me.

"Doesn't it ever get to you, how unfair life is? How some things go so well for some people, but not others?"

He shakes his head.

"So I left some comments, a few times, just gentle suggestions at first. But she ignored them. I suppose I was annoyed, and the comments got worse. Sometimes . . . when I was at home, drinking too much, I just wrote the first spiteful things that came to my head. The alcohol brought out the worst in me—I was trying to get her attention, but then all her fans ganged up on me, and it made me feel even more angry."

I feel sick.

"Do you ever feel like you love and hate someone at the same time? It made me feel better about my own parenting, seeing her get things wrong. I don't know. You probably think I'm an awful bitch. But I'm not, I promise. I just . . . I just lost all sense of what was appropriate."

"Jesus, Lily," Luke says.

"I'm sorry. I do know it all sounds crazy. It was just . . . it all started to run away with me. I was drinking too much . . . I don't know . . ."

"You're telling me," he says, sighing. "Jesus. You do realise your behavior . . . it's not normal? It's not rational?"

"I know," I say, desperate now. "It's just . . ."

"Why didn't you go and see someone about it?" he says. "Get some help?"

I look down.

"I don't know. I was too far in . . . But look, I've been trying to cut down on my drinking. I'm sorry about last night, it was a blip. I'm different from how I was back then. Back then I just didn't know who I could talk to, who would understand," I say. "But that's kind of what the charity does, ironically . . . helps single parents with practical stuff, but also . . . emotionally."

He looks away. I can't bear how uncomfortable I've made him.

"I'm sorry," I say.

"Let's eat something," he says, sighing. "And we can talk some more after dinner. I don't want to abandon you, Lily. But God. You should have told me. You should have trusted me to help."

I nod, pushing away the nagging shame that I still don't trust him enough to tell him *everything*, and I let the tears fall.

* * *

Luke is cooking again. The smell of spices coming from my tiny kitchen takes me back to a holiday I once had with James, in Morocco. Perhaps Luke and I will go on a holiday like that soon. And then, when the dust has settled a bit and our relationship is on more stable ground, I can tell him about Skye and my trip to the park, and what happened to Archie.

After the Skye incident, Violet sacked Mandy. She put an Instagram picture up of herself, her children tucked under her arms, explaining in vague terms how let down she'd felt, and telling her audience in no uncertain terms that approaching her children without her being around was completely out of order. I emailed her as soon as I saw it, saying how pleased I was she'd finally got rid of Mandy, and she replied and told me she'd report me to the police if I ever contacted her again. So I didn't. I couldn't take the risk. After all, I nearly lost Archie because of it.

I shudder, remembering the way he cried as I held him on the cold stone floor of our hallway. The bruise on his forehead that took a month to fade, a permanent reminder of how I had failed him as a parent.

I didn't stop watching Violet though. I was addicted to her, to her whole family.

I scroll through Instagram. I follow nearly five hundred people, and yet I probably only know twenty of them in real life.

I look through my posts. There are thirty-two in total, ranging back over the past year. I only joined Instagram to follow Violet and Henry's updates. My pictures are shocking, quite frankly. The early ones aren't so bad—pictures of Archie's little fists balled up around Bear as he sleeps, a few shots of the back of his head as he tackles the climbing frame in the park. But then it all goes wrong: blurry, out-of-focus selfies. The ones that gave me away to Ellie. Me in my bathroom, late at night after one too many, pouting at myself for no apparent reason. The pitiful number of likes—five at most. A few comments from random strangers with names like death2zorbs telling me I look fit. I'm so embarrassed. Then some boring shots of birthday cakes in the office. Who would be interested in this rubbish?

I sit there and methodically save each picture of Archie, then delete my entire account, before setting up a new one from scratch. The screen asks me to fill out my bio. On my old account there was nothing there. Not even my first name. Nothing else about me. I was an anonymous lurker, like so many others.

This time will be different. I use my real name.

Lily Peters, London. PR assistant @SupportingSolos.

A new start.

I reach forward to the coffee table, lifting up my glass of wine—just one this evening, I've promised myself—and then I pick up the silver coaster that lay beneath it. I turn it over in my hands, my fingers idly stroking the engraved design.

All I have left of Violet. I wonder if she's missed it yet.

VIOLET

I set up the camera in my new office. It's south-facing and overlooks the allotments in front of the trainline behind our house. A bit different from the view from our house in Barnsbury, but here I feel I can finally relax. This space is all mine.

I dig out my old ring light and reach down to plug it in by my desk. Then I turn it on, checking the screen on the back of the camera to see the difference as it illuminates my face. It's incredible, what a bit of lighting can do. Suddenly my face is lifted, the imperfections erased. But it's not real. It's not what I actually look like. I switch the light off, and before I have time to think, press record.

Testing testing!

My voice comes out hesitant to begin with, but I keep talking, to warm it up. I try not to imagine who might be listening. I try to imagine I'm just talking to myself, plastering a grin on my face and flicking loose hair from my eyes.

Hello chaps, if any of you are still out there!

So. Where to start . . . You might have noticed this is a new channel. I'll come to the reasons behind that in a minute. But things have changed a lot for me over the past year. First of all . . .

I pause, glancing over at the tissue box. I hadn't anticipated needing it so soon. I pull one out.

275

As you may already know, just before last Christmas, my daughter Lula had an accident. We left her unaccompanied in the bath, and she suffered a near-drowning. A near-drowning, for those of you who are not aware, is one stage before death by drowning. She was three, and we thought it perfectly safe to leave her splashing and playing in the bath for a few minutes while we went downstairs to answer the door.

I cough, imagining the comments rolling in already.

It never occurred to us that what would happen was possible. But somehow, Lula slipped beneath the water and when we found her, she was face down, not moving.

Did you know young children can drown in less than two inches of water? That in the time it takes to send a tweet, a child in a bathtub can lose consciousness? If you leave it just a couple of minutes longer, the unconscious child will undoubtedly sustain permanent brain damage?

I pause again, blowing my nose and wiping away the tears. The camera's red light blinks at me.

On the way to hospital, Lula's heart stopped twice. After thirty-two minutes of CPR, they managed to stabilise her. Once we were there, she needed a feeding tube and a breathing machine to keep her alive. She was in a coma for nearly three weeks. She lost control of her head and was unable to sit, roll over or speak. Her eyes weren't able to track objects, and it felt like she had turned back into a baby.

I keep talking. If I stop now, I'll collapse.

We were lucky though, that she didn't experience any seizures. She's had the best care over the past year and is recovering well, thanks to daily physical therapy, occupational therapy and speech therapy. We're hopeful there won't be too many long-term effects, but only time will tell. I cannot thank the doctors and nurses and experts who have helped her enough.

I lean forward slightly and take a sip from the glass of water on my desk.

Many people wondered why I deleted my social media accounts. It was a knee jerk thing. I don't even really remember doing it. I remember crying and shaking and screaming a lot as they worked on Lula and we waited for news. I didn't go to bed that night. I was so full of regret, for sharing everything. My precious daughters. I'd let the world have too much of them, and at that moment, I just wanted them back.

I look out the window, watching as a train trundles past. Then I take a deep breath and look back at the camera.

It was a horrific time. And since then, Henry and I have separated. It was a long time coming, and I'm not going to go into the whys and wherefores. The girls still see their father at the weekends and he continues to play an active role in their lives.

I sniff, pinch my nose.

So, you're probably wondering. Why am I here now? Why did I come back?

My break from YouTube made me think long and hard about what I was trying to achieve. It's a privilege, to have this platform. I want to make it count. I want to leave something behind that has meaning. I don't want to chase advertising revenues anymore.

I will no longer be featuring my girls. Not until they're old enough to truly understand and to consent. I won't be featuring my home, my handbags, my clothes or shoes. Because the last year has taught me how absolutely unimportant these things are.

Instead I want to tell stories. Of real mothers and their lives. Over the past year I have met so many different mothers, all with their own unique story to tell. Whether they're dealing with a sick child, or infertility, or—worse still—have faced the unimaginable and lost a child. I want to give these ordinary women a voice. To raise awareness of all the different struggles different women deal with daily, across the UK and beyond.

I hope that you'll join me in listening to them.

I smile at the camera, blink slowly, then reach forward to stop the recording. My heart is thudding in my chest. Who knows if this will work? Who knows if anyone even cares about what I have to say anymore?

Turning to my computer, I think of all the things I didn't say on camera. That Henry had cheated on me, then begged me for months to take him back. That I'd had a stalker who'd approached my daughter in

Regent's Park, trying to get information on us as a family. That I'd had to fire my assistant Mandy, because of what this woman had done. I'd wanted to tell the police about the woman—surely they could trace her through her emails?—but Henry talked me out of it. Looking back, it's clear he was worried it was his bit on the side that had been sending the emails, that she had talked to Skye in the playground. *Yvonne.* And he didn't want the police tracing her, and me finding out what he'd been up to.

That was so Henry, putting himself first, telling me that this nutcase hadn't technically done anything illegal, that we'd be wasting police time. He turned it into another one of our rows about my career choice. *"What did you expect?"* he screamed at me. *"You've been asking for it! Sticking our kids all over YouTube like that."*

I close my eyes. I don't want to think about Henry. It's the only way I can cope. By pretending he doesn't exist.

My eyes turn back to my laptop. The icon for my email account is bouncing up and down at the side of my computer screen. I click to open the message.

It's from Supporting Solos, a charity that supports single parents. I've been talking to one of their PRs about a possible collaboration once my new channel is live. The PR is very enthusiastic, full of ideas of how we can work together. We're meeting up next week. It feels like she really understands what I'm trying to do.

She's a single mum too. Her name's Lily.

She seems nice.

EPILOGUE

I was induced at thirty-seven weeks, thanks to pre-eclampsia, a side-effect of my age. In my hospital bed, I turned over all the awful scenarios in my mind, until the doctor agreed that I was also suffering from mild post-traumatic stress disorder from my previous experience, and consented to a Caesarean section.

It was nothing like last time.

They handed me the baby, and she was perfect. Bigger than I expected—so much bigger than Nathan—and strong too. She shouted at me when I first held her, great howls of anger at being plucked from my womb before she was ready. She was feisty already, and I was proud.

Simon cried, telling me I had made him the happiest man on the planet, and I didn't even care that it was a cliché.

When she slept, I studied every inch of her face, looking for similarities. She was fair, so much fairer than Nathan was. A fine reddish down covered her head. I stroked her tiny nose and realised that I would never know. And neither would she. We would never know either way, and I was fine with it.

In the weeks after Henry's visit, I was frantic. Not just for the scan at twenty weeks, for someone to reassure me that her kidneys were developing normally. But every morning I would wake up wondering how much longer I would get away with it all for. Thankfully though, as the baby grew, my anxiety shrank. With every passing day that I looked out of my bedroom window—wondering if Henry would be there, waiting to wreak revenge—and I didn't see him, I felt myself relax, just a little.

And then the time came when we got to take her home, and I was suddenly complete, my heart so full it ached.

We called her Daniela, after my mother.

*　*　*

Nearly a year after Lula's accident, Violet returned to vlogging as a single mother. A new channel; started from scratch. I watch the first few videos with interest; any feeling of antipathy towards this woman who replaced me, who for so many years had lived the life I thought should be mine, extinguished the second I held my baby.

She doesn't feature the children in her videos anymore, and the sparkle has gone from her eyes, but it's been replaced with a determined strength and altruism that I can't help admire.

Aside from his new single status, Henry's life doesn't change, as far as I can tell. But I try not to think about him, and I don't look him up online as I once did, so obsessively.

As the weeks roll into months, I come to understand that the look he passed me, out there on the driveway that night, was one of cold understanding, that we were finally even.

And of acceptance, that what he had done was his fault, and his fault alone.

I am grateful to him for that. For the only thing he has ever truly done for me: leaving Simon and me alone. To love our baby in a way he never could.

ACKNOWLEDGEMENTS

Writing this book was a completely different experience from writing my first. But one thing was the same—it wouldn't have happened without the kind support of lots of people.

First of all, a massive thanks to my agent, Caroline Hardman, for all her advice and opinions (no more books with bankers in I promise!), and for telling me she really loved it after I nervously sent over the first draft. She is ably supported by the brilliant team at Hardman & Swainson, who I would also like to thank. I'm so desperate to come and work in your office and chat about death too!

Then, of course, huge thanks to Cassie Browne and Rachel Neely for believing in my writing, and for pushing me to explore my dark side more (!) and also for all their intelligent and patient editorial advice and guidance. I have so loved working with the enthusiastic team at Quercus, and would also like to thank Hannah Robinson, Ella Patel, and Katie Sadler for championing my work to the world. Thank you too to Chelsey Emmelhainz and all the team at Crooked Lane Books for taking this book Stateside—the stuff of dreams! I really appreciate you wanting to spread Violet, Lily and Yvonne's stories far and wide, and hope US readers enjoy it as much as I enjoyed writing it.

Author friends are the best friends, and so I must thank all my fellow writers from my Faber Academy group, as well as the Savvy Authors, for understanding what this strange job is like and brightening the darker days. Special cheers go to my beta readers and dear friends Susannah Ewart-James, Victoria Harrison, Caroline Hulse and

Rebecca Fleet for listening to me whinge without complaint and for being brilliant writers themselves.

Thank you again to Alice Marlow and Claire Emerson for helping me with the medical aspects of the book. If I got anything wrong, it's my fault not theirs.

My family put up with my obscure witterings about writing/plots all the time—sorry and thank you. But the biggest thanks must go to Oli who can often be found patiently listening as I attempt to unravel a plot conundrum. You are such a support to me and I appreciate your unflinching belief in my work so much. Thank you to Daphne too, for telling everyone "my mummy writes books" and for bringing joy into every day.

A huge thank you to all the book bloggers who enjoyed my first book and spoke so enthusiastically about it online. Your love of reading is such a pleasure to see. I really hope you enjoy this one too.

And finally, thank you to everyone who has bought or borrowed my books. Writers wouldn't exist without readers—we owe it all to you.